CW00487193

I
Am
Multitudes

Published by Long Midnight Publishing, 2023

copyright © 2023 Douglas Lindsay

ISBN: 979-8858997580

www.douglaslindsay.com

I
AM
MULTITUDES

DOUGLAS
LINDSAY

LMP

for Kathryn

1

This is who fate has decided you will be. Just some fucking guy lying in a bed, a bit pissed, unable to sleep, next to a woman who picked you up in a bar. You can't remember her name. You would be pushed, at two-fifteen a.m., to say what day of the week it is. You hate yourself.

'They have to make James Bond a woman at some point, though, right?'

It's been a while since either of us spoke. And I mean, like an hour and a half, since just after we left the bar. We stumbled in the door, we slobbered a little over each other, we crashed into bed. We fucked. Self-loathing followed, like an equal and opposite reaction to ejaculation, but the sex was pretty decent. She came five times. I'm going to say she wasn't faking that, because why would you bother faking an orgasm that often? It's not like she's ever met me before and thinks she has to bolster my low self-esteem. And if she did know me, she'd know there's no correlation between Partner Orgasm Frequency and self-esteem anyway. Not in my head. There is literally nothing that could lift my self-esteem out of the abyss.

At least I still appear to know what I'm doing, but then, I reckon this woman could have an orgasm fucking Donald Trump, and it's not like anyone ever said *that* before.

Let's not think of such things.

'Where did that come from?' I ask.

I'm staring at the ceiling. So's she. I'm aware of her head turning to glance at me, I don't look at her, she turns away.

'Hmm,' she says.

I actually quite like her. Nevertheless, I should just get up and leave.

'You know how the brain works,' she says.

I make a small noise to accept the answer, and to not encourage further disclosure. Yes, we do know how the brain works. It's a cunt.

Turns out she's a talker. I guess I worked that out back in

the bar when she told me the story about her and three guys from a small village just outside of Milan.

'I was lying here thinking that was great sex,' she says. 'I mean, back in the bar I wasn't really thinking this was going to happen. But my God, have you ever looked in the mirror? Your eyes are something. Holy shit.'

She turns and looks at me again. I stare at the ceiling. She turns away.

'You must have seen some stuff, by the way. Maybe you killed someone. Hard to tell. That was what drew me in. And I thought, yeah, I'll have this guy.'

She pauses but we haven't got anywhere near James Bond yet, so she's nowhere near finished talking. I have nothing to say anyway.

'Can you go again, by the way?' she says.

'Can I go again? I haven't even left once yet.'

'No. Can you *go*, silly?'

'Right,' I say after a while. 'No. Don't feel like it anyway.'

'Yeah, too bad. I suppose that's the difference once you get to be an old guy like you.'

What is it exactly that's keeping me lying here?

I'm a bit drunk and a bit tired, and I can't be bothered moving.

'You were saying about James Bond,' I say, to move the conversation along.

'I mean, I don't want you to get carried away or anything, but you have that look about you, like you're haunted or something. Like there's a darkness. And you drink like, *a lot*, and can still go, and you were pretty good, and you don't say much, but boy you've got a tongue on you, if you know what I mean.' She pauses. I have nothing to say. The true measure of lack of self-worth is when someone blowing sunshine up your arse is utterly meaningless. One of Freud's that, I think. 'And I thought of James Bond, because, I mean, that's him, right? I mean, look at you, you have half a thumb missing, man. Who the fuck has half a thumb missing? And then I was lying here thinking, if I had to have one of those James Bonds, you know, which one would it be? Oh, yeah, and there's that, because all those guys seem so old, so that's something else about you. You're a little, you know, old.'

She stops talking again, though we all know by now it won't last. I don't ask which Bond she decided she'd go for, partly because I assume she's about to tell me anyway, but mostly because I don't care. There is, in all regard, only one Bond, and since he retired all the others, starting with Roger Moore, have just been filling his shoes with varying degrees of adequacy.

'Wait,' I say, a thought coming to me through the haze, 'aren't you like thirty-something? Daniel Craig must've been in his thirties when he started. He's not old.'

'Twenty-two.'

I stare at the ceiling.

Twenty-two.

Oh my Jesus suffering fuck.

Some things sober you up pretty fast, by the way.

Could have been worse. I could've had to arrest myself.

The distraction – albeit not one that I've welcomed – only works temporarily, and then she's back.

'Then I was thinking about who the next Bond should be, and then I was asking myself all these questions about his ethnicity and his gender and all that kind of thing. What d'you think?'

I don't care. I want to say that I don't care, but it seems churlish. If I had to talk about something, I'd rather talk about her. What is she doing sleeping with me in the first place? Because of my eyes? Really? Lots of people have eyes.

'No,' I say eventually.

'No?'

'I don't think James Bond should be a woman.'

'Well, I guess. Most of your generation think things should just be the same as they've always been, right? Like, you're still talking about the Blitz like you lived through it, even though you weren't born until the sixties.'

'Oh, fuck off.'

That was just up and out there before anyone could do anything about it. An alcohol fart.

She surprises me by leaning on one elbow, and looking at me. I glance. She's smiling.

'This sounds interesting,' she says.

'I don't think so.'

'Go on.'

I go back to staring at the ceiling. I'm tired and still a bit pissed, even though she's now holding me prisoner with inane chatter. I do kind of like her, though, so there's that.

'You want to go out for dinner tomorrow night?' I say.

It's a tactic. My interest in doing this is zero. This allows us to draw a line under it on her terms, which is fine by me. I ask, she says no, it creates awkwardness, I leave and everyone can move on.

Women always say no to me at this stage, regardless of their age.

'Sure,' she says. 'I know a cool place.' A pause, and then, 'But if you want to just come here and fuck, I don't mind. You working in the morning?'

Well that plan failed about as spectacularly as it could've done.

It's enough. I get up, wobble a little when suddenly finding myself on two legs, then regain my balance, bend down and quickly pull on my briefs and jeans. Nothing worse than some guy walking around with his dick out. No one likes that.

'There are already women playing Bond-type roles in cinema,' I say, pulling on my thin cotton jumper. 'Gal Gadot, Charlize Theron. They could be Bond. Charlize pretty much already played Bond in the movie *Atomic Blonde*. Exactly the same character, but there's your problem right there. The film business has no respect for women. She's a kick-ass triple agent, under-cover assassin or whatever, and they named the movie *after her hair colour*. It was dumb.'

She's smiling. I bend to put on my socks and shoes, and then I can be out of here.

'They need to conceive a new female character, throw a budget at it, and commit to a series. Sure, they could just make Bond female, but if you're going to create an iconic female lead, why land her with all Bond's baggage? Give her her own tune and her own opening sequence, her own supervillains, her own drink. Give it some originality, not just any old shit done on the coattails of men to generate a bit of media coverage. The Bond movies are iconic. It was an entirely organic thing that grew out of nothing. It happens. If enough decent quality, female-led cinema gets made, the same thing happens. Then you'll have your female Bond.'

I'm done.

Her eyes are a little wide, and then she laughs and starts clapping.

'Wow, I love that.'

I've said too much. Again.

'That was like a TED talk or something.'

'You really want to do this again?' I say, voice flat. We're done here. I'm due in work in… take my phone from my pocket, check the time, think, the Hell with it, no one bothers when or even if I turn up for work.

'I do.'

The smile dies away, we hold a look for a few seconds.

'You'd better give me your number,' I say.

'You could just come here at eight.'

'I'll take your number.'

She gives me her number. I type it in, and then stare at the screen.

'I don't know your name.'

'A better way to put that would be that you can't remember my name,' she says. She's trying to tease me. She's young.

'I'm not sure,' I say, walking to the bedroom door. 'I wasn't paying any attention when you told me, so I never knew it to forget.'

She laughs again.

'God, you don't give a fuck, do you?'

I don't. My face says as much in its blank way.

'Elise. See you tonight,' she says.

I nod, I turn away. Walking down the short hallway to the apartment door, I get the first feelings of alcohol-induced nausea.

Multitudes 1

'Why are you here?'

Fergus Hunt, dumped on the floor, chained at the wrists and feet, stared grimly back at his captor through the half-light of the basement.

'I don't know,' he said.

'Why are you here?'

'Fuck me.'

He could stare at his captor all he liked, but the guy was wearing a mask. A comedy horror mask of some sort, hard to make out, though when he spoke his voice was clear.

'Why are you here?'

'Because you're a prick,' said Hunt. 'What else is it you're looking for?'

'I want to know that you know why you're here.'

Hunt laughed. His voice was a little hoarse. While finding himself bound since he recovered consciousness, he hadn't at any point been gagged, and he'd screamed and shouted repeatedly for over an hour. His throat hurt, and if he was being honest with himself, he was just plain bored shouting by the time his captor appeared, turned on the low light, and informed him he was in a basement, beneath an old, derelict farmhouse, some way outside of Glasgow. No one within earshot. In any case, the wind was blowing, there were trees, there was no point in shouting. 'Obviously if there'd been a point in shouting, I would've gagged you,' he'd said, and Hunt had said, 'Well, at least it allows me to tell you to fuck off.'

'Really,' said Hunt. 'I don't know, OK? I mean, that's all I've got. I have absolutely no fucking idea why I'm here.'

Hunt didn't know what the captor's face was doing. He was sitting on a rudimentary dining chair, a couple of yards in front of him, hands resting on his thighs.

Hunt glanced at the phone that was attached to a stand, presumably filming him.

'Tell me,' said the captor.

'Jesus,' said Hunt.

'Tell me.'

'What's the point? What are you going to do anyway? Rape me? Some sordid shit to stick on some website somewhere? Jesus.'

'The bad actors always project.'

Hunt scowled, then he smacked his lips as though he'd finally realised he was thirsty.

'Get me some water.'

'No.'

'I need a drink, man.'

'No you don't.'

'Oh, fuck off. I'm thirsty, I need a drink.'

'No one needs to be hydrated in order to die.'

Another scowl, the harsh stare, and then Hunt couldn't contain the burst of anger, and he growled loudly, railing against his bonds, straining and pulling against them, cursing violently.

His captor did not move. Hunt continued. Both wrists started to bleed. Finally he cried loudly, an angry bark of an expletive, and slumped back against the wall, exhausted. He stared with hate-filled eyes at the mask of his attacker.

'Why are you wearing the stupid mask if you're going to kill me anyway? You worried I'll report you to, I don't know, the Heaven Police? You going to try to sneak a place in fu –'

'Why are you here?'

'I don't know!'

'Why are you here?'

'Fuck!' A pause, then again, 'Fuck!'

'Why are you here?'

Finally, Hunt slumped back in silence. He rested his head against the wall. Long breath expelled.

'How about you give me… a fucking… clue?'

'Abigail Naismith.'

The name, softly spoken, nestled into the dark silence of the basement, before being harshly broken by another barked expletive.

'You are kidding me! Really? You're kidding me!'

'Abigail Naismith.'

'Two words, numbnuts, two words. Case dismissed! Case fucking dismissed, you piece of shit. Now let me go, right now! Let me go! Let me fucking go!'

He was screaming. His captor sat perfectly still. When he

started speaking again, Hunt immediately cut him off with another strangled, ugly, enraged scream. 'Let me fucking go!'

'Tell me what you did to Abigail.'

Hunt spat, although his mouth was dry, and nothing much came out.

'Tell me what you did to Abigail.'

'Nothing! Nothing, you bastard!'

'This is how it's going to play out,' said the captor, and Hunt once again spat ineffectively in his direction, followed by a growled, 'Jesus Christ.' 'You will die. That is the only definite. You will die. How you die is still in play. You can admit what you did to Abigail. You can look at that camera there and you can say what you did. You can also say why you did it. You can also say if you have committed any other crimes, anyone else you might have wronged.'

'Oh, fuck off.'

'If you do that I'll kill you quickly. If you don't, you will suffer. Your choice.'

He was lying. Confession or not, Hunt would suffer.

He was met with a grunt, and then a laugh, and then a head shake, a low snarl.

'And don't lie. Don't lie to me, Mr Hunt. Don't say anything that undermines the video when I release it. If you tell one lie, it will put the agency of everything you say in doubt. It might make people think I coerced the truth from you, and you just said what you thought I wanted to hear. If you choose to die quickly, you will tell me the unadulterated truth of your actions. If I discover subsequently that you've lied to me, I will kill your son.'

'Don't you fucking dare!'

Another great tugging at his bonds, an angry scream against the constraints, again destined to get nowhere.

'And your son will die painfully. That is what awaits him. Tell the truth, tell the camera what you did, you will die quickly and your son will be unharmed.'

'You bastard!'

Another scream, another tug at the bonds, although this time the pain of the cuts on his wrists really began to bite, and he grimaced, his head twitching, and he settled back with another low growl, another expletive.

Silence. Occasionally, breaking through it, a heavy breath, a grunt from Hunt. The captor was unmoving.

Finally, 'Tell me what you did to Abigail Naismith,' and at last Hunt decided he had to play along.

Mind working. He would tell a long tale. Perhaps he would think of some way out of his hole while he talked.

2

I enter the station open-plan at three minutes past ten. At one time this would have been considered late, but not anymore. Now, no one cares.

There's a new detective sergeant in town, and I'm working out my last couple of weeks at the station more or less organising paperwork. That's it. That's all that's left of my police career.

I guess it's ironic. Yes, ironic. All the times I was kicked out, all the times I was suspended, all the times I nearly died, and then finally, finally my career is brought to a halt by a mundane reduction in police numbers across the entire force in Scotland. Some shitty, low-key redundancy payments offered. The day the e-mail went round I was at a low ebb. Well, fuck it, I've been at a low ebb since Detective Inspector Kallas went back to Estonia, never to be heard from again. It wasn't the worst parting – great sex, some misadventure resulting in me being in a coma, losing half a thumb and missing her actual, painful departure, and the sweetest, most beautiful leaving note you can imagine, the kind of thing a sad, lovelorn drunk can read in his darkest moments – but she's gone all the same.

Anyway, I sat here when that e-mail came in and I thought, fuck this. Let's do it. Filled out the form, walked through to see the chief and said, can you sign this, please, and I thought she was going to move quicker that Usain Bolt with a stick of dynamite up his ass, but she actually sat me down and asked if I was sure I knew what I was doing.

Well, no, I wasn't, but it happened anyway.

I might have changed my mind since then, if I'd allowed myself to think about it, but here we are. I'm leaving. It's done.

Then the station got offered Detective Sergeant Amanda Dale, and it was a take her now or lose her elsewhere, and of course Chief Hawkins had to take her, and basically I could have gone then, but I said I might as well work out my last few weeks, and here I am. Sitting at a desk at the back of the office, with no one for company, making sure paperwork is in order for all open investigations. 'The kind of forensic check we usually don't have time for anymore,' Hawkins said. She knew it was shit, but I was the idiot saying I'd stay until the end.

I go straight to the coffee machine. I turn and look around the room. A few empty desks, a few occupied desks. Dale now sitting in my old spot opposite Ritter. I'm pleased, at least, for DC Ritter. She always did deserve better than me.

I catch the eye of Sergeant Harrison, which isn't difficult, as she's looking in my direction. I lift a mug, and she nods, and then gets out of her chair and comes and stands by the coffee machine.

'Tom.'

'Eileen.'

'You look terrible.'

'You look gorgeous.'

'That's sexual harassment, but thank you.'

'Is it also sexual harassment if I tell you I slept with a twenty-two-year-old last night?'

She winces.

'Really? Jesus, Tom.'

'I misread the situation.'

The coffee machine spits and spurts in its way.

'You thought the two of you were going to bed to do her homework?'

'I thought she was in her thirties.'

'That's quite the lack of observation for a detective.'

'Poor, I admit.'

'Can I ask, given that you look every one of your fifty-eight years, what she was thinking?'

I hold up my left hand.

'She was attracted by the missing half-thumb and my haunted look.'

'Ah, nice. Can't argue with that.'

'She said I reminded her of James Bond.'

'Which one? Woody Allen in that spoof *Casino Royale* from the sixties? That would tie in with you having sex with someone a third your age.'

I can't help laughing. Me and Eileen are back, and all it took was DI Kallas leaving the country.

'You're funny,' I say.

'I know.'

I lift the two coffees, hand her one, smile and nod.

'Now, I have urgent police paperwork to do, if you don't mind,' and she laughs and ushers me ahead of her, and we go our separate ways.

3

I have eleven working days left, although my intention is to bow out a day or two early. I don't want an official last day. It's not like anyone's going to care, but I've a feeling the boss might at the very least get a cake in or something. I'll hate that. I don't want anything. And they might think I'll skip the last day and so they'll do something on the penultimate day, so I'll skip that one too.

And what if I came in on that last day and no one did anything?

Yeah, I'd kind of hate that too. I don't want to be the centre of anyone's attention, but the thought of being completely ignored is just as depressing. So, best I just go. Start whatever it is I'm going to do for the rest of my life two days earlier than billed.

The job the chief gave me, which is to be spread over these eleven days, could be done efficiently in two. Even I could do it in two and I hate paperwork the way I hate the tabloid press and raw onions on a burger. So I'm taking my time, reading over the details of some of these cases I'm going through.

Here, for example, we have a neighbourhood dispute, which began over one of the neighbours putting a No Turning sign beside his driveway. We should note here that they live on the edge of a housing estate on the hills to the south of Glasgow, on a road that loops around, so it's not entirely clear why anyone would need to turn in this guy's driveway anyway. Some people are just assholes, I guess.

The dispute started with a guy three doors down. This guy never needed to turn in the first bloke's driveway, but just started doing it out of badness. 'When you see one of those stupid signs, doesn't it make you want to turn your car right there, even if you don't need to?' he said to the first officer who went to his door to address his neighbour's complaint.

Now, normally, when someone complains to the police about a law they've created for their own property being ignored

– the horror – the police are going to politely tell them to STOP WASTING OUR FUCKING TIME! Or something like that. But the complainant in this case was a local councillor. The police said they'd have a word. They spoke to the neighbour.

Things escalated.

Guy starts turning in the other guy's driveway ten, fifteen times in a row out of badness. Another police visit. More turning. First guy dumps rubbish on second guy's lawn. Denies it was him. Security cameras are set up. A decapitated chicken is left by a front door, met with a disembowelled fox in retaliation. They have a rather pathetic fist fight. Car tyres are slashed. The wives have a stand-up row in the local Tesco. The guy who started it all, by one measure, by erecting the completely needless No Turning sign in the first place, gets the shit kicked out of him by two masked men. Broken cheekbone, broken jaw, broken nose. Two broken fingers. Bruised testicles. Seven broken ribs. Pierced lung. Bruised liver.

This is where we are. The neighbour who organised the hit is no Vito Corleone. He has no connections. He has no experience in doing something like organising a hit and leaving no trace. His fingerprints are all over it. He's been charged. His wife has left him. The house is up for sale.

The No Turning sign apparently remains in place. I am tempted to go there and turn my car. Just once, just for the hell of it. Might make it a squad car, see how he handles that.

I won't miss people.

4

Chief Hawkins appears at the door. She looks across the office. Both DC Ritter and DS Dale are at their desks. The room is quiet, no one on the phone. Hawkins has a look about her that attracts attention. She hesitates by the door, then approaches the detectives in the room. Well, the two active detectives. I'm now a detective in name only, my position being more that of filing clerk.

'You seen the Fergus Hunt video?' asks Hawkins.

They shake their heads. The guy was in the news – he'd very obviously murdered a teenager, but the police screwed up the investigation, mishandling several pieces of evidence, really basic crap like mis-labelling and mis-recording details, by a member of staff so junior they really ought to still have been in primary school – so even though the case never came anywhere near this station, we all know who Hunt is.

Hawkins makes a small gesture to indicate they should follow her into her office. As they get up, she glances over at me. We share a look.

'Sergeant,' she says, inviting me to join.

God, do I have a *what about me* look on my face?

I get up and follow the three women into the office, then she closes the door.

'Fergus Hunt's wife reported him missing yesterday morning. It wasn't really news. We didn't put out a report, his wife certainly didn't go calling any journalists.'

'Yeah, I saw the line,' says Dale, Ritter nodding along with her.

I don't comment that I missed it. I feel like such an outsider.

'This has just been posted online, the location communicated separately to the local station. Hopefully we'll be able to get the video taken down quickly enough, though it depends how widespread it's been posted.'

She presses play.

Fergus Hunt, the face we recognise from the news stories a few months ago, is chained to a floor, slouching against a wall. Looks like a basement or a derelict factory or something. It's dark, he's illuminated by a single light, filmed on a phone camera. He starts talking, occasionally looking into the camera, occasionally glancing to the side, presumably at the person who's trapped him here.

'I killed Abigail Naismith. Everyone knows it. The police know it. But they screwed up.' A pause, a glance at the captor, the eyes look into the screen, then drop once again. 'I used to see her walking home from school. Then during the holidays, going to meet friends, whatever. Particularly last summer... last summer she looked like such a slut. Cropped tops, barely covering her tits. I thought she must be having sex already. Look at her, I thought... I'm going to have her. I'll have her.' A longer pause now. Another glance to his left, obviously more urging. Gritted teeth, a swallow loud enough to get caught on camera. 'Jesus.' Another pause. 'I started working in my front garden. Spoke to her a couple of times as she walked past. When the sun was shining, I took to not wearing a top. Could tell she was in to me. Invited her in for a drink one afternoon. She was up for it. Went inside, and we fucked.'

There's a gap in the audio, though the video keeps running. He looks to his left, eyes filled with hate. Obviously receiving instruction, or threat, or something. Another scowl, and then he continues.

'All right, she didn't want to. I raped her. She cried. She was a virgin. She said it hurt.' A pause. 'I wore my gimp suit, wore a condom. Didn't want to leave anything behind. She cried. God, she was irritating. Stupid wee girl.' A pause. He doesn't lift his eyes, though there's a brief blip in the sound. 'I strangled her. Little cunt.' Another pause. 'She looked so fit lying there dead, the bitch. I fucked her again. I wanted to come on her and piss on her, but I couldn't risk it. I'd've had to make sure the body was never discovered then. So I stayed in my gimp suit, didn't leave anything behind. Billy was staying at his grandma's, Janice was in Paris for a couple of days at that thing, whatever it was. Probably fucking her boss. So I didn't need to get rid of the slut's body straight away. Stuck her in the bath. Washed her. Left her there. Banged her again the next day. Janice was coming back, so had to get rid of her. The slut I mean, not Janice.'

He stares darkly at the camera. He lifts a chained hand and raises the middle finger. The video fades to black. When it fades back in, a scene from a horror movie. Much of Hunt's body obscured by rats. His stomach appears to have been slit open. The rats are eating him. His eyes are still open, he is caught in the moment before death. Hawkins, who may have already watched it all the way through, looks away. Ritter and Dale each have a hand to a mouth, but they watch. I turn away. It's not like we don't know what happens at the end. I watch Hawkins.

She glances back at the screen at the right moment. I follow her look. The screen fades to black, and when it comes in again, the camera now shows Hunt dead, his body eviscerated, eaten alive. The rats are gone. Hunt's cold dead face has had a letter P branded on his forehead.

The video fades again. It's done.

A long, horrified silence could ensue, but there are some hard-nosed practical detectives in the room.

'We know what that is?' asks Dale. 'The P?'

Hawkins shakes her head. She stares at the screen for a moment, and then closes the application, sets the screensaver going.

Mountains. Forest. Snow. Very nice.

The three of us, having been standing to the side and behind her desk while we looked at the screen, now walk back round to the regular addressing-the-chief position in the middle of the small office.

'Where?' asks Dale.

'The basement of an old farmhouse out beyond Broomhouse. Nothing else within a hundred yards of it, so very isolated, at least by the standards of Glasgow. A vigilante killing, with the vigilante making sure he got the confession before killing him.'

'What d'you think he threatened him with?' I ask, surprising myself that I'm even remotely interested in this sordid bullshit.

'Will we ever know?' says Hawkins, making a small gesture.

No one says anything. Silence crawls across the room. Oh well, no point in us all just standing here.

'The film clip,' I say, indicating the back of the boss's computer, 'when you start watching it… you're not sure how much coercion's taken place. Someone points a gun at you, or threatens you with whatever, you're going to say anything. But you can tell. The look on his face, in his eyes, the *fuck you* in the voice. He was enjoying telling the story by the end. It's the first time he's actually admitted to what he did, and he loved talking about it. Probably had an erection by the end of that.'

None of the ladies comment. I don't leave this new silence resting for long.

'Eaten alive by rats? Got what he deserved.'

I don't say it with any relish. I mean, it's not like I *care*. But he did, no question, get what was coming to him if that's what he did to that girl.

Hawkins sort of nods, looking at Dale and Ritter as she does so.

'Well, I don't suppose any one of us will be saying it live on television, but yes, if he was telling the truth. Nevertheless, there is no place for the vigilante, and that's what we have here.'

'This isn't coming our way though, is it?' says Dale, being the practical grown-up in the room. 'You said the farmhouse was out Broomhouse way.'

'Oh no, not at all. I just… I thought you should see it, I thought we could have a chat about it, but, well, you were going to see it anyway. As is anyone who wants to. That video is all over the place. But the thing that's going to worry us, worry the centre, is not that Hunt's dead. Few will mourn his passing. It's that symbol at the end.'

'Like the guy's some sort of superhero,' says Ritter.

'Yes. There would seem to be a fair amount of delusion involved there. And if this starts to become a regular occurrence, then God knows where it could end up, who ends up getting sucked into it.'

'Not out of the question it comes our way eventually,' says Dale.

'Exactly. And given the nature of this, where it could be anyone from anywhere in Scotland who's outraged about the case against Hunt collapsing, it may well be we get someone from the centre on our patch sooner rather than later. Even on the basis of this, this is likely to be an all-hands type of situation. If this P character isn't done…'

Everyone bar me nods. I'm just thinking that if this does explode, I hope I'm out of here before it happens.

'OK, thanks,' says Hawkins. 'I'm sure we'll all see plenty more of this, through every imaginable channel, in the next few days. I'll keep you posted if there's anything specific to the station.'

We turn, we start to head off. Dale gives her a *thanks, boss* as she goes.

'Tom?'

I stop at the door. Ritter and Dale head off, I turn back to the boss. Here we go.

'How are you doing?' she asks.

'OK,' I say.

She indicates for me to close the door. I take a moment, as I only do this reluctantly, then with a small sigh I turn back into the centre of the office.

'How are you?' I say, getting ahead of the game. I'd rather this was about her than me.

'I'm fine,' she says, then undistracted asks, 'How's the job coming along?'

'You mean the paperwork job?'

'Yes, the paperwork job.' She smiles, I think sympathetically.

'It's dull,' I say. 'I should leave. I mean, I should retire. Bring it forward by ten and a half days. But... I suppose I'm aware I've got nothing else lined up for the rest of my life, so I might as well do this a little longer.'

She nods. Still with the sympathetic look.

Regular viewers may remember the boss and I had sex once. One of those things that just happened. If anyone had proposed that it should happen, it wouldn't have got anywhere near being put in front of the planning committee, never mind passing into law. But she is, just on pure American TV looks, possibly the most attractive woman I've ever been fortunate enough to sleep with. So there's that.

I recall she had a strange kind of grimace on her face when she came.

'What are you thinking?' she asks.

I hold the look. Time, I think, to make this conversation go away. I don't want her pity.

'About the time we had sex,' I say.

Oh. She doesn't say *oh*, but she has a definite *oh* look on her face.

'You broke the unspoken agreement,' she says.

'I did, didn't I?'

'First rule of Fight Club.'

'Exactly. But it's not as though I'll ever tell anyone else, so if I'm going to mention it to anyone…'

'Really?'

I shrug.

'You never told Kadri?'

My turn to do the *oh* face.

'And Eileen?'

'Weirdly never told Eileen.'

'Really?'

'I mean, I can if you want me to, but she might be jealous.'

'Of me sleeping with you? I don't think so.'

'Of me sleeping with you,' I say.

That takes a second, and then she nods. Maybe she actually goes a little red in the face. How wonderfully old-fashioned.

'I should go,' I say, and I turn away and walk back through to the open-plan.

As I sit at my desk and look at the spreadsheet of open case files my heart sinks, and I put my elbows on the table and stare at the computer screen like I'm staring into the pits of Hades. And the only thing that I can think of that would be worse than this godawful, stupid piece of drudgery, is sitting at home all day with absolutely nothing to do.

5

I arrange dinner at eight with Elise. No idea what I'm doing.

Nothing new on the Hunt murder by the end of the day. If it is to come our way, it's got some distance to travel just yet. The media not really talking about the full gruesome horror of the death, in their way, although of course millions of people will have watched the video, and everyone knows what happened.

Whoever this killer is, public opinion is on his side. Every clown likes a vigilante, right up until they get their facts wrong, take vengeance on the wrong person, and leave some poor sod dead in a rat-infested ditch when his only crime had been looking like someone else or being in the wrong place at the wrong time.

At the restaurant. I check my phone, glance around. I was a little early, but it's gone eight and she's not here. I start to wonder if she's thought better of it, or whether she saw me across the restaurant in the harsh light of a summer's evening and thought, dear God, this is going to be like having dinner with grandpa, then turned and legged it.

I already ordered a bottle of wine. Viognier. £27. Third cheapest on the list. Finding it agreeable, I always order viognier these days, regardless of the price. Take a drink, put my elbows on the table, clasp my hands, and rest my chin on the tops of my fingers. Close my eyes. Start to think that it will be best if she doesn't turn up, and then I can eat in solitude. Not really feeling an evening of idle chitchat, while making sure I get drunk enough to not care about how much of a sleazebag I feel sleeping with someone who's literally thirty-six years younger than me.

Ten days left at work. Minus the couple of days at the end that I intend to duck out of. And then days of wine and roses. Where does that dumb phrase come from? Anyway, we can dispense with the roses.

'Hey. Sorry I'm late.'

I look up, elbows off the table.

She sits, smiling at me. Oh my butt naked Jesus, she's young.

She looks a little uncomfortable, possibly because of the look on my face, and then she kind of shrugs. Looks at the wine. I lift the bottle, silently offering, she nods, and I pour the glass.

She's wearing a black dress, low cut, showing a lot of cleavage. Fake eyelashes. Eyebrows augmented by whatever it is they draw above their eyes. Too much foundation plastered on her entire face, after the fashion of the day. Maybe she looked like this last night, but I don't remember.

I want to tell her she's an attractive young woman and doesn't need all that shit on her face, but you're not allowed to judge people anymore, and that would just make me seem even more like her grandad.

We drink, we sit in awkward silence for a while.

'Good day?' I finally say.

Oh my God, who's writing this script? Can we get Aaron Sorkin in here, please?

She laughs, embarrassed for me and my clunkiness.

'Sorry, who cares?' I say.

'It was OK. Walked the dogs.'

She shrugs.

'You walked the dogs?'

'I walk dogs,' she says. 'That's my job.'

'Your job is walking dogs?'

She laughs.

'You're funny. I told you this last night. You really were hammered.' A pause, and then, 'Guess we both were. Which explains this…'

She smiles, and I kind of shrug, and it's probably best that we both recognise just how awful this looks.

Another silence. We hide behind our glasses of wine. Melancholy seeps over me, my old, familiar companion. My eyes drop. I debate, just as I did while lying in bed last night, how best to extricate myself from the situation.

'Are you ready to order?'

Waiter at the table. No artifice about him. No judgement. I mean, the guy's going to have seen more unlikely couples that me and Elise here in his time.

'You order for me,' says Elise. 'I'll eat anything.'

I glance at her, I want to get up and leave, I think she possibly wants to get up and leave, but neither of us wants the embarrassment of doing it live on TV in front of this guy, however little he'll actually care about it.

'Chicken Caesar salad, and the red prawn and courgette risotto, please,' I say.

He doesn't note it down. Hardly needs to, but he's one of those guys who could take an order from a table of eight and remember it.

'Anything else?'

'Can we have the Caesar dressing on the side, please?'

'Certainly, sir.'

He lifts the menus, he nods again, and he's off.

Uncomfortable silence resumes. I stare across the table hoping I don't look as wretched as I feel.

'What's that about?' she asks.

'What?'

'Caesar dressing on the side?'

'Sometimes the entire thing is clarted in too much gunk and it ruins it. Better to have control of the sauce.'

'Smarts,' she says.

Common sense rather than smarts.

'Speak to me.'

Oh God, we're doing that, are we? I kind of shrug.

'I liked you last night,' she says. 'I mean, look, we had stupid, drunk sex. It happens. But I mean I liked you afterwards. Usually I get boys, I don't know, they're just shallow, young, immature. They're practically asking to marry me when it's all over. But you didn't give a fuck. I liked that. So, talk to me. Say exactly what you're thinking, sitting there looking miserable, I don't mind.'

'You're far too young for me, and I feel like a sleazebag. I'm also a drunken piece of shit, and you likely deserve better than me. And the fact that you slept with me, coupled with your three guys outside of Milan story, suggests you put yourself around a bit, and maybe you shouldn't do that. Have a bit more respect for yourself.'

'How many women have you slept with in your life?'

'Lost count.'

'Hundreds?'

'Including ones I've paid for?'

'Well, yes, they exist as women, don't they?'

'Yes, hundreds.'

'And that's all right for you? A man. But I shouldn't be

doing it?'

'Does it look like I think it's all right? Do I look like it makes me happy?' A pause, she doesn't answer. 'I hate myself. Don't hate yourself, Elise, you're better than that.'

'Maybe I'm not. And maybe I don't hate myself, maybe I just enjoy it.'

I shrug. Take a drink.

'What else?' she asks.

'You don't need to dress like that, you don't need to put all that shit on your face.'

'I did last night,' she says, and she's laughing.

'I was too drunk to notice.'

She leans forward, relaxing. One elbow on the table, rests her chin in her hand. She smiles.

'I like the honest you,' she says. 'What is it you do?'

'I didn't tell you?'

'Nope.'

'Police officer.'

She embraces me with her eyes, as though this has actually impressed her. Sports fans, no one is ever actually impressed by the police as a profession.

'I'll be back in a minute,' she says, and then she lifts her bag and heads off in the direction of the bathrooms. Which I might add are in the opposite direction to the front door, so fairly confident she's not doing a runner. Not that that would be a bad outcome in itself.

I watch her go. I catch the eye of a judgemental old bastard across the restaurant and she looks quickly away.

I drink wine.

6

I get home a little after ten-thirty. As I open the front door I get the sense of someone else being here. Someone waiting for me.

Stop for a moment, halfway through the door. Listen for any sound. A moment of heightened tension, muscles strained, heart-rate starting to pick up. I think of the video we watched this afternoon, I think of the dumbass vigilante, the man who would take matters into his own hands. A slit-open stomach, the horror of being eaten alive by rats. There would be plenty of would-be vigilantes out there who'd think me worthy of such a fate.

From nowhere I recognise the faint scent in the air, and instantly relax. The moment passes. I close the door, light summer coat off and hung on the wall by the door, then walk into the sitting room.

Eileen stares back at me from the couch, looking like she just woke up. There's a half-glass of wine on the table.

'Hey,' I say.

'Hi.'

She sits forward, squeezes her eyes closed, tenses, stretches, trying to wake up.

'How long've you been asleep?'

'I don't know. What time is it?'

'Ten-thirty-five or thereabouts.'

'Shit. Sorry. At least an hour and a half.'

'You'll need this refreshed,' I say, lifting the glass.

I return a minute later, wine and water, lay the four glasses on the low table, and slump down into the armchair next to the sofa.

She's wearing the same clothes she was wearing in work. Guess she hasn't been home.

'Sorry, you hungry?'

'I might be at some point. Not at the moment. You were out for dinner?'

I take a drink of wine, lay the glass back on the table.

'On a date with Elise.'

'Who's Elise?'

I answer with a sheepish look, and she looks perturbed and concerned, and says, 'Really, Tom?'

'It just kind of happened, but we're cool.'

'You left her at home with the babysitter?'

'Everything's fine. She's my new twenty-two-year-old mate. You'd like her.'

'I want to say I don't want to know, but I kind of do.'

'Well, dinner shaped up to be pretty awkward, as you can imagine. Being drunk and falling in to bed can pretty much happen with anyone. But the cold light of day, with no inebriation? That's a wake-up call.'

'Which one of you woke up first?'

'I think it was mutual. Anyway, it allowed me to be honest, and I told her she was wearing too much shit on her face, and I guess I indicated, without actually saying it, that she didn't need to be showing the world that much of her chest, and then she retreated to the bathrooms and returned wearing no make-up, and a jumper, then we chatted, and we had a bit of a laugh, to be honest. It was nice. She enjoyed hearing my stories of law enforcement derring-do, and I enjoyed hearing her explanation of some of the genders no one knew existed until last Wednesday.'

'Sounds heart-warming. What does she do? O levels?'

'She walks dogs for rich people.'

'Gets you out in the fresh air.'

'That's what she said. Plenty of exercise, and since she only works for rich people, she charges twenty-five pounds an hour. And then she's happy walking like four different dogs at once, so she could be making a hundred pounds while she's taking those dogs for a one-hour walk. Averages two grand a week.'

'Oh my god. How many rich people are there?'

'As we know, a lot more of them now that so many people are poor. And by the way, why are you here? Don't get me wrong, you could move in and I'd be happy, but it seems odd, that's all. And how is it you're inside the house and not, I don't know, standing outside on the street pressing the buzzer?'

'Reasonable,' she says. 'I broke in with a lockpick, so that's fairly straightforward.'

'Nice. Is this the first time?'

'Nope, but the other twice… Doesn't matter.'

'Oh, you know, I think it does. It's my house, after all.'

'One time you didn't come home, and the other time you came home, but you were drunk and didn't notice I was here.'

'You were sitting there, and I came in and went straight to bed?'

'No. I was sitting on the armchair, and you came in here, stepped over my legs and fell asleep on the couch.'

'Well, that's embarrassing. When was that?'

'It was a while ago.'

'You weren't naked?'

'Really?'

'I mean, if that was the time you'd decided to finally give in to my charms, and I was too drunk to notice, I'm really going to kick myself.'

'You can be such an asshole sometimes, Tom.'

'Just saying.'

'Maybe I needed a friend, and you were too drunk to be one.'

Brutal, and bang on the money.

Hello darkness, my old friend…

She makes a small *don't worry about it* gesture, and we wave the moment away. Insomuch as one can wave away the darkness.

I drink wine.

'All I can be is here now, not drunk,' I say, and I ask the question with raised eyebrows.

'I worked late. Like, until just before eight. An e-mail came in. Apparently that round of voluntary redundancies that you pounced upon in a moment of weakness, they didn't get enough people.'

'Ah. They're doing another round and you're thinking of going for it. That'd be great. You can join me. We can walk across Canada together, or something. Or, you know, we could sit in an expensive Canadian hotel room, drinking wine, looking at some mountains. What?'

'Compulsory redundancy. I'm done. Two months' notice, though I can leave at the end of this month if I choose.'

'Shit.'

'Yeah. In fact, given the amount of leave I have, I worked out I can leave before you.'

'What are they thinking?'

'They're thinking I'm old, Tom.'

'You're not old!'

'I'm fifty-three.'

'That's not old! How are you feeling, anyway?'

'Hollowed out.'

'Shit.'

We share a look. I kind of want to give her a hug, but that would only really be comfortable if we were standing up. Jumping on the couch and wrapping my arms around her is unlikely to play out to anyone's advantage.

'If it was anyone else I'd be celebrating, but I know you actually like this dumb job.'

'Yes.'

'Crap. I'm sorry. Hey, at least you'll be able to come to Canada. We can stay in that big-ass hotel in Banff that you see on travel shows.'

'Where did this come from? This is literally the first time you mentioned going to Canada.'

I don't have an answer to that. I smile, she smiles with me.

From nowhere melancholy joins us. We've been at the same station, together, for almost seventeen years now. Our relationship has made its slow passage from being people who just happened to work in the same building, to close friends, with a few hiccups along the way. In fact, there've been quite a lot of hiccups in recent times.

I get up, deciding to make the journey over there.

'Nudge up,' I say, and she shuffles along a little, then I sit down beside her and take her hand. A quick glance, and then we settle back on the sofa and she kind of lays her head on my shoulder.

'It's not like the two of us are dying or anything,' I say. 'We just won't have this shitty job.'

'I have no idea what I'm going to do,' she says, refusing to accept my weak attempts at being upbeat.

'You can join the Women's Institute and the Women's Guild,' I say, and she laughs and sticks her nails into the palm of my hand.

'Bugger off.'

'Visit National Trust properties?'

'If you don't stop talking, I'm going to have to kill you.'

I squeeze her hand.

Silence comes, like lightly falling snow.

Multitudes 2

'Why are you here?'

Leanne Foster, dumped on the floor, chained at the wrists and feet, stared grimly back at her captor through the half-light of the room.

'I don't know.'

'Why are you here?'

'Oh, please. Why don't you fuck off?'

'Why are you here?'

'Really? Just get to fuck, and when you arrive, fuck off some more. You're not frightening anyone with this shit. When I get out of here, you're dead meat, bucko. I guess it was you who sent that stupid warning note. *Tick-tock*. Jesus.'

Different room, same set up. There was a phone recording everything, her captor was wearing the same mask he'd worn when he'd extracted the confession from Fergus Hunt.

'Everyone seems so angry these days,' he said. 'What happened to fear? What happened to respect for the kidnapper?'

'You want respect? Undo the chains and I'll show you plenty of respect.'

'Disappointing.'

'Fuck off.'

'This is how this is going to go.'

'You're such a prick…'

'This is how this is going to go,' he repeated, ignoring Foster talking over him. 'You're going to say to the camera what you should have said in court. This video will be released.' She continued to curse as he spoke, but not so much that she wasn't now listening. 'It will do nothing in the court of public opinion. Everyone knows you should have been found guilty. No one outside of that jury was convinced by your claims of mental health issues. And making the confession will do nothing for your long-term prospects in life, because you are not getting out of this place alive. You will likely die in the next half hour….'

'Then why am I confessing?' she screamed.

'Because if you don't, you will die painfully. Brutally. If you do your daughter one final good deed… in fact, if you do right by your daughter for the first time *in your life*, you will let the world know what you did. You will let the world know that I am right to have killed you, and I will do so quickly. I have a knife in that small bag there, and I will use it to slit your throat, and death will be more or less instantaneous. A failure to confess, or should you attempt to confess but lie while you're doing it, then death will be very, very unpleasant.'

'Ha! Fuck you.'

He wondered if it was hubris, or a determination to cling to life. It didn't matter that that extended period of life was going to be awful. Hunt, certainly, had pleaded with him to kill him once the rats had started eating his stomach. But before the awfulness has started, the human brain perhaps could not fully imagine the horror. One could visualise it, but until it's begun, one has no idea of the sensation of rats crawling over the stomach, tugging and chewing and biting at your internal organs, licking the blood off the skin, chewing pieces of flesh, chewing the genitals. That's when you scream for it to be over. When it's too late.

'We will not talk about this all evening, Mrs Foster,' said the man. 'I will give you one last piece of advice…'

'Fuck you.'

'You are going to die. You may want to cling on to life as long as possible, but when the brutal death begins, you will wish I had slit your throat. You will beg for me to slit your throat. And I will not slit your throat.'

'And I will give *you* one last piece of advice,' said Foster. 'Fuck off.'

7

We stop at the front desk on the way into the station. Eileen nods at Sergeant Ramsey, gives me a small wave and walks on.

'Stuart,' I say.

'Detective.'

Ramsey has been here longer than either Eileen or me. The three of us are old guard. No one else at the station has been here longer than fifteen minutes. Accordingly, Ramsey doesn't have any friends at the station. He and I always rubbed along OK, but we never got beyond that. It's been the same with him and Eileen.

'You all right?' I ask.

'Just tickety-boo,' he says, grimly, then he leans forward, elbows on the counter with a curious, amused look about him. 'That might be the first time in ten thousand years you've asked me that question. What's got into you?'

'Eileen got a redundancy notice last night,' I say. 'Thought I'd check up on you.'

She already cleared me speaking to him about it. Seems Eileen is seriously considering talking to Hawkins today, and then just walking out. I counselled otherwise. I suspect Hawkins will too. Either way, she sees no point in keeping it a secret.

Ramsey nods, rueful and defeated.

'Well, that's stupid.'

'You got one?'

'Aye. Wasn't surprised. To be honest I've been expecting it since I refused to refer to that rapist wanker Murray as a woman, and he sued us.'

'This sounds like a general clear out of the old guard, rather than something ideology-related.'

'I suppose. But what are they getting rid of Eileen for?' He shakes his head. 'I mean, I just stand here and speak to people, and organise shit, and do whatever. They can replace me with a robot. Probably already have in Japan. But Eileen is exactly, *exactly* what you want in a sergeant. Who're they getting instead? Some twenty-two-year-old dumbfuck who's done all the courses, and knows when a cat stuck up a tree actually just identifies as a pigeon?'

Ramsey has an axe to grind.

'How long have you got?' I ask.

'I could go today, if I wanted to take all my leave starting now. I'll see. But you know me, I may hate the police with every fibre of my being, but I won't let them down, I won't let the chief down, until I know she's got my replacement in hand. If it's tomorrow, then I'm gone. If it's two months, I'll wait. Either way, got a cruise booked in the Med for September, and that'll be the new start.'

'Nice,' I say, although I actually think going on a cruise ship in the Med would be worse than having your scrotum licked by Cocaine Bear.

Where in the name of Elrond did that come from?

We stand for a minute, but this is us, Ramsey and me. Bar the basics, we don't really have anything to say to each other. We share a nod, and then I turn away and head through to the open-plan.

8

What a dull end to a career.

Feeling maudlin. Staring at a screen, the initial efficiency of the morning long since having vanished. Have done nothing useful in upwards of four hours, bar have lunch with Eileen at the café in the precinct. Water and club sandwiches. She doesn't let me drink Coke Zero anymore. I mean, obviously she doesn't exert that level of control, but she's persuaded me otherwise. Wine would be nice, and it's not like I've never drunk wine at lunchtime when I'm working, but I think I can hold off that particular habit for another two weeks.

Lunch, nevertheless, was no fun. We wallowed. We were talking about old cases, people we knew, all that kind of thing, and it could have been fun. Should have been fun. But, like I say, it was maudlin, and by the end we were languishing in self-pity.

'Lousy job of cheering each other up,' she said, as we walked back to the station.

'This is why we need to book the fortnight in the Rockies,' I said. 'Give us something to look forward to.'

'OK,' she said. 'Bring me a costed proposal and we'll have a discussion.'

Nevertheless, she was rolling her eyes as she said it.

*

Two-forty-one, Hawkins emerges from her office. Seemingly attuned even more to her movements than they were yesterday, the two active detectives turn towards her, as if they instinctively know she's not about to head to the bathroom or grab a frappalappaccino. Hawkins nods, the invitation to her office contained in the spare movement.

She catches my eye. I don't care. I want her to give me a small head shake. The *don't worry about it. You're one day closer to walking out the door, so let's just leave it at that.*

She gestures for me to join them.

We stand in the same position as yesterday, looking at the same screen. Hawkins pauses, fingers poised on the mouse.

'This is a much shorter video. Different, if equally horrific. If you need to look away, no one's judging you.'

The video clicks on. There is a woman attached to the walls and floor, in exactly the same position as Fergus Hunt. The lighting feels a little different, but otherwise it could be in the same place. Except, it's obviously not.

The scene is fleeting. She leans forward, head stretched, face with the wrath of Al Pacino acting the shit out of a shouting scene. 'Fuck you! Fucking fuck you, you fuck!' Freeze frame. Nice directorial touch. The woman's face howling with rage and hate, contorted and vicious.

The freeze frame fades, to be replaced by the same woman towards the end of her life, in the act of being killed in the same manner as Fergus Hunt. Her viscera have been brought out of her body, but this time there are no rats. This time there are flies. She is howling, crying, screaming, wailing. It's a horrible sound, cut off by her mouth and throat filling with insects.

The flies are everywhere, a squirming, bloody, fevered mass. Tens of thousands of them.

The scene ends. Fades to black. When it fades back in there are fewer flies, but they are not completely absent. Again her forehead has been stamped with a branding iron, this time with the letter L.

The screen goes blank. The video ends.

Hawkins closes the screen, takes a moment, and then turns to look into the eyes of her detectives. Who's got the stomach for that?

'We must presume that Mrs Foster refused to confess,' says the detective sergeant in the room, who's far more switched on than I am.

'I think we can,' says Hawkins.

'I don't know this woman,' I say, happy to accept my place in the narrative as the guy who needs things explained to him for the benefit of the viewer. Like whatshisname in *Yes, Minister*. Bernard. Him. Senior civil servant, but every week he had to pretend to be an idiot so Humphrey could explain shit to him for the benefit of the audience.

Of course, I don't actually have to pretend to be an idiot. Occasionally cases that aren't mine worm their way into my consciousness, but far more often than not they pass me by, and I know nothing.

'Single mum. She was charged with killing her three-year-old daughter. Pretty brutal treatment over a sustained period. Her lawyer constructed a perfect defence, of doubt and hearsay, coupled with majoring on her mental health issues, putting the blame on pretty much every single other person in Scotland. Just not her. Just not the woman who actually systematically, slowly, brutally, killed her kid.' Hawkins pauses, but no one else picks up the baton, so she keeps talking. 'I don't know if the investigative team will've been compiling a list of potential vigilante victims after yesterday, after just one death, but if they have been doing it, she'll've been on it.'

'If they didn't compile such a list yesterday, then they will now,' says Dale.

'Jesus,' says Ritter, as though she's finally found her tongue after watching the video, and the single word isn't part of the conversation the rest of us are having.

'This is online?' I ask, and when Hawkins nods, I add, 'We've been pointed in its direction?' indicating the screen, meaning the location of the corpse, rather than the killer letting us know where we can download the video.

'Ten minutes away,' she says, 'but just the other side of the motorway, so not actually our patch. We haven't been officially called in yet, but can't imagine it'll be long before it happens.'

'Similar set-up to yesterday?'

'Not a basement this time. An old, abandoned house, but right next to the motorway. Not far from the landfill site. The victim could scream all she wanted, but she was bang smack, pretty much on top of the M74, so you know, no one's hearing anything.'

'And what about the sign at the end?' asks Dale. 'The L. Anyone got any ideas about that?'

'This hasn't been in long,' says Hawkins. 'They won't have had the time to analyse it yet. Not that they had anything after yesterday, but it's odd, either way. Does it point to this being the act of someone else, does it point to someone just playing a game? Are the letters supposed to mean *something*? Are they supposed to be some sort of idiotic superhero thing?'

'It's not like Batman isn't a vigilante,' I say.

'Slightly different methodology,' Dale feels the need to add.

'Hopefully,' says Hawkins, 'though I'm not that hopeful to be honest, but hopefully whoever's running the whole investigative shooting match has a much better idea of what's going on than is currently being communicated. My feeling is, however, that this is coming our way. If not today, then tomorrow, or whenever the next one of these abominations shows up. Just, you know, stay on top of this so that if we are called up, we're ready to hit the ground running.'

'Ma'am,' say Dale and Ritter in unison.

Hawkins and I share a look.

'What are you thinking, Tom?'

'Mind a blank as always,' I say.

'If they come calling, then I have to let them know that I have three active detectives on the books. If you don't want to get involved... well, no one will blame you if you want to take that leave you're owed.'

I hold the look, I can feel Dale and Ritter watching me. I glance at the screen, which has been returned to its natural state of a serene mountain photograph.

'I'm here for now,' I say. 'Let's see what happens.'

'Very well.'

She gives it a moment, ponders if there's anything else to say, and then indicates the door.

9

Two hours later and Detective Sergeant Dale has gone already. Called to the centre to be part of the investigation. The media have collectively decided that there's more than one killer involved, that we're dealing with a team of would-be superhero vigilantes – like Batman crossed with the Blood Countess – and that they should be known as the Rough Justice League. Speculation is rife about how many of them there might be, and who could be next in line. Speculation rife about what the initials could stand for. No one has any actual idea, and so it has become just another game, just another hashtag, for social media.

Given that the potential victims are all criminals, or at least are people assumed to have been criminals, there's not a lot of sympathy going for anyone. The term *this could get ugly* is flying around, albeit that is manifestly ignoring that this is already very, very ugly.

Sometime after Dale has left, I'm approached at my desk by Chief Hawkins.

'Amanda's been summoned, then?'

'Yes, she has,' says Hawkins. 'Take a wild stab at who's heading up the investigation?'

That doesn't require much thinking.

'Eurydice, is it?'

DCI Eurydice Hamilton. We have history. Not, as is so often the case, a history that involves sex, but in this instance a history that involves her kicking me off a case.

More than one case, actually, if I can reverse quote *Hot Fuzz*.

'Yes, it is,' says Hawkins. 'So, given what went before, I feel you won't be needed.'

'I don't know, boss,' I say, 'you can't fault my record.'

'Methods are terrible but you always get your man?'

'Exactly.'

'Not sure that's how DCI Eurydice will see it, but I'll let

you know if you get an invite.'

Silence returns. She stands there for a moment, she glances over her shoulder at DC Ritter, she turns back.

'Like I said earlier, if you wanted to get out right now, I wouldn't blame you, and neither will I stand in your way. However, should you want to hang around, then I wouldn't mind if you filled in for Amanda while she's out the office. And, you know, don't worry, if this thing isn't wrapped up, I won't be asking for you to stay on beyond the date you're due to be done. Actually, I wouldn't be allowed to, so it hardly matters whether I'd want it or not.'

'Sure,' I say, really just to stop her talking.

'You're sure?'

'Happy to help out.'

'Thank you. You can speak to Emma, she can sort you out with where we are.'

I nod, Hawkins thinks about saying something else, then she starts to turn away.

'Boss,' I say, and then I lower my voice as she turns back, though I don't glance across the office. 'You know Eileen and Stuart got their jotters last night?'

Hawkins doesn't look over in Eileen's direction either.

'Terrible decision. I did what I could, but there's this blanket thing going on. These people...'

'You've spoken to Eileen?'

'Of course. She seemed OK.'

'She's not.'

Hawkins holds my gaze, her eyes lower for a moment, she nods.

'OK, thank you, Tom.'

She looks to the side, she thinks it through, but she has nothing else to say, and then she turns away and returns to her office.

10

There's a street halfway up the hill above Main Street. One of those long roads with large Victorian houses built most of the way along, until it gets towards Burnside, and there the homes are small and newer and the feel of the old town is lost. The kind of road you drive along in any town anywhere without thinking about just how arboreal it is. Magnificent old oaks and fir trees, beach and birch, and that great import, the monkey puzzle.

There was a friend of mine who had one in his front garden when we were kids. His dad had planted it, and I can remember being taller than that monkey puzzle tree. Takes me back there every time I drive past it now. I mean, that tree is now absolutely gigantic, dwarfing the house my mate used to live in.

Like every single one of my childhood friends, I have absolutely no idea what happened to that guy. Lost touch during the high school years when I stopped going over to his house. Last I heard, he'd married someone in the Foreign Office and was travelling the earth going to cocktail parties, while writing shitty crime novels to pay for his breakfast gin & tonic habit.

Not that I'm a stranger to an alcoholic breakfast. And the thought of going to a government cocktail party makes me want to literally eat my own face.

Swing the car into a wide driveway, park on the slight slope, and then get out and take a look around. Large, detached house, on the south side of the road, so the upstairs rooms are looking down over the town, out across to Parkhead and the hills in the distance. One of the views of my youth. Not that I can see it from the driveway.

I ring the bell, stand back from the door.

I sat in Dale's chair, which had been my chair up until no time at all ago, and said to Ritter that she had the con. I'd do whatever she needed me to. She was completely matter-of-fact about it, because of course she was.

She asked me to take this missing persons case.

Sigh…

I mean, I know, I know how it is, sometimes the missing persons case turns out to be a rip-roarer, with mystery, covert ops, car chases, and explosions, but more often than not they are what they are. Someone left home. They didn't come back for… reasons. That's all. Because they didn't need to. Because they didn't want to. Because they thought of something better to do.

Until there's obviously criminal elements at play, we highly paid, highly qualified detectives wouldn't usually get anywhere near them. This missing person, though, works for Glasgow Council. Personally, I still think we shouldn't touch it with a stick, but it's another case where words have been passed from one person who knows someone to someone else who knows someone else, and it all comes down to this. Me, a detective sergeant, standing on a doorstep in uptown Cambuslang, waiting to speak to the wife of Menzies Warburton.

Door opens. A woman in her mid-twenties, with a greetin' bairn in her arms.

'Detective Sergeant Hutton,' I say, holding out my ID.

'Right, come in.'

She doesn't pay any attention to the card, and turns away with the kid, shouts, 'Sit in the front room,' over her shoulder, and then heads up the stairs.

I watch her go, then turn into the front sitting room.

A room like any other. A sofa, an armchair, a coffee table, a rug, a fireplace with a fake gas fire, a large flatscreen on a low unit, on the wall richly-coloured paintings of Venice and Florence and generic Italian seaside villages.

At the window another armchair, a table beside it, sort of a view out of the window, but largely you're looking at the house across the road. Perhaps we're in a watching someone in their bedroom situation. We get all sorts, of course, because every police force on earth gets all sorts. Humans are just so incredibly fucked up, in all kinds of ways.

When she comes back I'm looking at the painting of Florence. I don't know why I'm so sure it's Florence, because I don't know anything about Florence, but I must, somewhere in the depths of my brain, know it. Maybe Eileen and I could go there instead of Canada.

Ha, look at me. Assuming that Eileen and I will go off somewhere, when she may well have absolutely no interest in that. Why would she, just because we've done it once before?

It's not so long ago she wasn't speaking to me at all, although at least we managed to get over that, even if it was by pretty much ignoring the elephant in the room.

Really, that was because the elephant isn't in the room anymore. The elephant is back in Estonia.

'You ever been?'

She's standing behind me, arms folded. From above, the distant cry of the banshee.

'Never been to Italy,' I say.

'I love it. Too hot this time of year, of course.'

'Really?'

'God, yes. I wouldn't dream of it until at least September, and even that's potentially too early. Trouble is, Menzies hates it, and since Lizzie came along,' and she finishes the sentence with a rather hopeless shrug.

'You wouldn't leave her with your husband and go yourself?'

She laughs, a laugh knowing and rueful, then turns away and slumps down into a seat.

'Oh, sorry, I never offered you a cup of tea.'

'That's OK.'

I sit down opposite her, making a small head movement to indicate upstairs.

'Your daughter's all right?'

'Yes. Welcome to my life. She'll fall asleep in a while.'

'She cries all the time?'

'Literally. Doctor can't find anything wrong with her. Seen specialists. No one knows. There was one bastard looking at me like it was my fault, and I wondered, you know, I thought, if I push this, where is this going to go?' A pause, she remembers who she's talking to.

'We're not here to talk about your daughter,' I say. 'Tell me about Menzies. So far, I have absolutely nothing other than his name and address, so everything you've got, please.'

She talks for five minutes. I get the details. He's twenty-seven. First from Glasgow in town planning. Has been working at the council for six years. Unusually senior for his position. Plays golf up at Kirkhill, supports Cambuslang Rangers. (Found myself prosaically saying, *ah, he's the one*, and shut up thereafter.) He works until six every day, he comes home, they have dinner together, then he often works for another two or three hours in his office in the converted attic. He has a tendency to get angry when the kid won't stop crying. The wife does Pilates on a Sunday morning which is the only time Menzies has alone with the kid.

This woman's life sounds hellish.

'What did you do before you got married?' I ask, and she looks surprised. She has to think about it. She's so exhausted, she can't imagine a time before the child was born, and that's less than a year ago.

I won't miss this. Real life.

'Drank too much,' she says.

'You went to uni, you worked?'

'Is this relevant?'

'Probably not. Tell me the last time you saw or heard from Menzies.'

She leans forward, elbows resting on her knees. Pauses for a second at the silence from above, but it proves to be only momentary, and then the crying resumes.

'She does that every now and again. Lures you in, just so she can spit you back out again.'

She shakes her head, waves an apology. I give her the space. She'll get there eventually.

'Right, Menzies. Didn't come home last night. That's kind of weird. I mean, it's not like he *always* comes home or anything, but if he doesn't, he'd say.'

'What was your last contact with him?'

'Mine was when he left for work yesterday morning.'

'You don't text each other during the day?'

'Not usually. Was just expecting him home around six-thirty. Didn't happen.' She pauses, she stares curiously at the carpet. 'I guess I realised then how little I know about his work and who he works with. I mean, I know names and whatever, but I had no one to call. I called the council offices, but no one picked up, of course. I called his mobile, I called his work number. His mobile was unavailable, and no one answered at work.

'I went the entire night not knowing where he was. Kept expecting him to walk in, then suddenly I was waking up with Lizzie crying and it was quarter to six.' She snaps her fingers. 'I have no idea how that happened. I tried his mobile again, and still nothing. Left it until eight, called the office. He wasn't there. Actually, virtually no one was there. Called again at eight-thirty, and nine. Spoke to one of his colleagues who said he'd left at just after six yesterday, same as every other night.'

'When was the last time you spoke to his office?'

'Three this afternoon, maybe.'

'How are things at home?'

She wasn't expecting that question, and it takes her by surprise, and she presents something of the rabbit in the headlights look.

'How d'you mean?'

'Is he happy? Are you happy? Doesn't sound like you have much of a family life.'

She blurts out a strange sound, half laugh, half sob.

'Terrible,' she says. 'He hates it. I hate it. Jesus…' followed by another waved apology. 'Sorry, that's unnecessary.'

'Is it possible he's saved up a bit of money, and just left? Either for good, or just to go and have a holiday on his own?'

She swallows. She seems to be thinking about this for the first time.

'Well, yes,' she says eventually, 'but I don't think that's it.'

'Why?'

'He'd tell me. He had a long weekend in Amsterdam with some university pals last year. I was eight months pregnant. He didn't give a shit. Didn't ask if it was all right. Just went. And maybe just leaving for good would suit him, but it's inconceivable. This is his place. He'd ask me to leave. Well, he wouldn't ask. Me and Lizzie would be out the door.'

'You don't sound very happy with your husband.'

She stares at me deadpan. Another silence from above, and when the crying restarts it's with a little less force. The bairn must be getting tired. Maybe it's lying there thinking, why in God's name am I doing this? I'm even irritating myself.

'I couldn't muster the strength, if you're accusing me of anything. We're miserable. We haven't had sex since the night Lizzie was conceived, and even that was an aberration. But if you think I'm going to mess up my life even more for that man, you're wrong. He wouldn't be worth killing.'

*

Up the stairs to the loft. These are quality loft steps. Solid. The room looks neat and orderly. Polished wooden floor, a blue, Moroccan-style rug. Windows on both sides of the roof, with another at the gable end at the back, so the place is really bright.

All the windows have blinds.

There are two traditional filing cabinets, and a large desk with an iMac. The walls are plastered over, painted off-white, adding to the brightness of the space. There's no art. Between the filing cabinets there's a tailor's dummy, a red feather boa draped around it.

I look at the boa, I look at Mrs Warburton. At last, the house is silent. If it was me, I'd probably be worried the kid hadn't choked itself to death, but she seems quite sanguine, obviously more used to the routines of her bairn.

'Why?' I ask.

'There was some story from university. It was like some running gag between him and Charlie and Ben. I think they'd each worn one to some Pride march back in the day, and he kept it slung over there. He said it reminded him of *less vexatious times*.' The eye roll is in the tone.

'When was the last time you were up here?'

'Oh, I don't come up here.'

'Ever?'

'I came up when it had been completed. I mean, seeing it now, two years later, it looks exactly the same as it did back then. Nothing out of place, nothing dumped anywhere, everything in exactly the same position as it was the last time I saw it.'

'Including the feather boa?'

She smiles and nods, amused at my interest in the dumb scarf.

'You mind?' I say, indicating the filing cabinets.

'Go ahead. I presume they're locked.'

I try them, and they are. I go to the desk, and try the drawers. Also locked.

Just getting one of those strong uneasy feelings that you get in life. Along with it, a sinking feeling. This place, in all its order, feels sinister. There's something just not right with this guy.

'You mind if I try to force the locks?' I say.

I think of Eileen and her lock pick. I never did the lock pick course. I'm old school. Kick down a door, or jemmy a lock with a screwdriver.

She looks around the room, looking a little perturbed now. This is escalating.

'What are you going to force the locks with? Your mind?'

'Maybe you could get me a screwdriver or something? I don't know, anything I can stick in the gap and try to force a drawer with. Something that won't buckle.'

She's hesitant. She may think her husband is a bit of an arse, but this is raising the stakes. And he ain't going to be happy when he comes home.

If he comes home.

'I will one hundred per cent take the fall,' I say. 'If he's annoyed about it, we can say I did it when you were downstairs with Lizzie, and you didn't know it was happening.'

She looks uncertain, but then finally nods.

'OK, OK, I think I've got something. I'll, eh, I'll be back in a minute.'

She turns away, and walks down the stairs. I watch her go, and then I go back to the desk and turn on the Mac.

11

'So, you've got something going on?'

Have come into Hawkins' office, having already activated the search of the Warburton house. DC Ritter is out on other business. I called her, told her what I was doing. The relationship is a little odd, given that I was her boss three weeks ago and still outrank her, but I'm happy to defer to her, and she's happy to accept that I'm just some guy doing a thing.

'I walked into a beauty, I'm afraid.'

'Didn't take you long to get involved,' she says, and she sort of smiles.

'I'm cursed.'

'You certainly are. What have you got?'

'Missing person, up on Whiteside Road.'

'Warburton, the town planner? I saw you'd taken that.'

'Mum and young kid, kind of a stressy house. He has an attic office. She shows me up there. Weirdly well-ordered.'

'Always a sign of something,' she says.

I can't help looking around her office, the most neatly-ordered office in the whole of Police Scotland I'd wager. She doesn't follow my look, knowing well enough how high-spectrum tidy her office is.

'You were saying?' she says, an amusement about her. Jesus, she is so well disposed to me now that I'm on my way out.

'I ask her to get me a tool I can use to prise open the cabinets. She goes to get a screwdriver. I turn on the computer. Never going to be able to get in, but I can switch the thing on. The home screen is five guys in bondage. Like, you know, gimp gear. The wife returns, she stares at the computer. She is genuinely shocked.

'We've all seen fake shock, and this isn't fake anything. I've spent ten minutes with this woman already, and she is laid bare by the stress of motherhood. And that was the moment she realised her husband wasn't up there working every night.'

'Oh dear.'

'This goes way beyond *oh dear*. The bondage gear was in the first of the cabinets. Like, rammed full of it. Four drawers of rubber and plastic and chains and butt plugs and sex toys.'

'Not illegal, of course.' She's seeing the look on my face. 'What was in the other cabinet?'

'A lot of very nasty child pornography.'

'Jesus.'

She leans forward, elbow on the desk, hand over her mouth.

'You didn't show it to his wife?'

'I showed her one picture. She threw up on the floor. That was a bit of an event in itself, I have to say.'

'OK, we need to –'

'There's more.'

She takes a deep breath, indicates for me to continue.

'This was also his business cabinet. Two of the drawers were full of envelopes of various types and sizes. There were multiple copies of hundreds of photographs.'

'He runs old-school, mail order child pornography?'

'Yes.'

She sits back now, looking across the desk. I wonder if she's thinking the same thing that I'm thinking, but then she speaks, and it turns out she hasn't got there yet. She's just regularly sickened to her stomach by this guy.

'Where's his wife?'

'She packed her bag, and had already left to go to her sister's by the time I left the house.'

'How d'you know she hasn't done a runner? She kills her husband, she lets you find the stuff in the attic, maybe it was her business, or something they did together, she lets him take the blame for the porn.' She pauses, and then, 'We never see her again.'

'Even if there hadn't been pictures of him and small children, I would have made the judgement I made,' I say, and she visibly pales a little at that image. We're all hard as nails in the police, even the likes of the staggeringly attractive, never chased a drug-addled badger of a bastard down a street to have a knife fight, deskbound chief inspectors like Hawkins. Yet there's still something gut-wrenchingly sickening about child porn.

I sigh, and say the thing that I usually manage to avoid saying.

'I've been doing this shit for close on thirty years now. Even so, I think I'd've known this was nothing to do with her if I'd come across this in 1995.'

'OK.' She nods.

'I've spoken to her sister. The wife is there already. It's only just up the road, this side of East Kilbride. The sister was in a state of confusion, as Mrs Warburton is yet to explain the reason she and her screaming child have turned up at the house. I didn't enlighten the sister. I'll go round there later, maybe tomorrow morning, and speak to them both.'

'Where are we now?'

'The SOCO's are already at the house. Just a couple of them.'

'You left them the vomit?' she asks.

'I offered to clean it up before they got there, and they said to leave it, which is understandable. It's all evidence. They're used to worse, I guess. And Constable Cairns is round there in case Mr Warburton suddenly arrives home. We'll need the tech guys to get into the computer, and if they can... well, given what this guy was at the centre of, there is potentially an entire shitshow of information on there.'

'Oh, yes, there will be.'

She stares off into space for a moment, and then gives herself a metaphorical shake.

'Well, Tom, one last brutal hurrah for you. More engaging than paperwork, at least.'

I nod. Time to get down to that random thought I've had. I wonder if it might be a stretch, but damn it, it feels right. Things sometimes just fall into place, and for all the fact that I'm this wasted, useless, drunken shitburger of a cop, I've always been the kind for whom things happened. They just do.

'You're thinking something else?' she says.

'Yes. This thing that's going on, this guy, or these people, whoever they are.' I indicate her computer, as that is the means by which we've watched the all-new episodes of the Rough Justice League.

'It's very clearly known accused criminals that have been targeted,' says Hawkins.

'So far. And there have only been two of them. Our guy here, Warburton, is presumably anonymously online dealing. But it could be our killers have bought into his enterprise in some way, they've managed to locate him, and they've taken him out the game to enact justice. I mean, he is one hundred per cent the type of person they're going to go after. The only difference here is that he hasn't previously been charged with it and managed to escape justice. This would be the vigilantes cutting out the middle stage. It's not like our guys have a large body of work to consider, so that we can view this as a deviation.'

She's nodding by the time I've finished.

'You make a good case, Tom. Continue to do what you're doing for the moment. I'll call DCI Hamilton and see if there's anything she wants to do about it. One must presume they're already looking at all missing persons across the city in any case, and this is certainly the type of thing they'll need flagged up. I'll call it in now, but please, write up the report, give me as much to go on as possible.'

'Boss,' I say, turning away.

12

'Back on active detective duty?' says Eileen, summer coat on, heading for the door.

'Yep.'

'Uh-oh.'

'Right?'

'One last case. Too old for this shit,' she says. 'Odds no better than fifty-fifty you make it out alive?'

'That's about the size of it. On the other hand, when you're a functioning alcoholic, every day is pretty much fifty-fifty whether you make it out alive, so there's that.'

'One perspective, certainly. I heard about your guy.'

'Yeah, grim.'

She puffs out her cheeks, takes a glance around the office, comes back nodding. I nod along. Neither of us needs to say it. If the vigilantes have taken this guy out, well...

'You all right?'

'You know what it's like. Nothing quite knocks the stuffing out of you like child porn. These people. Anyway, on the plus side, such as there is with this kind of thing, by the time we've run facial recognition with some of the pictures, and if the tech guys can do their thing with his computer, hopefully it won't just be this Warburton guy who's getting found out for what he is.'

'Yep. Can't get too many of them. Of course, no reason why any of the others should be from around here. Or in Scotland or Britain even. Could be anywhere,' then she pauses before tagging on a, 'Don't work too late.'

'I'm more or less done. Spoke to someone in Warburton's office a while ago, but he didn't really know much about him. Everyone else has gone home. We're just going to leave it until the morning. It could always be, of course, that he's just buggered off somewhere, or that he comes home this evening. A lot of options still on the table. You want to have dinner?'

She looks at me warily. There's been an obvious softening

from that fairly brutal six-month period of little interaction, but we haven't done anything like go out for dinner yet.

'Why?'

'Harsh.'

She gives me one of her looks, which may or may not be designed to let me know how shit I can be at human relationships, but it has that effect, nevertheless.

'I enjoyed you coming over last night. It was nice. I'd like to do it again, if you're not doing anything else. Maybe some other night, if you can't this evening.'

'OK, you passed the audition. But wrap it up, I'm hungry. And you're paying.'

*

I'm obviously demob happy, and having casually tossed the dinner invitation out without much aforethought, we've ended up coming to a smart and expensive Italian place this end of Rutherglen, which is walking distance to both our houses.

Linguine with langoustine, tomato, garlic and sweet chilli for me, char-grilled mackerel, sweet and sour red onions, capers and mixed leaf salad for Eileen. A bottle of pinot grigio.

'You shaken it off yet?' she asks.

'The slime of busting a child porn ring?'

'Yep.'

'No. But talking about it won't help. I need to talk about something much more wholesome, like sport or your sex life.'

'You ain't going to change now, are you?'

'Sorry,' I say. 'My inner twenty-year-old cannot be contained.'

'That's not your inner twenty-year-old, that's just you being a man. Age has nothing to do with it.'

'Well, there's that.'

'Anyway, thanks for the brutal reminder,' she says.

'That you don't have a sex life?'

'Correct.'

'Still not feeling it? You said the HRT was kicking in.'

'Oh, the HRT has kicked in in all regards. Just, I don't know, haven't got back out there.'

'Well, maybe this vigilante case will come up trumps for you. Looks like Eurydice is back in the game.'

'She's been there the whole time, you know, and neither of

us has taken the opportunity to call the other, so that might be a thing.'

'Sure, but you know how it is. Out of sight, and all that. Maybe this Warburton fellow really will fit the bill, she comes by the office, you and her see each other across a crowded room...'

She's laughing as she takes a drink of wine.

'Well, I'll let you know if that happens.'

'I'm here for the news.'

We share the laugh, we eat. The waiter arrives and unnecessarily tops up our wine glasses.

'So, tell me, what's it like having sex with a twenty-two-year-old?' she asks.

There's music playing. Fifties crooning. One of those people that almost sounded like Frank Sinatra, but wasn't Frank Sinatra. Some of those guys might actually have been better than Frank, but no one would have cared, because they weren't Frank. That's just how it is.

'I really, genuinely, had no idea who I was having sex with at the time. Didn't know her age, didn't know her name. She was a body with great breasts. And she orgasmed very easily, so that's always a bonus for any man. Takes the worry out of it.'

'Must be tough sometimes.'

'Right? Nothing like a loud, shuddering orgasm to put you at ease. I could listen to that all night.'

'What was Kadri like?'

I hold her gaze for a moment, and then retreat to food. One mouthful, another on the back of it.

'Shit, sorry,' she says. 'That was just out there. None of my business.'

'No, it's OK.'

'It's not really.'

'It's fine. I've probably asked you that question about literally everyone you've ever slept with. Or, you know, that you've told me about.'

'I don't think...'

She stops, she takes some food, she waves away whatever she was going to say. I kind of want to let it stay waved away, but it probably is about time we got down to talking about this.

'Go on,' I say.

'It's OK.'

'We should talk.'

I get a familiar deadpan look across the table. I persevere.

'What don't you think?'

She takes another drink, she takes a moment, another drink, lays down the glass, leans into the conversation.

'I don't think I've ever had with anyone what you and Kadri had.'

Not sure what to say to that.

'The two of you... fizzed together. When she let it happen, I suppose. You had all the unspoken crap, the pain of her being married. There was a lot going on there. I've never had that much going on, that level of intensity.'

'The intensity was ninety-nine per cent agonising, of course.'

'I'm sure you had your moments. You had your occasional weekends away, even if that last time you did nearly get killed, and lost half your thumb.'

She smiles, but this is not a great subject for her.

'What other weekends are you talking about? I mean, that was it. What'd I miss?'

'She came up to see you in the Highlands last year, didn't she?'

'When?'

'That time you took a month off in Glencoe, or wherever it was you ended up.'

I shake my head.

'She did.'

'She really didn't. I would have noticed. As may have been reported in the press, or at least, as I told you over dinner, I slept with the local constable, but that was it. Why'd you think Kadri came up?'

'I thought...' She's looking at me curiously, then kind of shrugs. 'I just always thought that was why you went away for an entire month. It was like, you know, this really lame plan to fool people in the office. You took all that time off, and then when Kadri took a long weekend towards the end of that time, none of us were supposed to know she'd be coming to join you.'

'Wow.'

'Wow, everyone saw through the obviousness of your plan?'

'She went back to Estonia for her sister's wedding.'

She's staring across the table, looking a little perturbed.

'Sorry. Obviously jumped to conclusions.'

Am about to ask if she was jealous, but manage to stop myself. That would be an epically dumb thing to say.

'So, wait, why did you go for an entire month, then?' she asks.

'Just thought I should get away for a while after I sha –'

Uh-oh.

'You what?'

I take a drink. I take a mouthful of food.

Jesus, I'd be such a bad spy.

'Wait, was that going to be *shagged*?'

I nod, with a bit of an eye roll.

'Who the fuck did you shag?' Eileen never swears. There's been a breach in space-time. 'Sorry, didn't mean to swear. But really, who's left? No, you didn't do Emma, did you? She's still a virgin.'

'No she's not, and no, it wasn't anyway.'

Her brow furrows. The answer is obviously just too incredible for her to even consider it a possibility.

'The chief,' I say.

Her eyes widen. I would've doubted I could have shocked Eileen anymore, but there we go, I was wrong.

'You did not.'

'I did.'

Her jaw drops, she stares open-mouthed across the table. I reach across and do that performative thing of closing her mouth.

'Wow. I mean, just wow. How did that come about?'

'I did her a favour. Low key, no big deal, small policing job in Rutherglen for a family member of hers that the locals just weren't taking any interest in. I went round to her place to report, as I wasn't going to call or text. Should have left it until we were in work again, but it was a Friday, and I just thought, I'll let her know, get it out of the way. She asked me in. I'm not sure she was even being polite, I think she just didn't want anyone seeing me on the doorstep. Whatever. She was drinking wine, she'd made dinner. She offered me some of both.'

'Shit. And then?'

I shrug.

'I don't know, a tale as old as time, I guess. Food, wine, idle chit-chit. I have some stories to tell, and if I remember right, I told them. Before anyone knew what was happening, there was a second bottle of wine, and disaster followed.'

'Oh my God. What was it like?'

'It was… phenomenal. I mean, you've seen her.'

'Oh, yes.'

'She looks as amazing naked as you think she's going to. She knows what she's doing. She orgasms nicely.'

'Nicely?' She laughs. 'What does that mean?'

'I don't know. She kind of grimaced a little, but in an erotic way.' She laughs. 'I thought, uh-oh, but then she did it again. Hey, everyone has their face, right? And really, it was pretty sexy anyway.'

'Wow.'

She's got her chin resting in the palm of her hand, looking across the table at me in awe.

I like it. I like that I've managed to impress her.

'So you thought you'd get out of town for a few weeks?'

'Yep. And it worked.'

'Has there been a repeat?'

'God, no.'

'Have you ever talked about it, or have the two of you been wonderfully British?'

'The latter.' I take a drink. 'Until yesterday.'

'What happened yesterday?'

'Not really sure. I was in her office, and I blurted it out.'

'Broke the first rule of Fight Club, eh?'

'Exactly what she said.'

'Holy shit.'

'Yeah.'

Still got her chin in the palm of her hand. I'm sensing she's relieved I had sex with the boss rather than as part of my doomed, aching romance.

'So, how are we going to fix you up with Eurydice?' I say, to move the conversation along.

13

There's a guy in the building in Dalmarnock. Something of a computer genius. He was in the news when he was seventeen for successfully hacking into the Bank of Scotland. That was all that was reported. Turned out, once he'd been rounded up and all his equipment confiscated and examined, that he'd also hacked into seventeen national state security systems, plus numerous other international organisations. He wasn't even mischievous when he got in, it was all entirely done to see if he could do it.

Rather than lock him up, Police Scotland did the sensible thing and offered him a job. Snapped him up before anyone else got hold of him.

Our super-genius easily managed to open Warburton's computer, and now everything that Warburton did – all the people he dealt with and all the images he had access to, or that he took himself – is available to us.

When everything is in order, and all the paperwork is in place, there are going to be a few people surprised by a knock at the door. Knowing our lot, we'll likely do it pretty late at night, for full discombobulation factor.

The main hope I'm allowing myself here, and so far this hasn't been fully brought into the vigilante investigation, is that whoever is committing those crimes had managed to inveigle their way into the paedophile network in order to identify Warburton. This may then allow us to identify them.

Regardless, I'm not part of that investigation, and this isn't me looking to become part of it. I'll just do my bit over here, and if it helps them over there, then everyone's a winner. Except, of course, the vigilante or vigilantes. Although, let's not say too loud, there are plenty of people on their side.

'One of our best people.'

Sitting across the desk from the head of town planning at the Glasgow city council offices in the City Chambers in George Square.

'How does that manifest itself?'

Nell Lister. Her accent is southern African, perhaps. A little harsh on the ear, whatever it is. Broad faced, hair tied back.

'He has a first in, last out mentality. Never misses a day. We have trouble getting him to take all his leave, rather than being one of those who takes any opportunity to not be here, and there are plenty of those in the building. Menzies is working in the field he studied at university, and he's completely on top of his subject. He knows precedence, he's familiar with planning regulations, he's familiar with systems used in other towns in the UK, and across the globe. He's always first, and frankly, the best with ideas. If everyone on earth worked with the diligence, commitment and competence with which he worked, we would all be in a much better place.'

Well, this lady has got some major disappointment coming her way.

'Beth must be worried,' she adds.

Hmm. I think she might be hoping he's been crushed to death in an entirely random earthquake incident.

'Yes,' I say.

She smiles, shaking her head ruefully. She, at least, doesn't seem at all worried about Warburton at this point.

'I had no idea about this strange convention of not pronouncing the *z* in the name. And you get that with other names and places, Culzean for example, and yet it's not like you people don't pronounce the letter *z* when it's in a regular word.'

'Yeah, doesn't really make sense.'

'Oh, it makes sense,' she says. 'You should look it up. It's all to do with the letter *yogh*, its use in old Scots and the first printing presses. It's fascinating.'

I'll bet.

'D'you know if there's anyone from work with whom Mr Warburton was particularly friendly?'

'Dedicated family man,' she says. 'He came to a night out once, but in general, if there was anything going on, drinks, dinner occasionally, he'd cry off. Always wanted to get home and spend time with Beth and Lizzie. Far as I know there's no one here he particularly chats to. Takes lunch at his desk most days.'

'Does he ever do any work at home?'

'Definitely not. It's not encouraged at all, and frankly, he didn't need to. He had his brief, and he was completely on top of it. I mean, it's not like anything we do is top secret, and if someone needs to send work home to themselves, then that's OK. They do need to let us know it's happening though, and Menzies never asked.'

'He has his own desk? His own work computer?'

'Yes, of course.'

'We'll need to see that.'

'Why?'

'To find out if it contains any clues as to what might have happened.'

'I'm sure nothing's happened to him.'

'He didn't come home from work two days ago, Mrs Lister. Something's happened to him. We'll need to see his work computer.'

'We'll need to see the relevant paperwork first.'

'Of course.'

I'm not going to push that, or fall out over it. It barely matters, given what we do have access to. And hard to imagine the guy was dumb enough to commit any illegality on a work computer. And if he did, it'll struggle to be worse than what we've found elsewhere.

I nod a thank you and get to my feet.

'You'll call if you think of anything else, or if anyone at the office hears anything from him?'

'Yes, of course.'

'I'll leave you to your day. Thanks for your time.'

She nods, and then I'm out of the door, and quickly heading back down the stairs.

So this guy never went out with his work colleagues because he was such a dedicated family man, eh? If he does show up, and we find out who these vigilantes are, I might just give them his address.

Multitudes 3

'Why are you here?'

Lindon James, dumped on the floor, chained at the wrists and feet, stared casually back at his captor through the half-light of the basement.

'What?' he said. He almost sounded amused.

'Why are you here?'

'What does that mean? You put me here. Literally, it was you. It's not like you've just stumbled across me like, lying in your bed or something, and you're like, why are you here? You put me here.'

'Why d'you think that is?'

'So, wait, wait, of course. You *know* why I'm here. This is like a test. This is, why do I think you put me here? Why is it you have a grudge against me?'

The captor didn't answer.

'Nope, not helping me out, eh?'

Lindon James was bringing something new to the party, his attitude phlegmatic, as though some mild inconvenience had arisen.

'Maybe if you took the mask off I might know who you are, and might have a better idea what this is about.'

'You don't know me.'

'I don't? Then why bother with the mask, then? Thought for a minute you were going to turn out to be my dad. *It's about time someone taught you a lesson, my boy...*'

'It won't work,' said the captor, voice level.

'What? What won't work?'

'You're going to die. The only control you have is over how that happens. You can look into the camera and tell the world why you're here, and you will die quickly and painlessly. Or you can continue to pretend that you don't know why you're here, and you will die horribly.'

Soon enough victims in this position would know about the videos of the others, and have some idea of what was coming.

Lindon James had been tied to the basement floor for over forty-eight hours, however, and had no idea.

This was also why his captor knew he was putting on an act. No one held captive for two days in a basement, most of the time in complete darkness, crawled upon by spiders, hungry, thirsty, and sitting in their own soiled underwear, would feel a genuine lack of concern.

The news of his impending death made a small dent in James's composure, then with a shake of the head, he brought himself back.

'Seems harsh,' he said. 'I mean, is this because I never returned that copy of *Flowers for Algernon* to the school library? I might be able to find it in my parents' loft, if that'll help.'

'Last chance,' said the captor. 'It's your decision.'

Lindon James fake laughed.

'I mean, like what are my options here? This painful death, what does that involve? You going to stick Ed Sheeran on and bore me to death, or what?'

The captor stepped forward, a pair of scissors in his hands. James winced, then relaxed a little when he realised that he was only, in the first instance, cutting his clothes. T-shirt cut up the middle and then at the arms, then the soiled jeans and underpants. The captor wore gloves, and did not care about the recently urine-soaked underwear.

James was now naked, covered in goosebumps. It was summer out there, up there, wherever that was, but cold down in the basement.

'Freezing me to death, eh?' said James. 'I'll take it, I guess.'

His voice sounded strained this time, the façade beginning to crumble. Fear will do that to you eventually. This wasn't a movie, where glib one-liners could be tossed out in the certain knowledge that a last-minute escape had been scripted on his behalf.

Having laid down the scissors, the killer returned with a knife. He held out his right hand, palm up, and balanced the knife on two fingers. Eight inch blade.

'Ooh,' said James, 'a knife. Scary.'

He swallowed. The veneer, the attempted insouciance, was slipping.

The killer knelt down beside him, the knife still balanced on his fingers.

'Last chance,' he said. 'The camera there is running. Oh, this bit, the part where I'm talking, that's going to be cut out of the whole thing. People won't get to hear me talking. No one wants that, anyway, do they? They don't care who I am. What they care about is criminals who evade justice.'

'The fuck did I do?' snapped James, annoyance from nowhere.

'An interesting defence.'

'Oh, fuck off.'

The killer palmed the knife, gripped it firmly, and quickly thrust it into James's abdomen, just beneath the rib cage. A perfectly aimed and timed insertion, not penetrating too far. James ejaculated loudly, then winced, breathed hurriedly a couple of times, then realised that the knife had barely done more than break the skin, and that it hadn't, in fact, been anything like as painful as he'd thought it was going to be.

He swallowed, felt the cold shiver of sweat.

'I thought I told you to fuck off,' he said without conviction.

'OK, OK, I lied before,' said the killer. 'I said last chance, and here I am giving you another last chance. Obviously I need to think through my spiel to you people.'

'What does you people mean?'

James's eyes darted around the basement, what he could see of it, which was very little. He certainly couldn't see into the corners.

'Are there others?'

'Like I said,' said the killer, 'last chance. Look into the camera and explain what you did. Do that, and I'll slit your throat. Don't do it... death will be much more unpleasant.'

James gritted his teeth. The knife in his stomach was pressed in a little harder and he grimaced. The flippancy had gone, and now, having bypassed fear and panic, he found the hatred and contempt for his attacker that came more naturally.

'Now you're just peaking my curiosity, you stupid prick,' shot from his lips.

The killer firmly pressed the knife into the soft flesh, an inch, no more, and then brought the serrated edge quickly down through the skin and top layer of flesh, all the way to the pelvic bone.

James cried out, loud, pained, desperate, his breath hot and moist.

He laid down the knife, then carefully inserted the tips of the fingers of both hands inside the wound, and gently pulled the two sides apart.

James was looking down in horror, his mouth open, his face tortured, nothing coming from his throat bar a strange, strangled croak.

The killer gently eased his hands inside James's abdomen, positioned his fingers so that they were creating a ball of viscera in between his hands, and then, with James now desperately squeezing out the words, 'What are you doing?' the killer lifted out the bloody tangle of viscera, and set the coiled mass of organs and tubes down on top of James's slit open stomach.

He paused for a moment, still kneeling beside the bloody mess of a body, and then slowly got to his feet.

James was wide-eyed and terrified.

'You've got to call me an ambulance.'

Wide-eyed, terrified, and obviously not thinking straight.

'You're an ambulance,' said the killer, then he chuckled. 'Did that help?'

'Bastard!'

'Yes, you do that,' said the killer. 'Get agitated. And don't forget to smile for the camera.'

The killer turned, and walked away.

'The fuck? Come back here. You come back here!'

James was looking at his stomach, rather than the slow retreat of the killer into the darkness. Cold sweat dripped from his face. He finally lifted his eyes, searching the depths of the dim light for the killer's presence.

'The fuck have you gone?'

The lights went on, bold and big and bright.

The killer clamped his eyes shut, the brightest light he'd seen in forty-eight hours, muttering, 'Jesus Christ. Oh my God.'

Silence. Bar the heavy, desperate breaths of the victim.

He squinted. Through his mostly closed eyelids he saw the killer at the far side of the basement. Slowly he allowed in more light, slowly he took in his surroundings.

A basement, dirty, empty, expansive. Ceiling must have been twelve feet high. No flooring other than dirt on concrete. A string of bright lights attached rudimentarily to the ceiling.

'What?' he said.

The killer remained silent.

'What? What are you doing?'

He noticed the large box at the killer's feet. The killer bent down and opened up the front of the box. In the bright light of the room, the contents were immediately obvious. Four small dogs. Tiny. Little more than puppies. Shih Tzu Inu, they were never likely to grow very big in any case. They were scared and nervous.

'The fuck?' said James.

The dogs were reluctant to leave the box, until one of the ones at the back pushed another forward, out onto the floor, and then the four of them tumbled together out of the box.

They stood for a few moments, cowering. But these dogs, young and scared and nervous though they were, were also starving.

They smelled blood. They smelled a body split asunder.

They started walking slowly across the floor towards the prone figure of James, grotesque now, his stomach slit, his insides laid bare.

'OK, OK, I'll say,' he said, his voice strangely calm, as he looked up.

The killer was gone.

He looked frantically around, as though the killer might have blended seamlessly into the walls, rather than just walking silently up the stairs while James had been distracted.

'Where are you?'

The dogs hesitated every time he shouted, but they really were very, very hungry.

'Fuck!' shouted James, louder this time, directed straight at the dogs. 'Fuck off, you little bastards!'

They backed off, but only a couple of feet. A moment's hesitation, and then they started to advance again.

'Fuck off!'

A guttural roar, everything he could throw into the two words.

This time the dogs stopped, but did not retreat. And soon enough, as the sound of the horrible cry was swallowed up by the bare walls and floor, the dogs hesitantly advanced.

James frantically moved every part of his body that he could, instantly stopping at the discomfort, as his innards slopped around, running horribly down the side of his abdomen. Another strangled cry escaped his throat.

The boldest dog was upon him, sniffing, still nervous, still scared. Still starving, nevertheless.

It licked some blood from the floor. A moment, a pause, and then it took to it, licking along the line of blood. And then it was at his flesh, taking a first bite at a piece of nebulous, white tube.

'Aaaargghhhh!' he roared at it, but this time the dog was not nervous, and did not shy away. The dog had realised its prey was trapped, and it snarled back at him, snapping at air, and then when it returned to the feast it did so with more relish, biting into the warm, pungent tissue.

The pack was unleashed, and the other three dogs joined the fray. Two of them still a little nervously at the side, the other running up onto his body, and burying its face in the mass of viscera.

James tried, throwing his body around in whatever limited way he could manage. The dogs, however, were let loose, and they were feasting.

James's terror would not last long. He would die quickly. This was in sharp contrast to his wife, whose terror at his hands had lasted years, and who he'd finally beaten to death. The majority male jury had believed his claims of a marriage beset by violence on both sides, his wife the primary aggressor. He was found guilty of manslaughter and had avoided a custodial sentence.

In life, however, there is no avoiding starving Shih Tzu Inu puppies when your stomach's been slit open. So there was that.

14

A small house in a large housing development, built sometime in the last ten years. Several million houses crammed into what, until recently, would have been a couple of wheat fields. Built, no doubt, without the necessary add-on of a school or doctor's surgery, though naturally enough, the supermarkets will have come quickly along in the development's wake.

Well, that's just me being on brand, complaining about capitalism and government underfunding. That's not really why we're here.

Beth Warburton and her sister are sitting together on a sofa in the tiny front room. The television is playing, on mute. Some sort of late morning TV with which I'm not familiar. Beth has a cup of lukewarm tea in her hands. The sister, an air of wonderful suspicion about her, as though all this sordid shit is my fault, has her hands folded crisply in her lap. There is neither sight, nor sound of the wean.

'Tell me,' says Beth. 'Tell me everything.'

'That's not how this works,' I say. 'There's now an expansive investigation, and regardless of your relationship to the accused,' and the sister tries to cut me off with a scoffing, eye-rolling mutter of *relationship*, 'we're not in a position to divulge the details of everything we've found. Not yet. I shall just say that there is a lot more of what I showed you yesterday.' A pause, and then, 'A lot more,' for effect.

She closes her eyes, shakes her head.

'At least tell me this isn't going to be in the news.'

'I can't.'

'You bloody well can,' snipes the sister.

I give her a look, but I'm not here to get into any arguments, particularly not this sort. Nowhere for it to go except a trip on the ten-thirty-five to Ugly.

Yeah, OK, Aaron Sorkin still hasn't been taken on the payroll.

'Did your husband receive a lot of mail to the house?' I

ask.

An easy starting one. I mean, we presume not as we've already identified his PO box.

'Does anyone get any actual mail anymore?' she asks.

'Maybe not through Royal Mail, but there are several hundred other delivery companies.'

'No, nothing other than the usual.' A pause, and then, 'Hmm. He received a note, like a really small letter, a few days ago. That was unusual in itself. No idea what that was about.'

'He never said?'

'Really, we never spoke to each other.'

'You know if he took many trips to the Post Office? Did he leave the house with packages or envelopes, did any companies collect items from your house for delivery?'

She's looking at me like I'm asking why he orchestrated a coup in the Central African Republic the week before Christmas.

'No, none of that. I mean, what? Why are you asking?'

'He was running a mail order child porn ring, was he?' says the sister, her voice snarky.

'Were you aware of anything he did outside of the house, other than go to the office?' I ask Beth, ignoring the sideshow.

'He actually went to the office, did he?' she asks.

'Yes, he did. Model employee,' I say. 'Eight-thirty to six every day, never missed a minute. They speak very highly of him.'

They both snort at that one.

The sister has none of Beth's youthful attractiveness. There's a bitterness about her, the air of the kind of person who inhales raw, unfiltered twenty-four hour news, sucking in all the awfulness of the world, getting annoyed about every single damned thing that GB News wants her to get annoyed about.

'Apart from going to the office, d'you know if he did anything?'

Beth shakes her head. The derision leaves her, not having the mean spiritedness to maintain the anger of her sister.

'I did not exaggerate the awful state of our marriage yesterday,' she says. 'He could have been running guns to Castlemilk for all I'd have known. Looks like he was doing God knows what right under my roof and I had no idea. I presume you haven't found him yet.'

'No.'

Take a moment, a glance at the ill humour in human form

to her right, then turn back to Beth. There's something about her today. Yes, on the one hand, there's this piece of devastating, heart-wrenching, life-changing news. On the other, well, her awful marriage is over. She never has to see that man again. She might not want to move back into the house, but she'll be able to sell it and start up a new life somewhere.

And somehow, somewhere, her baby isn't crying.

'How's Lizzie?' I ask.

'She's asleep. She's fine.'

We look at each other. We've both been thinking the same thing, of course, though it's hard to know what he could have been doing to the kid that would have caused it so much grief that it was crying all the time, while at the same time no doctor ever spotted it.

'Are there pictures of Lizzie in amongst Menzies' things? You know… inappropriate pictures?'

'I don't know,' I say, not actually lying. I'd quite happily lie if I had to. I mean, there were pictures of babies, but I wasn't looking intimately at that stuff after all. That job, thank Christ, will be for others.

I get a snort from the sister, who thinks everyone is lying, all the time.

'Now that you know your husband wasn't working up there,' I begin, 'now that you know the kinds of things he was doing, is there anything that makes you think, now that you look back on it, *ah, right, that makes sense*? I'm one hundred per cent not suggesting you should have seen something, or been aware of it. The amount that goes on under the noses of people in their own homes is staggering, good or bad or whatever. No one's judging you.' Another snort from the cheap seats. 'But is there anything where you're now thinking, ah, OK, that's coming together?'

She's looking away from me before I've finished talking. Eyes staring vaguely at a spot on the carpet to my left. Getting lost in her past life for a moment. Given that her past life ended yesterday afternoon, she doesn't exactly have to search the deepest recesses of her memory. Momentarily she seems taken by a melancholic wistfulness.

The sister looks at her, her face briefly mellowing. It doesn't suit her.

'I'd decided he was gay. That's stupid, isn't it? I mean, I just thought, why was he interested in me one minute, and then the next… nothing? Must've been a reason. I was his beard, that's what I'd decided. Pretty embarrassing, I guess. I used to think, God, Mum'll love this, if he ever actually comes out. She'll probably blame me. If you'd been a better wife, he wouldn't have had to fancy men. That's what she would've been like. And I did wonder why he needed to be such an asshole about it. Thought I'd done him a favour, although I don't know why anyone would need a beard anymore. I mean, just come out, right? No one cares. But it was all I could think of.'

She looks at me now. Hopelessness in her expression, rather than wistfulness.

'Guess this explains it, though. All those shitty thoughts I'd been having, all those worse case scenarios. Peanuts compared to the actual explanation. Peanuts…'

I feel the eye of Sauron has been reactivated, and I look back at the sister.

'You finished?' she asks. 'You've already ruined Beth's life, what other damage d'you want to do?'

15

Sitting in the office a little later, back at the desk I vacated a couple of weeks ago. DC Ritter out and about, the open-plan with that quiet hum of low-level, understaffed activity. I've been told to expect a visit from DCI Hamilton. The team running the Rough Justice League investigation like the sound of our paedophile town planner, and the sordid business he ran from his attic.

Funny how the RJL moniker has taken hold. It was the Sun that started it, and now, as so often happens in life, where the press leads, the people in authority follow, and everyone, us included, is referring to these people as the RJL. There's always the possibility that it turns out to be the work of one person, of course, but the more we see of this, the more victims there turn out to be, the planning and aforethought that went into each revenge killing, the more it looks like there might be a team behind it.

We can hope. The more people there are to catch, the more chance one of them makes a mistake.

The chief appears at her door, takes a look around the office. Her eyes settle on me. Seems she's looking for a detective, and I'm the only one around. She makes a small gesture, a hopelessness about it, that I instantly take to mean there's another video. *Come and look.*

I walk through to her office. She sits down, and I take my place by her desk, looking at her monitor.

'Is it our guy?' I ask.

She knows I mean Warburton, and she shakes her head. She plays the film.

Again, as with the second victim, there is no confession, and we are straight to a barbaric scene, the victim chained to the wall and the floor, prostrate, his stomach split open, his viscera spilled upon his body.

Four small creatures appear, nervously, as though camera shy.

'What are those?' I say, unthinkingly.

'Shih Tzu Inu puppies,' says Hawkins, in a monotone.

'The little handbag dogs?'

'Yes, the little handbag dogs.'

'Holy shit.'

The volume is set low, but we can hear him shouting at the dogs, the dogs' nervousness is obvious, but eventually they are driven on, and now the shouting ends, to be replaced by the screaming. After another half minute or so, she turns it off, then we stare together at the wallpaper for a while, and then I walk away, back to the other side of the desk, think about it for a moment, and then, unbidden, pull a seat over and sit down.

We stare grimly across the desk at each other.

'There's a cumulative effect,' I say.

She continues to stare blankly.

'The first one,' I say, talking through the silence, 'there's shock and awe. There's something of a cartoonish, CGI horror feel to it. Maybe it's a one-off. Maybe all sorts of things. But now...'

I swallow. She finally nods.

'You all right?' I ask.

A moment and then she says, 'Not really.'

Aye, that's about the size of it. If you watch that shit, and you feel fine afterwards, then maybe there's something wrong with you. If you're the type of person who gets a buzz out of it, there's no maybe about it.

'How about you?' she asks.

I have nothing for a few moments, and then, inevitably, flippancy comes to play.

'Seen worse.'

She continues to stare blankly across the desk. She's not sure, although she knows enough of my back story to know that while that might have been something of a throwaway line, I have at least seen things just as bad.

'Those little fellas must've been starving,' I say.

'You get immune after a while?' she says in response, her voice expressionless.

'Eventually, maybe. Hey, we had decapitated heads in two of my last three big murder cases. It's a nasty world.'

'It seems to be, doesn't it?'

'We know who this guy is and what he did?'

'His name's Lindon James. Domestic violence case, I

think, but I don't know all the details.'

This would be the moment when one of us, if this conversation had been about which actor played whoever in the movie we can't remember the name of, would look it up. But this isn't our case, and we're looking at this thing with curious horror, I guess neither of us really wanting to know more than we have to, while unable to stop ourselves looking in the first place.

'You thought of getting out?' I ask, bringing up her career path out of nowhere, and she surprises me by nodding.

'I have, in fact,' she says. Holds my look, finally shrugs herself into acceptance. 'I've applied for a job at the WTO in Geneva. A little out of my comfort zone, but… well, I passed the first couple of stages already. Was aiming to go out there for an in-person interview at the end of next week. I guess this might get in the way.'

'Oh, God, don't let it. That would be fabulous.'

She nods.

'Not completely sold on the job, but the place looks nice.'

'You been to Geneva?'

'Nope.'

'Eileen and I had a night there. Ate dinner at this wonderful little steak place. That's the menu. Steak frites, nothing else. They bring you a small steak and a small plate of fries, and you think, OK, might have to fill up on water, but then, it turns out it's a dinner of two halves, and when you're done, they bring exactly the same thing again, and it's warm and fresh and… oh my God.'

'Well, that sounds perfect,' she says, laughing.

'And it's queued out the door every night. I'll find it on the web, get you the address. You can have dinner there next week.'

She smiles.

And there it goes, the good humoured, off-topic conversation drifting off into the ether.

'We should get on,' I say.

'Yes.'

'Oh, was there a, you know, calling card at the end of this one?'

'A.'

'A?' I repeat, with something of a shrug, and then I make a small hand gesture, like that Obama GIF everyone uses where he's looking around like, what the fuck, man. 'Avenger? Seems a little derivative, if that was it.'

'No one knows what any of these things are. I suppose we wait to see if there's a repeat. That's what everyone thinks is going to happen. This person does one thing, this person does another. Although, the killers are all obviously following the same pattern, maybe the first guy, the P, maybe he'll always use rats. Maybe he'll always go after child rapists.'

I nod my way through it. Frustratingly, as is invariably the case early in the first few days of any investigation, we have far too little information to make even an educated guess.

'OK,' I say, getting to my feet.

'Given that this has landed, I think perhaps our visit from Eurydice may be postponed. I'll let you know.'

'To be honest, our guy Warburton is a perfect sleazeball, and I couldn't give a shit what's happened to him,' I say, extracting maximum value from the words *to be honest*, 'but it would be nice if we could track him down, and not to some basement somewhere, and take ourselves out the loop. Much though I love working with Eurydice.'

Hawkins smiles now, a proper smile, something of relief in it, I think, at having the DS Hutton she knows and loves bring a little lightness to the conversation. Even if the lightness involves not caring whether your missing person gets his guts eaten.

16

DCI Eurydice Hamilton arrives at the office near the end of the working day. She stands just inside the door of the open-plan, surveying the familiar scene. Been a while since she was here, and I expect she's not so happy about being back. Our eyes meet, and we kind of nod at each other. Then she finds Eileen, they share a look, Eileen gets a smile because she's obviously the favourite, and then Eurydice looks back at me, indicates that she'll go and speak to the chief first, then she's across the office, has knocked at the door, and is gone.

I've now spoken to fourteen people who know Menzies Warburton. Work colleagues, family and friends. No one admits having any idea what's happened to him. No one has heard from him since he left work two evenings ago. And, without directly asking the question, I'd say no one has any idea of his illegal side hustle.

The more we learn, the more I believe he's quite likely to have become the victim of this RJL collective, but there's always the possibility that someone was blackmailing him, or was threatening to out him, and so he's just chosen to vanish. However, there's been no major activity in his bank accounts in the past couple of weeks, and nothing at all in the last two days.

My phone rings twenty-something minutes after Eurydice walked in to see Hawkins, the chief asking me to join them.

DC Ritter has not yet returned, the few people in the office quietly go about their business. I glance over, and see that Eileen has gone off somewhere, and then I'm up and back into the chief's office.

Eurydice is standing at the window, hands in her pockets. Hair the tousled blonde of old, a familiar white top, a couple of buttons undone, jeans.

'Sergeant Hutton,' she says. 'Where all roads in any major investigation soon lead, right?'

'Hopefully not in this case,' I respond, closing the door behind me. 'Although, the more we look, the more it feels right, unfortunately.'

'We're going to take this one off your hands, if that's OK.'

I stand in the middle of the office, looking at Eurydice. Chief Hawkins is a spectator, as she invariably is when Eurydice comes to play.

'He's all yours,' I say.

'Thank you. You'll understand if I don't ask you to join the investigation.'

'You'll understand I'm delighted you're not asking.'

We share the understanding smile.

'You'll send me through your notes?'

'Sure.'

'They're up-to-date?'

'Well, I could be offended by that, but it's a fair cop. And yes, they're up-to-date. The Shih Tzu Inu killer is all yours.'

'Let's hope that name doesn't catch on. I'll let you know what we turn up, and if we can rule Mr Warburton out of our investigation, the case will be returned to you very quickly.'

'Ma'am.'

I look at Hawkins, she nods in the direction of the door, and I'm gone again.

*

Eurydice stops at my desk on her way out.

'I sent the file already,' I say.

'Thanks. Have you noticed if there was a note amongst his things? One of our previous victims had a note in a drawer. *Ticktock*. That was it. It had a recent postmark. Feels like a warning, though we haven't found it with the others yet.'

'His wife said he got a small envelope the other day. Seemed a little odd. She didn't know what it was, and I don't think we've found it.'

'He could have put it in the bin, of course. As could anyone.'

'Yes.'

She takes a moment, glances round the office, turns back.

'You're getting out at last,' she says, and I don't reply. 'Amazing, if you don't mind me saying, that you're leaving of your own volition, and haven't been forcibly ejected.'

I can't help smiling, and she smiles with me.

'Apologies, Tom, that was a little rude.'

'Accurate, nevertheless. I'm waiting for Netflix to approach with the offer of a six-part docudrama of my career.'

'Six-part? Multi-series, I think, with a hell of a lot of cliff-hangers.'

'That's an option.'

A moment, another smile comes to her face, then she tosses, 'Perhaps Pornhub might be more appropriate than Netflix,' into the mix, and I can't help laughing.

She has a nice smile. She always did, though she doesn't use it much.

'Talking of which,' and she glances over in the direction of Eileen's desk, 'any sign of your fellow sergeant?'

'Think she's out on a call. Stuart on the front desk will have a better idea.'

'OK, thanks. You haven't made an honest woman of her yet?'

Once again, since my audience is different, I do the Obama what-the-fuck-is-happening gesture.

'Am I the only one who knows Eileen's gay?' I say.

She smiles, she nods, she taps my desk a couple of times with her knuckles.

God, Taylor used to do that. Jesus, don't put that back in my head.

'Love knows no boundaries, sergeant,' she says. 'Tell Eileen I was asking for her, eh?'

And with that, she's gone. I watch her out of the office, then the door closes, and I turn back to my near-empty desk.

Love knows no boundaries. Kadri also said that about Eileen and me. It's like Eurydice just turned up to deliver the greatest hits of my ex-bosses, whose departures I lament in completely different and equally devastating ways.

I shake it off. At least, try to. Stare blankly at my computer.

Eight days to go, the one major case I'd picked up now taken away again. I glance at the time, and realise that the working day is done should I want it to be. The one thing I had to do is gone. Freedom awaits.

I open my inbox, scan quickly through, there are a couple of mentions of the RJL in messages being circulated throughout the force, and then I close the page, and log off. Glance over my shoulder, Eileen still hasn't returned from whatever's taken her from the office. I have a glorious night on my own, with my self-loathing, a six-pound bottle of Viognier, a microwave dinner and no live football because it's mid-July.

The thought of calling my new twenty-two-year-old chum flashes through my head, and thank God, equally quickly vanishes, along the way multiplying that self-loathing by two thousand, three hundred and fifty-six.

The chief emerges from her office, and comes straight over, sitting in DC Ritter's seat on her way by. She's wearing her light coat, has that large handbag she carries around with her.

'You heading off,' she says.

'Yeah, if that's OK. Now that I've had the Warburton case taken off my hands,' and I make a gesture to indicate that there's nothing much doing.

'Emma hasn't asked you to take care of anything else?'

'Nope, albeit she doesn't know about losing Warburton.'

'You can talk to her in the morning,' she says, nodding, and then, surprising even the usually unshockable me, she says, 'Want to go for a drink?'

I take a moment to look curiously across the desk. I feel the pull of the glance into the side-on camera, but decide that might be a little obvious.

'The chief never asks me out for a drink at home,' I say.

'That's right, Tom, I don't. And I'm not sure I'm entirely on board with how you said *asks me out for a drink* there.'

'You don't mean this in any kind of romantic way, then?'

'Not so much. More of a work colleagues who have faced a certain level of trauma together taking the time to decompress. But really, don't worry if you don't.'

'I'll get the first round,' I say. 'Where d'you want to go?'

And I'm standing up, jacket off the back of my chair and thrown on, with all the panache of President Bartlett, and if she'd been about to try and back out of the enterprise, I've cut her off at the pass.

17

At some point early on I get her to openly admit she's feeling much better disposed towards me as a fellow officer now that I'm leaving. She then goes on to list all the times she's contemplated suspending me, which includes several occasions when I wasn't even aware I'd done something overly stupid, and finally gets to the point where she says she likes me despite herself, and all this before she's even drunk.

I think she's likely aiming not to get drunk, and perhaps she won't, but after two drinks we start discussing food, and then I say that my place is within walking distance, and she, giving in to a police officer's natural curiosity, accepts the suggestion, and we stop off at a fine establishment called the Orient Express on the way home, and buy a variety of tasty, and obviously very healthy, Chinese dishes.

*

'It's going to be a hell of a memoir,' she says.

I've been going over some of the highlights of my career. I should note that she keeps asking. Every time I've asked her anything about her career she's batted it aside, making a much better job of not talking about herself than I am.

Sitting at the small dining table by the window, listening to some old-time Hadda Brooks blues.

'Who was your first chief?' I ask, and she once again waves the question away with a pair of perfectly held chopsticks.

'Some boring guy in a suit, a leftover from the old days. Considered women to be new-fangled things. He was barely worth remembering, and… sure enough, I don't recall his name. That's a bonus.'

She stares off to the side, shakes her head, dismissing the thought, takes a drink of wine.

'You've got to tell me more about the Bob Dylan murders

guy. I mean, what the …?' and she says *fuck* by making a head explosion kind of gesture.

'Nah,' I say, 'I think we're done.'

There is no way I want to talk about the Bob Dylan murders guy. Just as there's no way I want to talk about the Plague of Crows. Both the work of Michael Clayton, who will hopefully die where he currently rots.

'Disappointing,' she says.

'I don't think so. You'd make a good spy.'

'Really, why?'

'You keep turning everything back to me. You've lured me in with alcohol, you allowed me to bring up the suggestion of food as though it might have been my idea, and you deflect every question, while expertly probing me for information along the way.'

She smiles kind of sadly, and then shrugs.

'I suppose I just don't feel like my career's been very interesting. I'm an administrator. I might as well have been working at the local council.'

I have no pep talk to hand, not being a pep talk kind of a person.

'You think being an administrator in Switzerland might be more interesting?'

'God knows. It'll be different. Get away from Scotland, there'll be international work colleagues at least, that should be fun. I'll get to use the French and German I've barely touched since I left university, and there'll be skiing.'

'You might be swept off your feet by some Swiss gazillionaire,' I say, because it's the kind of lightweight, small-talk bullshit you say in these situations. Not that she's wrong about all the other cool stuff about living in Switzerland, particularly when you're working for an international organisation and someone else is paying the rent.

'I don't think I'm the Swiss gazillionaire's type,' she says, taking another mouthful of noodles, slurping them up, running her tongue along her lips to lick off the juice.

Uh-oh.

'Of course,' I say. 'You're ballsy, smart, multilingual and gorgeous. Men hate that. Particularly those Swiss gazillionaires, they don't like their women being too attractive.'

She laughs, self-consciously takes a drink of wine. Quite a long drink of wine.

Hmm. She's beginning to let go.

We may be headed for a Code Red.

Awooga! Awooga!

A variety of bullshit lines form in my head, all fortunately rejected by the Executive Committee in Charge of Erotic Entanglements. Silence, as ever, is best.

She takes another mouthful of noodles. Sucks 'em up, licks her lips, dabs at her mouth with a napkin, takes another long drink of wine. Glass nearly done. I dutifully lift the bottle, and hover it in her direction. She looks at the bottle, she looks at me. Boy, there is a tonne of shit going through her head. Let's not try to untangle it.

I pour her another glass, and top up my own.

'I told Eileen about you and me and the sex, by the way,' I say.

'I knew you were lying.'

'I wasn't. I told her last night.'

Elbow on the table, she rests her chin in her hand.

'Now, why would you do that, detective sergeant?'

I take a mouthful of Szechuan chicken and a drink of wine.

'She asked me why I took that month off to go to the Highlands, and I wasn't prepared mentally. I can lie, obviously, having been married three times I have that natural ability, but I wasn't ready for it.'

'Hadn't she asked you before?'

'Nope. Turns out she always thought it was some over-elaborate plan for Kadri and I to have a weekend away together without anyone noticing.'

'Really?'

She ponders this, very possibly considering that she'd thought, up until now, that Eileen was the sensible one.

'So,' she says, on the back of another slug of wine, and through another unintentionally erotic mouthful of noodles, 'if I can be so bold as to ask another probing question which is, this time, I admit, none of my business…'

'Those are the most interesting ones.'

'How many women have you slept with since then? Since you and me.'

We hold the stare across the table, then she reads the surprise in my eyes and immediately waves away the question.

'Sorry, that is…' and she lifts her glass and hides behind it for a moment, and then lifts a prawn cracker and takes a noisy crunch.

'Hard to be definite. Fifteen, maybe. I mean, I usually know about it at the time, but sometimes they blend together after a while. The insignificant ones.' We stare. 'The significant ones I remember.'

'Fifteen,' she says. 'Gosh. I can't imagine.'

'It wasn't all at once.'

She laughs.

Fuck it.

'What about you, then?'

I get a little bit of an eyebrow in response. She doesn't look at me. More food, more wine.

'None,' she says, without looking up.

I stare at her. This time I lean on my elbow, chin resting in the palm of my hand. Unlikely I give off quite the same vibe.

She finally looks up.

'None?'

'None.'

'That seems a waste.'

'Of what?'

Another significant look across the table. In unison we lift our glasses to take a drink.

*

I think of it lying in bed. P – L – A. The letters branded on the foreheads. It's ludicrous, and yet entirely on brand in its absurdity. And as soon as the thought appears, I can't imagine why it never came to me before. It's obvious.

Those last two questions that the chief threw in about my career. The Plague of Crows. They're staring me right in the face. The grotesque playfulness of them. Going so far, taking care not to kill, and then unleashing creatures of nature upon the incapacitated victim. Straight out of the Crows' playbook. There were no animals used in the Bob Dylan murders, but the same macabre humour was in evidence. The work of someone who enjoyed planning an execution, and who took delight in executing the plan.

Michael Clayton.

Of course, Michael Clayton is in prison. I know he's in prison. I don't get regular updates or anything, I certainly don't go visiting him, but I would've heard if he'd been moved, and I would know if he'd been released. But he's due never to be released, so that can't have happened.

And so I lie awake thinking I'll need to check when I get into work tomorrow morning, and until that happens, and until I know for sure he's still in HMP Shotts, I'm going to think the worst.

After all, the guy always did know how to use a high-priced lawyer as a cudgel against the system.

Fuck it, they would have told me. That's what happens. And Jesus, with that fucker, it would've been in the news. That's also what happens. The fucker is the Plague of Crows. He's the Bob Dylan murderer. If he doesn't die in prison, people are going to be talking about it.

Not, of course, that anyone's officially allowed to call him the Plague of Crows. That was never proven, and he ain't officially admitting it. But we know. We all know.

I glance at the time on my phone. I forgot to dim the screen light before coming to bed, and so the three a.m. darkness is briefly illuminated, then I quickly turn it off.

'What time is it?'

Shit.

I continue to stare at the ceiling.

'Three o'clock. Sorry, didn't mean to disturb you.'

'It's OK, I wasn't sleeping. Lying here thinking I ought to get up and go home.'

I don't say anything, then she adds, 'It's hard getting out of bed in the middle of the night.'

'My alarm's set for six,' I say. 'Get some sleep, you'll have time to go home, get changed. It'll be daylight by then, easier to get up.'

She doesn't reply. I feel her move a little, and when I glance over, she's on her side, facing me, her eyes closed.

Her orgasm face was just as I remembered it. I remembered the taste of her as well. And that thing with her tongue and her lips at the base of my cock.

I close my eyes. I try to think of what we've just done. Try to picture her lying back, her breasts almost flat against her chest, me kneeling between her legs, thrusting into her, trying to fuck her as hard as possible, but to not come too quickly. To keep going, because it felt so damned wonderful. Stopping, so I could last a little longer, going down on her, giving her another orgasm with my tongue, doing everything I could to spin the magic out for another few minutes. As long as I could make it.

But I can't. I can't think of the chief, and her wonderful, strange, pained orgasm face, I can't think of her breasts, or her fabulous tongue, because all I can see is Michael Clayton, and I feel the fear of it, and the horror of it, in ways that never crossed my mind while watching that video this afternoon.

Multitudes 4

'Why are you here?'

Menzies Warburton, dumped on the floor, chained at the wrists and feet, stared grimly back at his captor through the half-light of the basement. He didn't answer.

'Why are you here?'

Warburton had no idea what had happened. One minute walking along the back lane he took between his work and the spot he'd found to park his car for free every day, the next he'd woken up in complete darkness, chained to a floor, cold and hungry and needing to use the toilet.

He had shouted for a few minutes. But he had some level of common sense. He knew there'd be little point. His abductor would come when he would come. If he'd been somewhere in the vicinity, perhaps a shout or two might have alerted him to the fact that Warburton was awake. That aside, it was apparent that if there'd been the slightest possibility of alerting an outsider to his presence, he wouldn't have been left ungagged in the first instance.

'Why are you here?'

'I appear to be being held in a similar position to the man who was eaten by rats,' said Warburton. His voice was low and calm. Deadpan. Zero expression. Watching that film clip online had been one of the last things he'd done before he was taken. 'So, you've brought me here to make a confession.'

'Very good. At last. Someone who's not an idiot.'

'I don't know what it is you think I have to confess,' said Warburton, his tone the same.

The man in the mask allowed his shoulders to drop a little.

'How disappointing. We'd been doing so well.'

'How was it you got whatever that guy's name was to admit to anything?' asked Warburton. 'Did you promise him a clean, quick death if he confessed, and then killed him horribly in any case? Or did you threaten his family? His children. Did you threaten his children? People do anything for their children, don't they?'

Warburton wasn't even looking at him. He's given up, thought the killer. Interesting. He's accepted his fate. He knows what's going to happen to him, and he knows there's nothing that can stop it. That had been the trouble with Fergus Hunt confessing prior to being eaten by rats. Perhaps, in retrospect, he ought to just have slit Hunt's throat.

Too late now.

'And if I threaten your daughter, Mr Warburton, what then?' asked the killer.

'I don't have a daughter.'

Warburton stared straight ahead. He was here now, and he had no agency to change the outcome of what was about to happen. He was determined not to beg.

'Interesting,' said the killer. 'What does that mean?'

'The kid isn't mine. Beth slept with me to cover for fucking some guy at her office. I knew it as soon as she got home. Could smell it on her, and she wore her guilt like a veil. Then, like two weeks later, she was all over me one night. Like she was gagging for it. I thought, God's sake, all right, whatever. Thought she'd been watching porn or something. Soon as she said she was pregnant, I understood.' He paused, and then added, 'I never did tell her I'd had a vasectomy. Stupid bitch.'

'Well, you really are a deceitful and cunning fool, aren't you?'

Finally, Warburton roused himself to stare at the killer. Everything about him might have suggested he'd already conceded defeat, but he still managed to regard his killer with contempt.

'Fuck you.'

'I see that threatening you with the murders of your wife and daughter will be of no use. As, obviously, will threatening you with a more painful death. Entirely due to my own miscalculation, I'm afraid. So, what are we to do?'

'I presume it was you who sent that stupid note. *Tick-tock.* Jesus. You probably got that from the Hardy Boys or something.'

'Yes, yes, very good.'

The killer stood over him, looking up and down his body. Warburton was already naked. His skin cold and blue and covered in goosebumps, his penis and testicles small and shrivelled.

'Well, you are tedious, Mr Warburton, but I suppose I only have myself to blame. I expect, at some point in the middle of the night, I'll have some brilliant idea of how I could get you to confess, but we really do need to get on now, if we're going to keep to the schedule. As it is, the police are already all over your house, so I think we know what that means, and your wife and her child by some other father have already moved in with her sister.' Warburton sharply raised his head at that piece of information. 'Already the police will know who you are, and when this murder gets revealed, the police will very *reluctantly* allow the information to be released. As if. They'll be desperate to let the public know that the people in general, the magnificent hard-working populace, needn't be concerned, and that this particular victim absolutely got what he deserv –'

'In the name of God, can you just shut up and get on with it? Do what you will, you limp-dicked, anonymous little fuck monkey.'

The killer quickly got to work.

18

Breakfast.

Two cups of coffee. A glass of orange juice. A glass of water. Two fried eggs on a slice of sourdough toast.

Eileen, who now eats the healthiest diet known to humans, tells me that drinking orange juice is of no use to you whatsoever. She heard it on a podcast. The very act of squishing the orange pretty much instantly renders it as nutritionally useful as a deep fried Mars Bar. You have to messily eat the orange in its natural state, or else you might as well drink melted butter.

I continue to largely ignore Eileen's diet advice, though I do think of her every time I drink orange juice, so that's nice.

Unexpectedly, the chief and I had coffee at six a.m. before she went home.

'I hope you don't think I used you,' she said, looking troubled.

I managed not to spit my coffee out.

'Never crossed my mind. But if that's using me, feel free to keep doing it until you move to Switzerland.'

We smiled. The smiles held the unspoken fact that this was a one-off. Well, it was the second one-off. A thing that happened.

We chatted amiably. She left. *See you in a couple of hours.*

And the door was closed, and I went for a shower, and then I made breakfast, and now I'm sitting here, and I'm searching the Internet for word of Michael Clayton, which is not something I've done in a long time, and there's nothing. Barely a mention of him anywhere since he was convicted and sentenced to life imprisonment, and any discussion of him that there is, is all in the past tense. There's no news of his life of incarceration. I mean, that's fair enough, the fucker shouldn't have any life to report. Nevertheless, he's a manipulative bastard, and he'll have been doing *something*. The fact that whatever that something is has never drawn any attention to him is far more worrying.

I search, I find nothing, I eat breakfast, I determine I will call the prison when I get into work this morning.

19

'Hey.'

'Morning.'

'What'd you do last night? You look tired.'

'Mind working overtime,' I say. 'Didn't sleep well.'

'Looking into your retirement with dread at a future deprived of meaning?'

'Thinking about Michael Clayton.'

That puts a quick end to the familiar morning chitchat.

Standing at the coffee machine, me and Eileen, traditional first thing in the morning formation. I expect the same people who advise Eileen not to drink orange juice, would also advise me not to drink four cups of coffee in the morning, but here we are, on the fast train to oblivion. Coffee is good, alcohol is good, sex is good. Nothing else matters.

She touches my arm. The machine spits and gargles its two cups of Americano with milk.

'I thought you didn't do that anymore.'

I look at her. I squeeze her fingers, and she squeezes my arm and removes her hand, with an instinctive quick glance around to see if anyone's watching this unexpected moment of intimacy.

'Well, people have started dying in inventively cruel and horrible ways,' I say. 'It seems kind of obvious now that I've thought of it.'

'He's in prison.'

'He should be.'

'What does that mean?'

I shrug.

'I presume he's still in prison,' I say. 'I'm just going to check.'

'The man is still going to be in prison. This killer, these killers, whoever they are, it's not him.'

She squeezes my arm again. I watch the coffee splutter to its conclusion. I can feel her looking at me. Her concern is nice, yet meaningless. I've thought myself into a hole here, and I'm not sure what the way out's going to be.

'Tom?'

I lift the coffees, and hand her one of the cups.

'I'm going to call Shotts just to make sure. Trouble is… even if he's still there –'

'He's still going to be there.'

'Even if he is, doesn't mean he's not orchestrating this from inside. This has his name written all over it. The more one thinks about it, the more one examines the methods, it says its him. From the delight in the grotesque, to his choice of victims. Look at him. He's killing people that the general public are going to be quite happy are dead. A *lot* of people are going to be on his side.'

'He's in prison.'

'He never actually carried out the Plague of Crows business, did he? He did all the, you know, he planned it, and he taunted us, and he took care of the online element, but he got someone else to carry out the murders. When I got…' I swallow, take a moment. Jesus, this stuff really messes with my head. 'When I was there, when I watched whatever that guy's name was, when I watched him die, when she started to cut into my skull with the thing, the bone saw, that wasn't Michael Clayton, was it? That wasn't Clayton taking a bullet. And you know what? Maybe some of those dumb Dylan murders that he did, maybe some of them weren't him either. Who knows? We didn't have direct evidence of him for every one of those deaths. It would've been entirely on brand for him to have been coercing someone else into active, bloody participation. He coerced the psychiatrist in that case, didn't he?'

Take a breath. Jesus.

This time, Eileen takes hold of my hand. Her fingers are cool.

'As we say in Glasgow, calm the fuck down, man, calm the fuck down.'

She smiles, I smile with her. My heart going. She's right, of course. With the exception of twenty minutes talking to the chief this morning, I've been thinking about this shit for five hours now. Your brain will really mess with you when you worry about the same thing for that long. Every single apocalyptic eventuality courses through your mind, each one horrifically worse that the one before.

I start walking to my desk, and Eileen comes with me. DC Ritter is not yet here, and Eileen sits down opposite me. I look at the phone, check the time. Decide that I'll leave it until after nine to call the prison. I can wait that long. Of course, prior to that, I can go into our systems and see if there's any mention of the deviously sick bastard.

'So, let me ask you a question,' says Eileen.

I smile, take a drink of coffee. It's not awful, though not as good as the one I make at home.

Maybe that's something I can do in retirement. Be one of those people who spends hours every day making the perfect cup of coffee. I can learn to use one of those Italian Moka pots. I always see those wee things and think, the fuck do you do with that? Can't be that complicated.

'Go on.'

'Is this your case?'

'That's not the point.'

'Is this your case?'

'No.'

'Why don't you alert Eurydice to your concerns. I mean, I do see your point. There are similarities here. If our man wasn't in prison, then you know, you might be right. This has his name written all over it. So, in fact, it's reasonable to pass it on. For all that Eurydice knows just how much of a giant fuck-up you can be on an investigation,' and we smile grimly together at that, 'she'll also know she can weirdly, and conversely, trust your instincts. You may well be right. She'll check. She *will* check. It's her case. Let her make the enquiries. You don't have to go anywhere near this. And if she decides there's anything needing doing, if she decides Clayton needs interviewed to try to establish what kind of contact he has with people on the outside, then it will be her that does it. Not you. After all, you call Shotts, what are they going to say? Hmm? Why are you asking? That's the first question. And you don't have an answer, because it's not your case, and you can't say it is. So... leave it to Eurydice.'

I stare across the desk. I nod. I put the coffee cup to my lips, take a drink.

'You're going to call Shotts, aren't you?'

I don't reply, which is, of course, a reply in itself.

Eileen sits back, though she's not relaxing into the seat. She's done her bit, she's given me what is, by any measure, very good advice. I get a familiar look, then finally she stands.

'Let me know when you need me to pick up the pieces,' she says.

'I'm fine. I'll be fine. I just need to check. And if, you know, if there's anything to be passed on, I will call Eurydice. I promise.'

'Of course.'

'Maybe he died and we never heard. So there's that.'

I get her look of concern, and then she turns away from the desk, coffee in hand, and heads across the office.

20

'I'm sorry, that prisoner is no longer held in HMP Shotts.'

I finally get my call put through to the liaison officer in charge of police visits, and after the basic opening pleasantries, she whacks me over the head with that.

It *needn't* be bad, of course. Prisoners move prisons on a regular basis. But not people like Clayton. They should go to Shotts, and they should stay in Shotts.

'He's no longer there,' I repeat, my voice deadpan.

She sounds officious. Or perhaps I'm just reading that into the tone. But I need to not sound as judgemental as I know I'm about to feel, or her officiousness will be off the scale.

'No.' There's a pause while she waits for my next question, and while I hope she's just going to explain why he's no longer there without me having to ask.

I win this tiny-assed battle of wills.

'Ms Clayton was transferred to HMP Cornton Vale eighteen months ago.'

I stare straight ahead. DC Ritter arrives in the office, disposable coffee cup in one hand, backpack held in the other. She nods across the desk, drops the bag on the floor and kicks it beneath her desk, pulls out the chair and sits down. Blows a couple of loose hairs off her forehead, which of course makes no difference whatsoever, then takes a drink of coffee, pushes her hair back, then leans into her desk and turns her computer on.

'That didn't happen,' is weirdly the only way I can think to respond to this prison update. As I say it, I know the words are useless. I obviously don't know this woman at all, but she is highly unlikely to have made that shit up.

'January seventeenth, last year. We have the paperwork. You should contact HMP Cornton Vale if you would like to speak to the prisoner.'

Emma has noticed the look on my face, and mouths, 'Everything OK?' across the desk. I kind of nod, in a way that she'll know means that it isn't, but there's not a lot to be said about it at the moment.

Another movement across the office, and the chief arrives. She nods at Emma, acknowledges me in a totally innocent, there's-no-way-we-slept-together-last-night-I-don't-know-what-any-of-you-are-thinking kind of a way, and then she's into her office. She starts to close the door, then thinks better of it, and pushes it back fully open, then she's out of sight as she goes to her desk.

'Are you aware of how that came to be?' I ask.

'You mean, the particulars of Ms Clayton's transfer to the female prison?'

'Yes.'

She pauses. I get the sense she's reading notes on a file, rather than taking the time to consider how to answer, or perhaps even considering not answering at all.

'Ms Clayton started transitioning four years ago, and petitioned via her representatives to move to the female prison three years ago. This was granted eighteen months ago.'

'He started to transition?'

'She.'

I have nothing. Emma catches my eye every now and again.

'Ours is not to judge, Detective Sergeant Hutton,' says the woman on the phone, surprising me a little. Perhaps, in the gentle admonishment, she is not judging me as much as I suppose she would.

'Is it recorded in your notes there, how far Ms Clayton has transitioned?'

'Ms Clayton had not, at the point she left our facility, undergone any surgical procedure, but had started on a basic program of hormone therapy.'

'Did this really happen?' I ask. It's a stupid question, but this feels so absurd I can't help asking it.

'Yes, of course.'

'It would've been in the news, surely. I mean, I just…'

Heart rate starting to pick up. I mean, ultimately, it shouldn't make any difference. It's not like Cornton Vale has an open-door policy. Nevertheless, we can see where this is going. Someone as cold and calculating as Clayton, is going to have thought this through to its natural conclusion, one that is to his great advantage.

'There are currently eleven transwomen prisoners in

Cornton Vale. The ones that make the news are the violent sex offenders. Ms Clayton is not, nor ever has been, a violent sex offender.'

'He was literally a serial killer!' I can't help saying way louder than I ought, unintentionally rising a little out of my seat.

Heart thumping, skin beginning to crawl.

'I'm only reading to you what's in the file,' she says. 'I wasn't here at that time, but obviously, even if I had been, the decisions taken in relation to this prisoner would've been nothing to do with me. Reading between the lines, and really, this is between you and me, Ms Clayton clearly has very good legal representation. While everything with the prison transfer appears to have been above board, and of course, entirely in line with Scottish government policy at the time, it would seem that Ms Clayton's lawyers ran an aggressive campaign to ensure the media were either not made aware of the transfer, and if any by chance did find out, they were threatened with various actions to ensure their silence.'

'Fuck me,' is just out of my mouth before I can stop it. I wave a silent apology, which is completely lost on her, obviously. Perhaps Emma thinks I'm apologising to her. Once again she mouths a question, though I can't make this one out.

'That's all I have for you, detective sergeant. If you require any further information, you should contact Cornton Vale.'

'K, thanks,' I say.

We hang up.

Emma and I stare at each other across the desks. She asks the question with a what's up gesture.

'You know who Michael Clayton is?' I say.

'Yes, of course.' A pause, her face darkens. 'Wait, he hasn't done something, has he?'

'He changed his gender, got moved to Cornton Vale eighteen months ago.'

She opens her mouth a little wider than is normally considered decent, giving me one of those young persons' looks they all learned from watching People React To videos on YouTube, which is a thing that someone my age cannot begin to understand. People React To Finding Out Bombay Duck Has No Duck In It. *Whaaaaaat?*

'You are not serious,' she says, not so far removed from placing a full stop at the end of each word.

'Yes. I doubt anyone can possibly believe that, but that's

where we are.'

I hold her look across the desk, and then push my chair back and get to my feet. Lift the cup of coffee, take a long drink.

'I'm not going to call them,' I say. 'Just going to head out.' I nod in the direction of the boss. 'It's not a secret, if the chief comes asking.'

She gives me another concerned look, but it's not like DC Ritter was around back then. All she knows is what she'll have seen on the news, and what she might have read in the files. I've never spoken to her about it. I've never dropped into conversation that he haunts me, that he's so far inside my head he's a brain-sized malignancy, and that some nights, when I lie awake, I wish to God I'd just put a bullet in his face when I had the chance.

I turn away, consider just walking out, but stop at the door, and then turn back to speak to Eileen. I owe her far more than just this.

'He's in Cornton Vale,' I say, standing at her desk.

Eileen, likely even more shocked than Ritter, gives the more traditional reaction of her age. A look of despair, disdain, and then the withering eyeroll. 'You have got to be kidding me.'

'No one is shocked. Indeed, ought to have seen it coming.'

'How long's he been there?'

'Year and a half.'

'Jesus. And it wasn't news because he's not a rapist, and he has good lawyers.'

I tap the side of my head.

'Wise beyond your years, I've said it all along.'

'Where are you going?'

I answer with a small shrug.

'You are not.'

'I have to.'

'Tom, seriously. You promised.'

'I have to. No one knows him like I do. I'll just have a wee chat, nothing, you know…'

'Tom, the man messes with your head without going anywhere near you,' says Eileen, 'do not put yourself through this. Eurydice is good. She can handle him. Leave the man alone.'

'He's not a man anymore. It's a completely different ballgame,' I say glibly. Superficial bullshit, of course, as every fool knows. 'I'll report back in.'

Her eyes widen as she starts to object, and then I turn away and walk quickly from the office.

21

Sitting in a small office, waiting for the deputy governor. I've got this far into the facility, which is unusual in itself. Prisons don't like police officers turning up without an appointment, which is understandable.

So far, no one has told me anything. I have no idea if I'm about to be admitted to speak to Clayton. Of course, ninety-nine point nine (infinitely repeated) percent of me hopes they say no. I *want* them to say no. I was driven to come here. I had to. I *have* to sit in a room with this bastard and look him in the eye. I need to know whether he's got someone on the outside doing all his outrageous dirty work for him. And sure, of course he could just stare blankly back at me, deadpan and dismissive, and say he has no idea what I'm talking about. But my conceit is that I understand him. I know him. I'll be able to read him like a cheap paperback.

Michael Clayton. Or, as I've been informed, Alice Clayton. *Alice.*

Jesus.

The door opens, a man in his late thirties enters. Shirt and tie, sleeves rolled up. Not sure what I'd been expecting, but this guy has something of the Westminster first term Tory politician about him. Still thinks he can change the system, still thinks he can bend the party to his ways, still thinks he can make a difference. This man has another thirty years of work ahead of him, during which time his aspirations will be crushed, and he will either die unfulfilled and unhappy, or he will slowly, over time, be subsumed by the bubble, and become what he currently despises. No other options available.

'Detective Sergeant Hutton, thanks for coming over,' he says, as he takes his seat. I nod. I have a feeling I'm not going to find it easy to speak. I mean, apart from saying things like *you have got to be fucking kidding me*, which I predict I'll find coming to me very easily. I should probably try to keep this guy on board, however.

He opens up a thin brown folder, scanning quickly through a couple of papers. Hard to believe that any folder with Clayton as its subject could be that thin. Possibly, of course, he's looking at a report on something else, just leaving me hanging here until he's done.

He looks up.

'You were one of the arresting officers when Ms Clayton was originally detained?'

I nod again.

He nods in return, something annoying in it, then he lowers his head, looking back at the file, this time softly tapping the edge of the desk with both hands.

'Without paperwork or proper authorisation,' he begins, 'and without Ms Clayton's lawyer having been appropriately notified, under normal circumstances this request of yours would, I'm afraid, have been summarily rejected.'

Oh, shit. Under normal circumstances. Those words just come out of nowhere and bludgeon me over the head. *Under normal circumstances.*

He stares at me expectantly. It would appear he's waiting for me to ask about these circumstances everyone's talking about. There ensues a peculiar battle of wills, with me unable to speak, and him waiting for me to enquire further. However, when it comes to being interactionally weird, I am always going to kick this guy's arse for him. I can do weird in ways this guy can only dream of.

I possibly shouldn't have stopped off at home to have three shots of vodka on the way here.

That happened.

'Ms Clayton was released on parole three months ago.'

Oh.

Well, I win in the game of silence. He cracked. He said the thing. That pyrrhic victory aside, I lose at everything else.

I swallow. My insides curdle. If I couldn't talk before, I certainly can't do it now.

He licks his lips in a curiously reptilian way, then looks back at the file.

'Alice was the most cooperative, the most helpful prisoner any of us have ever seen here, I believe. In her short time, she gave of herself quite fully to the betterment of others. She helped everyone, prison guards included on more than one occasion, at any opportunity she received. You may recall the early parole scheme the government introduced last year. A rather blatant attempt to reduce the prison population, and not at all popular, of course. Naturally, given the crimes for which Alice was imprisoned, she was not eligible for the scheme. However, she was able to successfully bring a case against the government and the parole board, so that her application was at least considered, and from there, well she was, as any of us who knew her knew she would be, quite exceptional in the presentation and execution of her case. The parole board were quite taken with her.'

'Where is he now?' I manage, the first four words to crawl unhappily from my lips.

'She.'

Take a moment.

'Where is she now?'

'I believe at her home in Glasgow. I'm afraid it will not be up to me to supply you with those details, however. You'll need to contact the relevant authorities.'

Something snaps in my head. Words start appearing in my mouth, when before they seemed so unlikely.

'How is it,' I begin, and now I'm having to stop myself, and then I think, whatever, this is just some guy whose jurisdiction over Clayton has long since ended, so what difference does it make, 'how is it that this *fucking* guy, the most notorious fucking killer in Scotland in the last twenty years, how *the fuck* can he get released without the police service being notified? How the fuck did he get released and it wasn't in the news? I mean, *the news*? Those fuckers have sensationalist bullshit coming out of every orifice, how the fuck could they not have picked up on this?'

His shoulders have straightened a little. I'd say he doesn't like it up 'im.

'I'm a very busy man,' he says, closing the file and getting to his feet. He indicates the door. 'I've told you all that I can for the moment. Ms Clayton is not here. I'm sure there are people who will be able to satisfactorily answer your questions, but it is not me. Good day.'

I'm not so close to his desk that I can't lean forward, elbows on my knees, and put my head in my hands. Jesus. I can feel the shakes coming. The fear and the horror building inside, like my body is about to start quaking, like it will shudder so much it will end up breaking apart, exploding apart, bursting into a thousand, horrific bloody pieces.

'Sergeant?'

I take a deep breath. Ladies and gentlemen, I'm going to need a bigger bottle of vodka.

22

I walk into the chief's office. First time we've spoken to each other since the amiable chat over coffee this morning. That seems a lifetime ago, a light year away. Another world. A simpler time. Albeit, by then, I'd already started thinking about Clayton, I was already starting to put the pieces together.

I stand inside the office for a moment, as we stare silently at each other, and then I close the door and walk further into the room.

'You're not all right,' says Hawkins, and I kind of shake my head. 'Have you heard? I'm not sure how you –'

'Heard what?'

'You were right about Warburton. The video of his death just came in. The same set up.' A pause, and then, 'This time his insides were eaten by what appears to be a wolf. God knows where the killer got hold of a wolf. It was, as you can imagine, particularly savage. The address has been given, Eurydice is on her way, I believe. They will have to be particularly careful, given what they're dealing with. There will be a team, naturally, instructed to shoot the wolf on sight. They did it with the Shih Tzu puppies after all.'

'The letter at the end of the video, stamped on the forehead,' I say. 'It was G…' I add, just as she's saying, 'G this time,' and she straightens her shoulders a little, her brow furrowing, looking at me curiously.

'I'm not sure I like the sound of you having worked it out. Go on.'

'He's spelling out Plague of Crows. Or plague, at any rate.'

She holds my look for a few moments, and then, as I knew she would, she starts shaking her head.

'No, no.' A pause, and then, 'No, I don't think so. It can't be. He's in prison.'

'He's on parole.'

'He can't be.'

I indicate her monitor.

'You have more access than me. Check the parole records. But don't look for Michael Clayton, look for Alice. Alice Clayton.'

She holds my gaze, curiosity still on her face, and then she turns to the screen and starts typing quickly.

She swallows loudly. Colour draining from her face. She reads all she needs to read to confirm what I've just told her, and then she swallows again, her eyes drifting off to the side. Her brow starts to knit together. Thinking through the whole thing. The murders, and the killer's delight in the grotesquery of them. The P and the L and the A and the G. They don't mean PumaMan and LobotomyGirl and Absolute KnobheadGuy and GigantaPrick, like the press have been hypothesising. And not just the press. There's been plenty of that shit going on in the offices of Police Scotland. But here we are, and everything seems to be falling into place.

'Don't do anything,' she says, a note of determination finding its way into her voice.

'Don't do anything?' I say, unable to stop the laugh. 'What is it you think I'm about to do?'

'Go round to her house.'

'It's *his* house,' I say. 'This man is a cunt. This man is playing the system, because he is the kind of person who always plays the system.'

'We don't know that,' she says, holding up a couple of placatory hands.

'We know all we need to know about this guy.'

'OK, Tom, fair enough. We can agree to disagree on how she should be known, but you are not going anywhere near her, do you understand?'

'I won't.'

'Good. Leave it with me. I'll call Eurydice. It'll be up to her to do with it as she thinks best. Given the nature of what's been going on here, I can imagine she'll take the suggestion of Clayton's involvement seriously, but it will be up to her to find her and interview her.'

I lift an accepting hand. Fine, whatever. Put whatever procedures in place that you want, chief. Safeguards and barriers between me and him, but now that it's started, I know. It ain't finishing until he and I are alone in a room, and this time if the bastard has the chutzpah to put a gun in my hand, I'm using it. Which means, of course, that we know he won't.

We hold a look across the desk, the urgency and potency going out of the discussion. A return to the more nuanced, closer feel of the chat we had at breakfast this morning. Or perhaps, the chief is just remembering what she learned on some course on dealing with troubled members of staff.

'Perhaps... perhaps you should go home,' she says. 'This horror story aside, things are quiet around here. Emma is more than capable.' Another pause, and then, 'Perhaps you ought to just start your retirement now, as previously discussed.'

Standing here, it seems pointless. If he's out there somewhere, and he appears to be out there somewhere, then he has my name on a list. He can't not have. He did before. He killed several people just to taunt me, after all. If he's at it again, there's no way he won't, at the very least, be including me in the hit list.

'This just you trying to get rid of me because we had sex?' I say. 'I can bring a case of constructive dismissal.'

She smiles, and shakes her head.

'No, you couldn't, and you know that's not it.'

'I know.'

Deep breath.

'Maybe I'll go,' I say, 'but not just yet. Call Eurydice. If she thinks there's anything in this, then I might as well be here to speak to her about it. She can get from me what she thinks she needs, and then she can decide if she's happy for me to go. Because, once I'm gone...'

I shrug. Once I'm gone I'll head home via the off licence and drink myself into oblivion.

She nods, reluctantly I think, and then indicates the door.

'You've got things you can do?' she asks.

'Always.'

I kind of smile, and leave her to call the DCI.

23

'OK, we'll do it.'

I look at Eileen over the top of my club sandwich. Pleasant early afternoon, sitting outside in the precinct just below the first floor offices of the police station. Club sandwich each. Eileen has water, I have Coke Zero. She frowned. I said it's this or wine.

What I really want is more vodka. I think she's sitting here with me so that I don't go home, unaware that I'm dutifully holding off in case I'm needed.

These days I tend to drink wine rather than vodka. Some shit about a maturing palate. That'll be it. But all it means is that when I do turn to vodka, I could drink the entire bottle. Did pretty well to just have those three shots before I drove out to Cornton Vale.

I'm going to need to see Clayton at some point, regardless of what any of my authority figures say. Probably today, now that it's out there. Tomorrow at the latest. I believe it's something that'll best be undertaken at least a little inebriated.

I look curiously across the table at her. I could probably work out what she means if I thought about it, but I'm distracted, so don't even try.

'Sounds great,' I say. 'What is it we're doing?'

'Going to Canada.'

I smile sadly, and take a bite of sandwich. This is my usual, and favourite lunch, but I'm barely tasting it today. It's a stomach-liner.

'You realise I'm a detective and can work out what you're doing here?' I say.

She nods. She smiles.

'I get that.'

'You're willing to retire a week or two ahead of schedule, and come on holiday with me, just to stop me doing anything stupid?'

She nods through a mouthful of sandwich. We hold the

look. One of those looks we'd lost for a long time. One of those looks which I always feel I don't deserve from her.

'I mean, don't get carried away here, chum,' she says. 'If these bastards don't want me, I might as well just leave, right? And it's not like you're asking me to go to a one-star dump in the shittiest part of Transnistria.'

'You've been looking at the hotel in Banff?'

'Yep.'

'Draws you in, doesn't it?'

'Yep.'

'I've never looked at the price, to be honest.'

'I did,' she says.

'Go on.'

'We can afford to have a cup of tea, though a piece of cake might by tricky without dipping into our pensions.'

'What about staying the night?'

'Maybe if I mortgage my apartment.'

'You could sell it and move in with me.'

I get the sudden sense that the conversation has hit the point where it's become a little too uncomfortable. Maybe we've both thought at some point of moving in together. That it might actually be a long-term option.

Have I ever thought that before? No, perhaps not. I don't know. But suddenly it feels like something that one of us might have seriously considered, while at the same time thinking there's not a snowball's chance of it actually happening.

'You really check how much it is for a room?' I ask, to return the conversation to some sort of equilibrium.

'We can get a small suite for a couple of grand a night,' she says. 'Next week.'

'That sounds doable. Business class flights to Calgary?'

'Oh, didn't check that, but it should be fine. How expensive can a long-haul business class flight be?'

I pop the last of the sandwich into my mouth. That settles it. I'm not sure what settles it, but something does. I need to go home and drink vodka. If Eurydice is at hand when I get back to the station, fine. If not, then she'll know where to find me.

I look away from Eileen, straighten my shoulders as I'm aware of slouching, nod to myself. Can feel that old, familiar creep of fear and self-loathing. I need to drown it out.

'Some other time,' I say after a few moments.

I don't look at her. I can't. I can't have her care too much about me, not when I'm just going to throw it back in her face.

She reaches across the table. Not all the way, placing her hand there if I want to take her up on the offer. The supportive finger squeeze. The affirmation of affection, and intentions well meant. Perhaps more than that.

I can't have her offering more than that. I'm only going to fuck it up, fuck her up, the way I've always done in the past.

I look at her at last. I can't stop myself placing my fingers lightly on her hand.

'I need to go home.'

We both know what that means. She has nothing to say.

*

My work here is done. My to-do list has become very simple.

One. Get drunk.

Two. Go and see Clayton.

The jury remains out on whether number two on the list is going to happen while drunk, or while hungover and feeling like the vomited remains of a rancid dog's dinner.

Is it the dog or the dinner that's rancid? Hmm...

Walk back into the office to get my car keys, close the computer down. Tell Emma that I'm off for the day.

Eileen walks away from me without a word. She wasn't being serious about Canada – I'm pretty sure – but whether she was or she wasn't, she was quite literally reaching out to me and I responded with my usual narcissistic bullshit. It's about me destroying myself, not about her trying to care for me.

We both stop at Eurydice emerging from the chief's office, like she knew I'd just arrived. She first catches Eileen's eye and they share a nod. Like, a knowing sort of nod. My detective smarts say there's something going on there, but I'm too eaten up by my inner call to self-destruction to really care, and then Eurydice is looking at me, indicating for me to join her in the chief's office.

Now Eileen and I look at each other. One of those many-layered blank looks that one has in life, that sometimes it's best not to over-analyse, and then I turn away and walk through to the boss's office.

There are two seats set up by Hawkins' desk, but as I close the door behind me, it's apparent that no one's going to be sitting down. The chief is standing behind her desk, Eurydice to the side.

'You've been working outwith your remit, I hear,' says Eurydice, to get the ball rolling. There's no harshness in her tone, nevertheless.

'Yes.'

'You went to Cornton Vale? That must've been popular.'

'Not so much.'

'The repeated use of the word fuck maybe wasn't great.'

'Word gets around, huh?'

She folds her arms. Here we are, me and Eurydice where we usually end up when we're working on the same case.

'We're already aware of Mr Clayton,' says Eurydice. 'I know his whole story was pretty much kept under wraps, and no one was talking about it. And I know he's somehow managed to weaponize his mental health and his claims of gender transition in a quite spectacular way, but it's not like we haven't been aware of what was going on. We knew he moved prison, and we knew those absolute clowns on the parole board saw fit to release him. This is the world we live in, and we have to adapt. Nevertheless, as soon as this first murder video dropped, we were looking into his movements. We have him covered. He is not the killer.'

'You have him covered?'

'Yes.'

'Where is he?'

She pauses. Hawkins is a spectator, but I don't think she'll mind not having a part to play, particularly now that her days in Police Scotland are hopefully numbered.

'At home.'

'And you've got him watched twenty-four-seven?'

'Yes.'

'How many people?'

'How many people are watching him twenty-four seven?'

She doesn't answer.

'It's not enough,' I say anyway. 'You've got a huge hunt on here for what, according to everyone, is potentially a group of vengeful killers. Many or one, it doesn't matter, we're in a sadly all-too-familiar all hands on deck situation. There's no way you can afford to have someone at the front of his house and at the back of his house, and making sure he doesn't nip out under the cover of darkness and scurry through the trees of that big garden of his and nip over the fence. And in the last few days, I can't believe you'll have had the resources to set up cameras or drones, even if you weren't too damned pusillanimous to do so, because this man can use a lawyer the way other criminals use machetes, and sometimes it's like he owns the police. And I like you, and you seem to be pretty decent at what you do, but you're liable to be in thrall to this guy same as everyone else, and you can't afford to be *seen* to be watching him, which means you won't be watching him closely enough.'

Silence, borne of her knowing I'm right, because that's just how it is.

'We have someone at the front of his house,' she says after a few moments.

'Are you going to go and speak to him?'

More silence. This one, I must admit, I'm not sure I'm able to decipher. She's liable to not tell me either way.

'If you do, can I come with you?'

'No.'

'I know him.'

'I know.'

'I know him better than you. When you're speaking to him, I should be in the room.'

'You're a liability, detective sergeant. I've asked you in here today to pick your brains, to see if you have any advice regarding this man, but you are not *on the case*, and you will not go anywhere near Mr Clayton.'

'What's with the Mr Clayton, anyway? Are you not obligated to bow at the feet of his gender reassignment claims?'

Her face is hardening. Taking it a bit more personally now, as I, reckless and feeling the need to get home and get the vodka production line up and running, seek to push her away, into the corner with all the other well-meaning suits and do-gooders.

'I am,' she says, her voice getting colder by the minute. 'To no one's surprise, since maintaining his gender reassignment wasn't part of his parole stipulations, having decided he was more likely to achieve parole if he changed gender, and having behaved impeccably at Cornton Vale to gain his release, he immediately gave up the pretence upon returning home. I'm sure the parole board would be shocked at the suggestion they might have been played.'

She says the last line with perfect, dismissive scorn.

I don't react. I mean, come on, we all knew.

Eurydice and I silently hold a look for a few moments, and

then I turn to Hawkins.

'I'm going home, boss,' I say. 'Sorry.'

'You don't have to –'

'I doubt I'll be in tomorrow.'

I turn away, and as my fingers touch the door handle, Eurydice stops me with, 'Give me some advice. As you say, you know him better than anyone. You also know it would be disastrous for the police and for you personally if you were to go anywhere near him. So please.'

I've listened to her with my head down, frozen in the act of opening the door. Take a moment, and then turn.

'Go round there right now and take him into custody. Find something. Anything. Don't be scared of his lawyers. Be the police officers everyone thinks we are. Have no fucks to give. Don't let him contact anyone. Find something, anything to hold him, see what effect it has on this murderfest. Maybe it proves nothing. Sure, even if everything stops, it doesn't *prove* anything. Even if it continues, perhaps he's just doing what he did with the Crows business and he's got someone else doing the dirty work for him. But that man should not be out of prison, and if you can use this as a reason to get him off the streets, even if he's got nothing to do with this bullshit, then you should take it.' A pause, she doesn't leap in to fill it, and so I say, 'He one hundred percent has something to do with this, and the P-L-A-G crap is him taunting us. You. Me. The entire force.'

She still has nothing to say, and then, with a final glance at the boss, I'm out of the office, walking quickly to my desk, and, with nothing bar a regretful glance in Eileen's direction, I'm gone.

Multitudes 5

'Why are you here?'

Margaret Stillwood, dumped on the floor, chained at the wrists and feet, stared grimly back at her captor through the half-light of the basement. She didn't answer.

'Why are you here?'

'I'm not scared.'

'Interesting.'

'Is it?'

'No one seems to be scared anymore.'

She stared dimly at him. As soon as the killings had started, she'd wondered if this would happen. After all, some would consider her worthy of such a punishment. Accused, obviously guilty, allowed her freedom by a system skewered curiously in favour of the perpetrator. She hadn't physically hurt anyone, of course, but this was Britain after all, and most people weirdly considered hurting dogs to be an even greater crime.

She'd thought of running. It would've made sense. But then, it didn't matter how logical it was for her to be taken by what she presumed was the Rough Justice League, and how much sense it made for her to run, because at the same time she'd been gripped by that other great conceit of humanity. *It won't happen to me.* Bad things happen to other people. And the *tick-tock* note? That had been easy enough to ignore, even when the police started talking about it. She assumed thousands of people had probably received one.

'You know how this plays out already.'

'Yes.'

'So there's no point in offering you a deal?'

'I don't know what that would be.'

'Confess on film and I won't kill your father.'

She laughed. A rueful sound, the killer almost found it attractive.

'If you didn't already know, I'd give you his address,' she said. 'He's all yours.'

The killer stared grimly at her, an air of defeat having come upon him. He was unfamiliar with the feeling. He'd enjoyed this process, the series of grim murders, up until this point. He'd made this miscalculation, however. His methods had been worked out, people knew what was coming. There had only been one confession, and there were unlikely to be any others.

At least there would be deaths. So, there was that.

He turned away and walked out of the pool of light, so that he was lost in the darkness beyond.

Margaret Stillwood stared after him, into the space where he'd been a moment earlier. From nowhere she felt butterflies, an unexpected anxiety. A strange laugh appeared in her throat, echoing briefly into the empty basement, bouncing off the walls.

Movement, and then he was back, the knife in his hands.

'You're boring me,' he said.

'Oh, God!' she said, her voice finally infected by fear.

He plunged the knife, a little further than usual, into her abdomen just beneath the rib cage.

24

The phone rings.

On the way home I bought more vodka, tonic and crisps. Actual scientists say that crisps are the most important food group. On this occasion, black pepper and sea salt.

The tonic is my one concession to common sense. Don't just drink shots. Don't tip the vodka straight into your stupid mouth from the bottle. Sure, the bottle's getting finished, and the next, but let's at least try not to complete this journey in half an hour. Let's spin it out until this evening before you collapse.

The phone's still ringing.

I rolled the crisp packet up and stuffed it against the other arm of the sofa when it was about half done. Got myself some chunks of cheese and a few olives. That'll do. Thought about making toast, but couldn't be bothered, and also, I'm not that hungry, it being not so long since the lunchtime club sandwich.

It's been a while, vodka and tonic, my old friend. You have not lost your magic.

'What?'

I put the phone on speaker, leave it lying on the sofa next to me.

'Sergeant Hutton?'

Eurydice.

Now, don't say anything stupid. Focus. You probably have to say *something*, but, you know, try not to be a complete moron.

To avoid saying something stupid, I mutter incoherently.

'You may be right,' she says.

I don't speak.

'We've just been round there. Looks like Clayton's cleared out. He'd managed to get his GPS bracelet off, left it for us sitting on a table.' I still don't say anything, and so Eurydice talks through the silence. 'We can't leap to conclusions necessarily, but we definitely need to find him. We would be looking for him anyway, obviously, but we'll ramp this up under the circumstances.'

I stare at the television. I'm watching lesbian porn, because fuck it, if you're going to give in to one of your addictions… Look, could be worse, right? Could be Fentanyl or crack cocaine, and then I would barely be able to answer the phone.

'Can you come into the office? We could do with picking your brains.'

Stupidly, for a second, I contemplate it, then the word, 'No,' just takes control and emerges of its own accord.

'You've been drinking?'

'That's correct, defective.'

'Detective,' I add after a second.

Jesus, what was that? Are you playing a comedy drunk in a Carry On movie?

There's a hesitant silence from the other end of the phone.

'Maybe you'll be able to come in tomorrow.'

I have nothing to say to that. I stare at the ladies on the screen. I searched "MILF lesbians real tits." Only one of the three women onscreen has not had work done on her breasts. I'll need to complain to the algorithm team at Pornhub.

'I doubt it,' I manage.

Well, that was better than what I was actually wanting to say. Which was *bugger off, you had your chance, what did you think was going to happen when I walked out of that station?*

'You're still a police officer, and lives are at stake.'

Nice try.

I manage not to say that either. But a variety of bold declarations, ranging from the glib to the downright offensive, are beginning to form a queue, so I do the sensible thing and end the call.

'Fuck off,' I say to the dead phone.

*

Phone rings again a while later. I'm now, and this may be too much information, naked on the sofa with an erection. Vodka tonic in one hand, hard, damp cock in the other.

This is my life. Never have to go back to work, decent pension, mortgage paid off, I can sit here every day like a bum, drinking and watching women fuck on the TV. That's a life, right? With the bonus that you don't get into any emotional entanglement with any of these ladies.

I look at my phone.

Elise.

Hmm.

This might go better if I wasn't drunk. And erect. Turned on, under these circumstances, is not good.

'Hey,' I say.

'What's up?'

'Why are you calling?'

Well, that's a solid start. Aiming to take none of her shit.

'Wondered if you were doing anything tonight?' she says.

I forgot she views my curtness as performative indifference. Her generation have taken ownership of the notion that everyone can be themselves, everyone is free to express their inner identity without fear of judgement, everything is real.

'What are you watching?' she asks, with a laugh in her voice.

I turned the volume off for Eurydice's call. Didn't bother this time.

'MILF lesbians.'

She giggles.

'Aren't you at work? Or is this work, and you're investigating some illegal lesbian porn scam?'

'I don't know what that scam would be,' I say, 'but I'd happily investigate it. But no, I'm at home. Afternoon off.'

'Ooh, nice. And you're watching porn?' She laughs, like watching porn while drinking vodka is not a perfectly solid way to spend an afternoon. 'Can I come over?' she tags on to the end of the laugh.

At this point I probably ought to finish masturbating, and then use the juxapositionary post-ejaculation moment of self-hating satisfaction to say no.

'Sure.'

I give her the address. She says, 'I'll be there in ten. Save some for me.'

She laughs again and hangs up.

I take a shower.

*

We watch porn and drink vodka tonic. She says she likes watching gangbangs, as long as the woman looks like she's not being exploited. Even drunk I think I have something to say about that. She sees the look on my face, and says, you know what I mean. As long as they look like they're into it. She finds a gangbang video she likes. She says one day she'll give being gangbanged a go, but she's not sure how one actually finds oneself in a real-life gangbang situation, not without some level of threat or abuse attached to it. I point out she had sex with three guys in Milan, and she says, 'I mean a *real* gangbang.'

I guess, so far, me and Elise is the real-life equivalent of watching porn. Emotional attachment seems as likely as getting emotionally attached to one of the fake-breasted women on the screen. She's having a laugh, and seems impervious to everything bad about me. Not because she loves me or any of that crap, but because she doesn't give a fuck. And neither do I.

We fuck on the couch to the background of the onscreen sex. I'm not as interested in it as she is. She comes a lot, again. I'd forgotten how easily she manages to do that. When I come, finally – and alcohol is good for some things, I suppose – she's sitting on top of me, facing away, my hands on her breasts, grinding her pussy into me, moaning and crying out, now like she's finally having to really work for her orgasm, an almost pained quality to her euphoria when it arrives.

She laughs when it's all over. She slumps back, softly running her hands over my legs. I know I'm going to be asleep in minutes. Seconds.

At some stage I'm aware of my legs being moved, and Elise saying she's going for a shower.

25

It's dark when I wake up, although that fact in itself takes a while to filter through the awfulness of how I'm feeling, and is told to me in the merest flickering of my eyes, which I close again. The television's still on. Been playing all this time. I can hear someone in the kitchen, the kettle rumbling to a climax.

Do I feel sick? Yes, it's there somewhere. The nausea. Though I'm lying still and my eyes are shut, so there's that. Let's see what happens when I try moving.

There's a blanket over me, which is why I'm not cold. The girl has stayed all afternoon, watched porn all afternoon, and is domesticated enough to put a blanket on me and get the kettle going.

No, that's not right. Doesn't make sense. I feel warm under the blanket, so it's been on a while. The fact that I never woke up cold, in fact, says that Elise put the blanket on some time ago. But she wouldn't have been watching porn all day. I mean, let's not get carried away about how well I know her, but still.

I swallow. Coming to terms with the fact that more than likely someone other than Elise is here.

Who's your money on?

Eileen is favourite. We've already established she can let herself in. And she has a long history of looking after me when I've fallen into the wastebasket of an alcoholic stupor, thankless a task though it's been for her.

But Eileen would also have turned the porn off.

And I doubt any of the other women at the office who may have some level of affection for me, or at least don't absolutely hate me to quite the level I deserve, would pitch up here and use their police skills to break into the apartment. But if they did, they too would have turned off the sex.

Who does it leave?

I can feel the fear. Just the inkling of it at first, as the thought forms. The creep of goosebumps across my skin. The tingle at the small of my back. The dry swallow. The first twisting in the stomach.

Really?

You're still drunk, remember. You're incapable of any cohesive thought, so why should any of the conclusions you've just come to make any sort of sense?

Come on, genius boy, open your eyes. See what you've got. See who it is who's just walked into the room. Where are your balls?

A cup is set down on the coffee table, then the soft pad of footsteps, and then someone taking a seat in the armchair, another cup set down.

I am, in my naked drunkenness, too scared to open my eyes.

What the fuck? I mean, seriously, what is the worst thing that can happen here? He kills me? Bring it on. We fight, he wins, I end up manacled to a wall, my stomach slit open, and get eaten by, I don't know what, vicious kittens, or worms, or baby red pandas. Fine. Bring it all on.

I think of Elise. Maybe she's in on it. No, don't be stupid. He would hardly need her. But maybe she was still here when he arrived.

I open my eyes.

Michael Clayton, sure as eggs is eggs. Sitting in my apartment. On that seat right there. Watching the television.

I look at him for a few moments. He hasn't changed, at all. I follow his gaze. There is a horrible scene playing out on the screen. That poor lassie is getting exploited like fuck. This is not the kind of gangbang that Elise goes for. I reach out to the TV remote and turn it off.

The room is lit by the small lamp by the table. The curtains are open. Interesting choice, if he's going to murder me where I lie.

'Oh, I was enjoying that,' says Clayton.

He leans forward and lifts his mug, taking an intentionally loud drink of tea, settling the mug back down with an equally loud, 'Ah, splendid.'

'You're breaking the conditions of your parole,' I manage.

I think I'm going to be sick. I suddenly wonder if he's manacled me to the chair in some way I hadn't realised, make a quick check of all my limbs, and determine he hasn't.

'Well, those conditions are so barbaric, aren't they? I mean, really. We both know I'm better than that.'

I look at him. I'm still lying down, naked beneath this blanket. I want to sit up. I want to get dressed. The fear that came crawling in behind closed eyes has gone, and now from nowhere, in my part drunken, part hungover state, I have the desire to nab him. Sure, I'm convinced he's this week's vicious killer, but even if he's not, he certainly belongs back in the slammer.

But if I sit up I'm going to heave, and that won't be compatible with making an arrest.

'What are you going to do?' I ask. I realise how thick my voice sounds.

'How'd you mean? Oh, you're not drinking your tea. I didn't poison it, don't fret.'

'You're going to stay on the run forever? What's the point? You got out. You played the system. Why didn't you just do what they asked?'

'God, it was so boring. Anyway, I have plans.' He chuckles. Fucker. 'You'll laugh. The very same plans I had to get away after our last escapade. They're all still there, still in place. Obviously, I've had to renew my plane ticket.' He laughs again. 'But that gorgeous Mediterranean villa is still waiting for me where it's been all this time. Those islands are quite beautiful, aren't they? And the colour of the water! I mean, people are complaining about the heat these days, but I *love it*.' A pause, and then, 'This time next week, although let's see how events play out.'

We look at each other. The stare across a couple of yards. God, I fucking hate this guy. Just get up and do something! What difference does it make if you vomit everywhere? Vomit on the prick. Put your hands to his throat and squeeze your thumbs into his trachea. He deserves no more.

I lie there, incapacitated by vodka. Even the thought of moving makes me want to throw up. And the notion that I could actually get off this sofa, butt naked, with any sort of urgency is laughable.

I swallow. Might as well extract a confession while I'm here, for what it's worth.

'You behind all this crap, then?'

'If you mean the rather splendid work of this team of intrepid vigilantes, then no, I'm afraid not. Call me a fan, though. What sterling work.'

Lies, as they have always done, pour from his lips like raw

sewage from the mouth of a Tory minister for the environment.

'Why are you here, then?'

Close my eyes. Vomit is on its way. Little to be done about it at this stage. Shit, shit, shit. I don't want to be sick. I hate being sick. And definitely not now. Swallow again, long and hard.

'Thought I'd pop by, see how my old friend is doing. I'm sad to say I'm a little disappointed in you, sergeant. You've had so many great triumphs in your career, and this is you. Last couple of weeks on the job, and here you are, practicing for your retirement. Drinking vodka, sleeping with someone who seemed, from a bit of a distance I must admit, to be dangerously young, and watching rather grotesque pornography. It's all rather seedy.'

I don't rise to it. I mean, I really don't have two fucks to give about this prick and his fake judgement. But I can't allow myself to get too defensive on behalf of Elise, in case he turns his attention to her. I can't mention her again, and will need to ignore it if he does.

'The fuck are you doing?' I say. 'You're literally spelling out PLAGUE with those stupid symbols you're leaving at the end of each murder.'

'Oh, that?' He laughs again. 'Much though I'd love it, I'm afraid I don't have a monopoly on the word. There are so many plagues these days. If you ask me, these geniuses, whoever they are, are more than likely spelling out some other kind of plague. I don't know, how about a plague of do-gooding lawyers, who manage to get these vicious scum found not guilty. Or somehow manage to make sure they don't get charged in the first place. A plague of well-meaning liberals, with their soft touch, and their concerns for the mental health of the criminal. How about a plague –'

'You just exploited the do-gooding liberals of the parole board.'

There's no viciousness in my tone. I can't manage it. Words just spoken, while behind them lies a great torrent of vomit waiting for me to give in to it.

'Exactly. I mean, look at it. Look how broken the system is. It's utterly ridiculous. But, dear God, what do you do if you're a voter? On one side you have these absurd do-gooders and their complete nonsense, giving in to every single special interest group who sticks their nose above the parapet to say they're upset about something, while on the other, you have those deplorable, Oxbridge, pig-fucking hedge fund managers. Excuse my language. But really, there is literally no one to vote for anymore. That's why I'm leaving. And, I'm afraid, I just couldn't get on that plane to the Med while wearing that ridiculous ankle bracelet. It had to go. But, you know, in the meantime, don't worry about me, I have somewhere to stay.' He laughs. 'That's not why I'm here. I'm not looking for a bed for the night.'

He really laughs this time, the idea obviously amusing him greatly.

The vomit wins.

I throw off the blanket, his eyes widen in fake comedy at me naked, and then I dash through to the bathroom, and my hands are grabbing the seat, my forehead rested against the back of it, and all the vodka and the tonic and the crisps and the Coke Zero and the club sandwich, and God knows what else that I certainly don't remember ever eating, is coming back up, exploding loudly into the toilet.

*

When I walk back through, some minutes later, wearing a pair of boxer shorts and a T-shirt, he's gone. Thoughtfully, he put the brutalist porn back on the TV, just to remind me of who I am.

26

I stand at the coffee machine watching the spit and cough and the splutter of the milk. No one else here yet, bar Ramsey on the front desk.

'You came,' said Ramsey, as I walked past. I didn't stop to talk, though I noticed he cut off a wince as he spoke.

'You too,' I observed, and he shrugged.

Coffee made, I walk to my desk and sit down. It's not my desk. It's Detective Sergeant Dale's desk, that I will now use, as an interloper, for the last week and a half. Or for my last day. Perhaps this will be my last day. I don't know.

I feel like shit. I look like shit.

I vomited on five more occasions. Kept drinking water, kept throwing it back up. At some point, I drank vodka from the bottle to see if that would help, but God, that was horrible. Everything about it was horrible. Drinking it, swallowing it, the feel of it, the retch of it, it barely stayed down for twenty seconds, and then it felt absolutely horrendous on the way back up.

Nice that my stomach, my literal stomach, has more brains than my brain.

Slept fitfully. Fell out of bed at some point dreaming I was having a fight with a spider. Not sure how I was having a fight with it, because in the dream it was a giant house spider on a curtain, not Shelob. But the spider and I became entangled, and in the process, I fell out of bed. Banged my head, bruised my back. Could have been worse. After I'd hauled myself back into bed, I had to get up again to go to the toilet to throw up, discovering when I got there that I'd neglected to flush the toilet after the previous occasion.

Still feel a little nauseous, but the worst is past. Can drink without bringing it back up, at least. Haven't eaten anything yet. The thought of vodka or wine makes my stomach turn, but I know that by mid-afternoon that will have passed. Tonight will be the same as last night, though hopefully without anyone turning up at the house. Not that I should shoehorn Elise into the same box as Clayton, but her intervention in the evening was also unwelcome, even though it proved a lot more enjoyable.

I feel empty. I breathe fire.

The door goes, Eileen and a constable, whose name I have shamefully forgotten, enter chatting amiably in the way that people do. I'm not sure I have any conversations anymore that aren't completely weighed down by life, but Eileen is still capable. She nods at the bloke as he trundles off to his desk which is somewhere behind and not in my line of vision.

We stare at each other, Eileen and I, she thinks about it, and then she comes and stands by DC Ritter's desk. She doesn't take a seat.

'Didn't think you'd make it,' she says.

No words form in my head in reply.

'You look terrible,' she adds, in response to my silence.

Another moment, and then I can see the precise second the aroma of stale alcohol reaches her. No number of minutes standing in the shower, no amount of litres of mouthwash can do anything about that.

She doesn't say anything. The shadow passes. I can see her thinking *are you sure you should be in*, and then not saying it.

'I need to speak to the chief,' I say. 'In fact, I need to speak to Eurydice, so perhaps I should just have gone to Dalmarnock, but I'm here now.'

There's something else subtle in her look when I mention Eurydice. I don't mention it.

'What's up?' she says.

Conversation coming in stutters. Every question asked, every answer given, carefully considered. Not because either of us is choosing our words, but because neither of us really want to be having the conversation in the first place.

I feel now, as I have several times in the past, that the friendship between Eileen and me has grown so close and involved that it could easily spill over into enmity. If that happens, it'll be my fault, which means it's on me to make sure it doesn't.

'Clayton came to see me last night.'

That shadow across her face again, but this time with good reason, and now she pulls out Emma's seat, and leans into the desk.

'How are you?'

'Too hungover to care,' I say.

'Tell me.'

I sigh, contemplating whether I want to revisit the evening. Take a drink of coffee. Stare at Eileen the entire time. Suddenly wonder if my life, all this shit and all these murderers and all this stupid crime, is all just subplot. All the sex and affairs and infatuations, has just been bullshit. My life, this entire time, has been a romcom. Me and Eileen are the stars, and rather than just put us together at the start of the movie, thereby completely nullifying the point of the thing, the screenwriters have devised a series of plot twists to keep us apart. But rather than the conventional misunderstanding, or one of the protagonists being lined up to marry someone else, or an initial meeting that pits the couple against each other from the beginning, we've had serial killers, sex addition, alcohol, lesbianism and fuck-witted stupidity.

She looks at me curiously, which is a familiar look, but not one that's in keeping with this morning's stilted discussion.

'What are you thinking, Tom? You're drifting.'

I'm not sure what to say, suddenly overcome with affection for her. I've been so foolish and such an unredacted moron towards her for so long I feel there's no point in just blurting out something that is liable to be dumbly romantic or something.

'Sorry, trouble focussing,' I say, weakly.

She looks curiously at me, asks the follow-on question, or indeed re-asks the previous question but with her hands.

I sigh. I look apologetic.

'I got drunk. I watched porn.'

'Lesbians?'

I smile sadly. Eileen and I have watched lesbian porn together before. We have that happy, erotic remembrance in our arsenal at least.

'Elise called.'

I pause to allow her time to look disapproving.

'She's not becoming infatuated with you, is she?'

'I didn't think so. I thought she was just wanting some fun. But now that you mention it.'

'Well, you were drunk and watching porn, no one's expecting you to say no at this point. Oh, God, Clayton didn't turn up in the middle of it, did he?'

I shake my head. I think of how it played out.

'No,' I say. 'She called me. She came over. We had sex.

We did, you know, we did whatever. I fell asleep. Not sure how much later it was I woke up, but it was more than a few hours. I mean, it was afternoon when she came by, it was dark when I awoke. He was there, Elise was gone.'

'You think possibly she's not infatuated, and she's working with the enemy?' asks Eileen.

'Not out of the question,' I say. 'I mean, I don't actually think that, but…'

Eileen puffs out her cheeks, lets out a long breath.

'I don't know, Tom. Well, you've met her. I mean, you've actually talked to her when you were both sober. What d'you think?'

I look away finally, a vague stare into the corners of the office, while I consider the dinner spent talking to Elise.

'She seemed young, normal. Nice sense of humour.'

'Did she ask you about your career?'

'Sure, but then… don't you find the same thing? Don't people always ask about our careers, looking for cool details about arrests and murders and drug dealers?'

'Did she look for more specific details once you'd mentioned the Plague of Crows?'

I stare deadpan across the desk, and she nods.

'You didn't mention the Plague of Crows,' she says, not asking a question.

'That's correct, ma'am. I mean, I don't usually.'

'Well, what d'you think?'

'I think she's not involved. I think she genuinely, for whatever reason, wanted to sleep with me. More than once. Even if that doesn't make sense.'

'You need to look in the mirror and see beyond the self-hate sometimes, my friend. Regardless, you might want to mention her to Eurydice and let her make the final decision.'

I give her another deadpan stare for that.

'Moving on,' says Eileen. 'Mr Clayton turns up. I take it he wasn't wearing a dress and nice lipstick?'

'No. He was just sitting there watching me, waiting for me to wake up.'

'In your bedroom?'

'I was sleeping naked on the couch. Someone, I presume Elise, had placed a blanket over me.'

'Thank God. So what did he say?'

'Said this isn't him. These murders, they're not him.'

'That sounds implausible in itself. Why was he there?'

I think about the conversation. I don't recall.

'Not sure. He said he had a couple of things to do and then he was going to make his way to some house he has in the Med. And retire.'

'What couple of things?'

I try to recall if he said anything, but I've already thought about it. If he did, and that seems unlikely, then I don't remember.

The door opens, the chief enters. First thing she does is look in my direction, hesitates in her flowing walk through the station, then gives me a five-minutes sign, and walks through to her office, unusually closing the door straight from the off.

'She looks happy to see you,' says Eileen.

'We're good,' I say. And then, because my defences are down, and I feel nothing anymore, I can't help saying, 'we had sex again the other night.'

The slight frown, the curious smile.

'Jesus, Tom, when did you have time?'

We hold the look. She does not seem at all judgemental about all this ridiculous fantasy sex I've been having. She stands, she nods to herself.

'Onwards and downwards,' she says.

27

Here we sit, in the HQ in Dalmarnock. Me and Eurydice, in her office. Kind of hoped I'd never be back here again, to be honest. Getting dragged into a city-wide investigation was not on my list of twenty things to do before leaving the police.

The list only had one thing on it, and it involved not doing much of anything. Nevertheless, I doubt Eurydice wants me here anymore than I want to be here, so no one's happy. Circumstances have included me in this shitshow – indeed, Michael Clayton's very existence has included me – and this will be played out until it's over.

This time it has something of a him-or-me feel to it. Well, so did the last one, to be fair, and that didn't pan out. However, as previously noted, I'm still kicking myself about that, so we can't let the same thing happen again.

Clayton found me easily enough last night, and I have no doubt he'll do it again.

I've told Eurydice everything there is to tell, including all the relevant information on Elise. She's staring at me across the desk. There's no judgement in her look.

'I take it you don't believe him,' she says, just as silence has begun its invasive creep across the room.

'Not sure. There was always something about him, though. He was big on the lies of omission. So perhaps he's not actually carrying out these murders, but it doesn't mean he's not behind them, at least.'

'How did he word it?'

'I don't remember.'

'You think it'll come back to you at some point?'

'I wouldn't count on it,' I say. 'But if I think of anything...'

'We shan't make the case dependent on it. Anyway, if what we have to do here is get this guy off the streets and back into prison, he's removed his parole bracelet, so we have just cause.'

'All you need to do is catch him again.'

She admires my deadpan delivery.

'You think I should speak to this woman?'

When I say I told her all the relevant information, I neglected to mention Elise's age. Not that being twenty-two doesn't make her a woman, but I feel when Eurydice learns this, the word woman will not be getting used in the conversation.

I let out a bit of a sigh, but I don't really care if the relationship between me and Elise is messed up by Eurydice asking her if she's working for the bad guys. And then there's the other thing. While some women would be offended by the suggestion, I suspect Elise will love it.

'Yes,' I say. 'I'll give you her details.'

'Don't let her know.'

'I won't.'

'What does she do?'

'She walks dogs for rich people. Makes two thousand a week.'

'That's what she told you?'

'Yes.'

'Did you believe her?'

'I've seen her three times. Twice we had sex and once we split dinner. I don't know why she'd lie about the money she makes, she can't think I'd care.'

'Maybe she considers you a catch, and wants to lure you in,' says Eurydice, with none of the tone one might expect when stating such a preposterous hypothesis.

'I don't think so.'

'Why? Three women have married you before, and you appear to have an endless queue of them happy to sleep with you.'

'She's young. She's seen my apartment. She already lives in a nicer place than I do. She has nothing to get from me other than… Well, she seems to enjoy the sex.' I shrug.

'Young?'

'Yes.'

She asks the question with a silent look across the table.

'Twenty-two.'

'Oh my God. Aren't there women your own age?'

I have nothing to say.

'Jesus. OK, give me her details, I'll call the crèche, see if they can get her to the phone.'

I have nothing to say to that. I suspect I'll hear from Elise soon enough afterwards. Unless, of course, she's working with Clayton, Eurydice doesn't get out of there alive, and Elise goes underground.

'When was the last time you looked at a file on Clayton?' she asks.

'I checked quickly yesterday morning before going looking for him, but that aside... I don't know. Not since the trial and his sentencing. There's been no reason.'

'I'd like you to go through his complete file. I know it inside out. I want you to go through it, and I know you'll have written a lot of it, but I'd like you to go through it and add in any thoughts. Anything you left out at the time, for whatever reason. There are always reasons. Anything that someone else added to the file, or that came up in the trial, that you think is just plain wrong, or which you have some comment on.'

I stare grimly across the desk. She gives me a pair of raised eyebrows, asking whether this is fine. It's not fine. Reading that man's file, and my extensive part in it, will be like thrusting a burning hot screwdriver into my eyes.

'I'd rather not.'

'I understand that, but I need you to look at it. If you need to take a drink beforehand, well, not something I should recommend of an officer at any point, particularly one who suffers from alcoholism, especially when you smell like this, but really, I don't care. Do what you have to do. Find a desk out there, open the files, get stuck in. Do it as quickly as possible. And while you're doing it, give some thought to what Clayton might be doing now.'

Well, I've already been doing that, of course. How else am I going to get to kill him, if I can't find the bastard? I have, nevertheless, absolutely no idea where he might be now.

I nod. Meekly and pathetically. Because I know she's right.

'Anything else?' I say.

'I think that's enough for the moment. Read the file, make notes, come back to me. If it was by lunch, it would be good. And if you find anything that appears revelatory, let me know asap, please.'

That's all. I have nothing to say.

I stand up, another small nod, and then I turn away and walk from her office, back out into the Dalmarnock open-plan.

*

I don't take up the opportunity offered by Eurydice for a pre-work drink.

The file reads like the haunted inside of my brain. I sit at a desk in the main open-plan office on the third floor, a young constable opposite ignoring me. She obviously doesn't realise that I'm a celebrity police officer, whose every action is worthy of record.

Soon enough I'm sitting with one hand worrying my forehead, the other with a pen poised to make notes, while scrolling and clicking through the file. I read all my old work. My old reports. I hate them. Badly written garbage. If I read this crap from a fellow officer I'd likely think they were an idiot.

And, just like Eric Clapton can tell that those albums he made in the seventies and eighties were recorded drunk, I too easily spot the tells of my inebriation, and the occasional moments of sobriety.

It doesn't take much for me to hate myself, it doesn't take much for me to plunge into the abyss. And there is nothing more likely to do it than reading files detailing how shit I've been. And it's all there. From the first hapless and hopeless chase of Clayton, when he gave DCI Taylor and me the run-around, to my part in the capture of the Plague of Crows – or, at least, the capture of his sister-in-law, the woman who was doing his bidding – amounting to little more than allowing myself to get picked up in a coffee shop, and then being caught completely unawares during intercourse. From our total inability to see Clayton coming when he laid all those preposterous clues for us during the Dylan murders, to me once again walking straight in to a sex situation, all at Clayton's orchestration. The latter, of course, leading to the sex video that has remained on the Internet pretty much ever since.

Whatever.

I read the file. Time passes. I make few notes. I want to kill myself.

28

At some point the next video is released. The victim is named Margaret Stillwood. This very fact makes me more certain than before that this is the work of Michael Clayton. It also becomes more certain that eventually this thing, this awful horror of a ritualistic shitshow, is going to end with me dead. Or being arrested for killing Clayton, and obviously I'd be the bad guy in that.

Stillwood was one of ours. Not singularly my case, but it was in Cambuslang, there were a few of us involved, and Emma and I both handled the detective branch side of it.

Margaret Stillwood was a cunt, and I'm sure she remained a cunt right up to the moment her splayed innards were eaten by a Great Dane. We all get what's coming to us, eh?

She killed dogs. A lot of dogs. Like, every dog in the neighbourhood, one by one. Now, me, DS Hutton here, I don't care about dogs. But people who own dogs care about dogs, and she killed them out of badness. We know she did. Everyone knew she did.

Zero evidence. And she wouldn't admit it, of course. Not an outright, signed confession at any rate. But she complained to everyone in her scheme about their dogs – and if someone didn't have a dog, she'd complain to them about everyone else's dog – she would threaten to have dogs killed, and was oblivious to any anger she received in return, and then all the dogs in the scheme died over the course of a few weeks. Poisoned mostly. The owners all thought it was her. In discussion with anyone other than us, she wouldn't deny it; with us, she pretty much answered every question with the words, 'fuck off.'

I'm quick to accept the blame for most of the things I've messed up, but on this occasion, there really wasn't anything else that Emma or I could've done. We did what we could. It was just that the system is there to be played these days, and Stillwood played it like Tiger Woods in his heyday walking down the eighteenth at Augusta with a double-digit lead. She also, just as the dog slaughter was picking up pace, got herself a puppy, so that when we went to talk to her, she could say, *but I love dogs! Look at my little fucking dog!*

She wasn't fooling anyone, but it was all part of the plan. If she hadn't been so small-mindedly evil, I might have been impressed with her ability to avoid comeuppance.

Some might think that being put to the sword and eaten by a Great Dane is a little harsh for being a dog-killer – it's not as though she'd have had all that much of a prison sentence had we managed to get a case to stick – but they would be in the minority.

Either way, this one is a little closer to home. The victim's initial crimes were close to home, and the body was found in an abandoned warehouse just down off Clydeside Road.

And, to the surprise of no one anywhere, the killer left an all-new, exciting symbol to his identity, this time a U. Already we've seen news feeds claiming that this means we might well be looking at the fifth different member of the Rough Justice League, which is just dumb, frankly. The Usurper, one suggested. Another, the Unicorn.

Aye, well-known vicious killers those mythical unicorns.

Idiots.

The Great Dane was wearing a collar, with a small name tag.

Scooby Doo.

Ruh-roh.

*

Mid-afternoon, back at the station. Like a normal, weird, sort of working afternoon. I did not envisage this day when I started out on it this morning. The day was mapped out in uncomfortable bullshit, lurching from one unpleasant interaction with someone who saw right through me to the next. And, to be fair, that's what happened this morning. And yet, here we are, we come to the afternoon, and I haven't gone home, retreating to my familiar haven.

Nevertheless, working life is a holding pattern. There's no way the chief is giving me any responsibility. We had a brief discussion in which she said she didn't think it appropriate that I, under the circumstances, continue to work in detective branch. 'Emma can manage fine on her own,' she said.

The circumstances, one should note, being that I'm wrung out and ready to rage quit, not that I have the spectre of the evil demon on my shoulder.

There was some discussion on whether I should just go home, but then given my close personal attachment to the multiple serial killer, she thought it best if I hung around, during working hours at least, in case Eurydice, or anyone else on her team, decided I could be of use.

So here I sit, the bum in the corner, a stale alcohol exclusion zone around me. No one speaks to me. Not, of course, that I want anyone other than Eileen to ever speak to me, and she's been out of the office all afternoon.

I stare at the screen. It shut itself down more than half an hour ago. The screen saver plays, a variety of pictures of Yosemite bouncing from one side to the other. It's kind of annoying and hypnotic at the same time. Staring at it certainly beats working.

I rouse myself to look at the time. Gone three. Jesus, what am I doing?

I close the computer down, push my chair back, go to the chief's office, knock and stand in the doorway.

'I'm going insane. I'm just going to go home, I'll be back tomorrow morning in case anyone needs me, and then… I should probably call it the last day, just get out of everyone's hair. Feels kind of pointless.'

'One of DCI Hamilton's team might have some questions about Margaret Stillwood,' says Hawkins, though there is no judgement in her tone.

'Emma got back twenty minutes ago.' I glance over my shoulder at her, turn back to the chief. 'I don't know if she's going out again, but she knows the case as well as I do. They know where to find me if anyone feels a peculiarly urgent need.'

She takes a moment, but is nevertheless going to agree with this. We hold the look.

'OK,' is all she's got when she speaks.

I don't immediately move, thinking there ought to be something else. But I don't know what that is. And if she has anything in mind, whether it be censure or support, she decides not to say it. I am released.

Silently I turn away, hesitate for a minute as I look around the office, and then walk quickly to the door, past Ramsey on the front desk without a word, and on out of the building.

29

I walked in at six-forty-five this morning, and so I walk home. I suddenly feel this strange sense of freedom, like I wouldn't have imagined. Even though we're in the middle of a case. Even though the chances of me getting caught up in it again have got to be pretty high. Despite that, I still get the sense that I'm done. My work here is finished. My time in the saddle is over.

I walk along this blasted main street, which has been redesigned into a town planning hellhole over the years, and imagine I could play golf, or do that walking across Canada thing that people in my head have been talking about. Or, since it's a big old world out there, I could go and look at any part of it I choose. Pyramids and oceans and jungles and exotic animals and God knows what else. All sorts of glorious wonders, the likes of which we don't have in Scotland. Though we do have the Falkirk Wheel, so there's that.

I break into a run. Don't know where that comes from. I mean, it's not like I'm even running to get to the off licence before it shuts. I'm running for nothing, on a road to nowhere, in my black Oxfords and my nothing-grey suit. And, befitting someone with the pickled internal organs of a specimen in a jar, I don't get very far before my lungs start screaming at me.

Nevertheless, I'm at the far end of the town, and down the hill, after pounding along empty pavements and across the intersection at the top of Bridge Street, before my lack of fitness catches up with me, and I stop running, slowing at first to a quick walk, and then giving in to the inevitable, and slumping against a fence, bent forward, panting, hands on my knees, breaths coming in ugly rasps.

Jesus. Got that uncomfortable feeling in my throat that comes when you sprint after years of no effort. God, I'm so unfit. Might have to practice walking *anywhere* first, before Eileen and I walk four thousand miles.

Something makes me turn, and I look back up the hill. There's someone else there, standing in exactly the same position as me, bent forward, hands on her knees. She's wearing a dark trouser suit, and has police officer written all over her.

I don't know her, but you don't need to be a genius, thirty-year detective like me to know what's going on here.

I start walking back up the hill towards her, still struggling to get enough air. She notices me coming, and casually straightens up – as best she can, as she's obviously as unfit as I am – and takes her phone from her pocket so that she can assume the innocent position of our times. Neck bent, looking at a screen, texting one of your mates or posting something on social media.

I stop beside her. Still breathing hard, but managing not to sound too awful. She looks disinterestedly up from her phone.

'DS Hutton,' I say.

She stares at me, then remembers to use her acting – like Gary in *Team America* – and she kind of looks disinterested and shrugs, then says, 'What? What have I done?'

I stop myself laughing, shake my head, take another moment or two to get my breathing regulated. We look at each other the whole time. Her acting isn't terribly good.

'You're following me,' I say, hoping to get to the bit of the conversation where we accept who everyone is and why they're playing a part in the drama.

'Why would you think that?'

'No one expected me to start running there. Took myself by surprise, to be honest. So, I'm guessing DCI Hamilton asked you to keep eyes on me. I take off, and maybe you thought I'd spotted you and was trying to run, but either way, you couldn't let me get out of sight. You don't know me, you weren't to know I'd get five hundred yards and nearly die. So you had to keep up, even though you're no more of a runner than I am.'

Her face is expressionless. I mean, I've done her like a kipper, but she's not ready to admit it yet.

'So what instructions did Eurydice give you, then? Keep your distance, make a note of everyone who comes to see me?'

She still holds my gaze. Perhaps it's hardening a little. She slips the phone into her pocket.

'Yes,' she says, finally.

'How exactly are you going to do that? I live in an apartment. How are you going to know if someone arriving at the block is there to see me or someone else?'

A moment, while she works through the fact that she's

been busted in the first five minutes of her assignment.

Well, I say that, but maybe she's been following me all week.

'Are you specifically on the lookout for Michael Clayton?'

'Yes.'

'This isn't about protecting me, it's about using me as bait, hoping that Clayton comes to see me again.'

'Yes.'

'Seems like the smart thing to do,' I say. 'But I think you'll be disappointed.'

'Why?'

'He's not an idiot.'

She doesn't have anything to say to that.

'You don't know anything about Clayton?' I ask.

'Just the basics. I've seen pictures of him.'

'Including what he looked like when he was admitted to Cornton Vale?'

'Yes. Is that one of his things? Disguises?'

'Completely fooled me once before,' I say. 'I wasn't expecting him at the time, but nevertheless, even though the guy haunts me, he managed to stand right in front of me, we talked, and I had no idea it was him.' A pause, and then, 'He's good. Pretty much good at everything.'

And that's that for conversation. Breath recovering, with her just a gasp of air or two behind.

'What's your name?' I ask.

'Julia.'

'Julia? You don't have a surname and a rank, any of that?' I say, and when she looks blankly at me, I throw in my regular, 'Are you a Brazilian footballer?'

'I don't know what that means.'

'I'm going home. You can follow me, and sit outside, if you like, although to be honest, that feels a little weird, or we can walk together, and you can come in for a cup of tea if you like.'

What are you doing, Hutton? I don't want someone coming in for a cup of tea. I don't, myself, want a cup of tea. I want wine. That's all. There's a viognier in the fridge. Crisp and fresh. Might stick it in the freezer after I've taken the first glass, get it even crisper, even fresher.

Talking of crisps. I'm out of snacks. No, don't fret, friends, there's cheese, and some bread that might be a little on the stale side, but I don't think it's actually mouldy yet, so it'll make passable toast.

'You're very intense,' she says. 'I wasn't expecting that.'

Jesus.

'Come on. This way, fifteen minutes. I'll get the kettle on.'

Multitudes 6

'Why are you here?'

This one was different. This was go-big-or-go-home taken to its extreme. It would perhaps appear a little clumsy in its exposition, but the python had died, and so he'd had to combine the day's intended solo murder, with the following day's slaughter. Those thirteen victims and their planned method of execution had been added to today's single victim, so that there were fourteen of them in the cold, damp, rat-infested basement. Dumped on the floor, chained at the wrists and feet, staring grimly back at their captor through the half-light.

None of them answered. They were all asking themselves the same questions.

How the fuck had they allowed this to happen?

How the fuck had one person managed to put them all there?

How the fuck were they going to get out of this?

Nevertheless, none of these fourteen, despite all the evidence to the contrary, thought it was too late. They had numbers on their side. Even if one of them was thinking to themselves that they didn't know a way out of this godawful mess, one of the others would. Surely. There were thirteen others. Someone would have something. One of these geniuses.

'Fuck off.'

The killer's shoulders sagged a little. That answer was becoming very predictable. He preferred silence.

'Really?' he said. '*That's* all you've got?'

There was one of the impending victims set apart from the others, a few yards from the end of the line. The other thirteen, so closely packed, were more tightly bound than the killer's previous victims. Since he was about to walk down the line, knife in hand, slitting open every stomach, he couldn't afford anyone in close proximity to interfere with his work.

The one who was set aside had been the head of the drug network. Not for much longer, but still, at that moment, he remained in charge of the gang, if not exactly in charge of the situation.

'Fuck off,' he said again.

'I'm tired of you people,' said the killer. 'You're all getting what you deserve, but you act like *I'm* the bad person. This is for the greater good, that's all. You know that per capita Scotland leads Europe in drug-related deaths?'

'Fuck off.'

'Of course you know that. Everyone knows it. Everyone in Scotland, everyone in the UK, everyone in Europe. Governments all across the continent, when criticised on their drug policies and the number of addicts dying on a weekly basis, can at least point to Scotland and say, we're not as bad as them.' He paused, and looked along the row of scowling faces. He saw one look of fear, one other of remorse. 'But you people don't see a health crisis. You don't see a public scandal. You see an opportunity. And the police, for God knows what reason, lack of will or lack of resources, or hamstrung by the liberal elite in the justice system, do nothing about you all. Well, the system, those in power might not thank me for this, but the people will. The general population. I'll have pre-Iraq War Tony Blair level popularity.'

He giggled.

'Fuck you,' came from four different voices in the row, mixed with a, 'Fuck off.'

'None of you, huh? None of you want to salve your conscience a little by making a confession?' Silence. 'I will be honest, it won't actually do you any good. Not here and now. You all know the score, you all know what's about to happen. I shan't spoil the surprise, though.' He laughed again, made a game show host hand movement, and said in an affected voice, 'What exotic beast will be the means of your destruction?'

He got no response.

'What about God though,' he said, his voice dropping a tone. More serious. Colder, as if he meant what he was saying.

He didn't mean what he was saying.

'Maybe God would appreciate a confession. That's what they teach you in chapel isn't it? There are at least three of you still go. Think about that. You three, sitting in chapel, your prayers and responses, all the chants of your cult. And then you leave with the blessing of Christ, and go out into the world and aid the addicts of the land to kill themselves and ruin the lives of their families.'

He looked directly, in turn, at the two men and one woman he knew to attend chapel.

'None of you? None of you think it worthwhile making your peace with the Lord before dying?' then he added, 'No one else?' looking along the line.

Weird, thought the killer, how the mention of Christ seemed to quieten everyone down, bringing a little guilt to the party. And yet no attempt at redemption. No penitent men or women kneeling before God.

Well, fuck 'em. It's not like it would've done any of them any good in any case.

'Oh well, friends, time's up. Let the challenge begin!'

And he approached the leader of the pack, knife in hand.

30

Sitting at the table, a cup of tea and two Lu *le petit beurre* biscuits each. Sure, there's nothing to stop me helping myself to a glass of wine or a vodka. The hangover has passed. The period when just thinking about vodka induced a feeling of nausea has passed. The need for alcohol has returned, as currently I exist in a time when there is no middle ground. There is no life without alcohol. There is either feeling its adverse effects, or wanting more, with nothing in between. And yet here I am, with Constable Rowan, and there's something about her that makes me defer the first drink of the day.

'So how come you got this shitty job?' I ask.

You're thinking, who would play Constable Rowan in the five-series show on Netflix? I'm going to say Melissa McCarthy. I mean, facially not so much, though there might be something there. And while I don't think this cup of tea is heading in the direction of the bedroom – because actually some people don't automatically have sex with everyone they meet – I'm here for it if that's how it pans out.

'And,' I add, when she doesn't immediately answer, 'not just shitty, but also potentially dangerous. If this is the work of Clayton, and he's back for me, to toy with me and do whatever, then you're in the firing line. Sure, he may be targeting specific individuals this time, but the man will not mind a bit of collateral damage.'

She takes another drink, sets the mug back down.

'I just got the job,' she says, with something of a sigh.

'You just got the job?' I can't help laughing. An engaging laugh, all the same, not designed to draw her in, but I know it will. 'You must have done something to get the shitty job.'

I laugh again, mostly with the eyes this time. Like Paul Newman multiplied by Brad Pitt. Women find it irresistible.

'The DCI said you had a thing.'

'A thing? This sounds interesting.'

'Hmm.'

She seems reluctant to say it. I wouldn't usually care, but possibly because it's coming from Eurydice, I'm in the mood to hear it. I continue to give her the Paul Newman-Brad Pitt look.

'She said you have a sex addiction.'

I take a drink of tea. Lay the mug back down. Weirdly, just the mention of sex from a woman's lips has me getting interested. Can feel it at the back of my throat. Elsewhere, too.

'I don't believe that's a thing,' she says.

'You don't think you can be addicted to sex?'

'Not really. I mean, you're a man, right? You want to have sex with women? Oh my God, quick, stick a label on it, it must be a condition.'

Can't help smiling.

'You may have a point,' I say.

'Seriously, don't all men just want to have sex? All the time?'

'I don't know.'

'You never discussed it with any men?'

'Nope.'

'You don't have any male friends?'

'Not really. Even if I did, I wouldn't want to talk to them about sex.'

She lifts her first biscuit, takes a bite. We look at the few crumbs that have fallen on the table.

'It still doesn't explain why women sleep with you, although the DCI did say you have something about you.'

'Really?' This I'm here for. 'What exactly did she say?'

'I just told you,' she says, though she thoughtfully leaves the dumbass off the end of the sentence. 'You have something about you. She didn't go into specifics.'

'So, d'you see it? The something.'

She rolls her eyes at me, takes the rest of the biscuit, glances at the crumbs on the table, decides not to do what everyone on earth would do at this point which is dab them up with her fingertips – which, given it's not her house or her table is fair enough – and then she takes a drink of tea.

'So, she picked you for the job, and warned you about me so that you could make sure to have your shields up and phasers set to stun, then sent you off to deal with the notorious fake sex addict?'

'Do you see me as a challenge?'

'No. I have no self-belief. And I hate the sex addict thing

anyway, though possibly it's a convenient diagnosis to hide behind. You're probably right, though. Man wants to have sex. Big whoop.'

I take a drink of tea and look over my shoulder in the direction of the fridge. Maybe I could get the wine in the freezer as preparation for my first glass when she's done her tea, we've said all we have to say, and she goes to watch the front door of the building.

'You do jigsaws?' she says, deciding it's time to move on, having noticed the small pile beneath the table by the door to the kitchen.

'My daughter gets them for me,' I say. 'I did the first one, and now it's her go-to present.'

'That's nice. I imagine you're hard to buy for.'

'Sure.'

'You've done them all?'

Small talk. Not usually my strong point.

'There's one more I bought off Amazon. Weirdly, buying it for myself made me kind of lose focus on starting it. Maybe I will.' A pause, and then I add, 'I like doing jigsaws of works of art.'

'Nice. What's the one you got for yourself?'

'Tassaert's *The Cursed Woman*.'

'I don't know that. What's she cursed by?'

'She's having sex with three men.'

She stares vaguely in the direction of the jigsaw boxes, though it's not lying on the top of the pile.

'Doesn't sound so much like a curse,' she says.

'That's what I thought.'

'I'm a lesbian.'

Well, that came out of nowhere.

'That's why Eurydice gave you this job?'

She doesn't answer.

'She was worried a straight officer might fall prey to my amazing personality?'

'I don't know.'

'Why did you tell me you were a lesbian, then? I mean, I can accept when someone doesn't want to sleep with me. Scientific studies have shown that more women than not actually don't.'

She smiles along with me.

'I guess if the DCI is looking at your file, or hearing stories about you… well, she's not going to hear stories of you *not* sleeping with someone, is she? She's not going to have seen videos of you *not* having sex. She sees the bad stuff. Or the good stuff, if that's how you'd put it.'

'Definitely the good stuff.'

'And, like I say, she says you have something about you, so, I don't know… Have you and the DCI…?'

'Nope. She's spent more time being annoyed at me than anything else, so I'm not sure it's on the cards.'

'Well, you never know. I hear stories of the DCI, and her husband didn't divorce her for nothing.'

As soon as she says that she feels the icy grip of the guilty gossip, and waves it away. Takes another quick drink of tea, shakes her head, then pushes her chair back.

'I have a job to do, and I shouldn't be doing it sitting here. I'm going to go to that apartment right there,' and indicates a window across the road on the same floor.

I look across, then look at her.

'You're kidding me.'

'Nope. I should go.'

'How did you just get a room in that apartment?'

'As far as I'm aware, it was available.'

'That's convenient.'

She shrugs.

'I don't know what else to say. I don't think you've been getting watched by your own force all this time. It does seem sensible under the current circumstances, however.'

'You've been over there already?'

'No.'

I look over at it. Try to think of who it is who lives there, but I can't. Despite sitting at this small table when I do my jigsaws and when I eat dinner and drink wine, I don't pay any attention to anyone across there. Maybe I've just never noticed because it lies empty. I can be, after all, very unobservant for a police officer.

'Thanks for the tea,' she says.

'Be careful.'

'I'll be fine.'

'When you get over there, make certain you're alone, and make certain the door's locked, bolted, chain across, whatever. If you're spending your day looking over here, you don't want someone coming in from behind.'

'I'm fine.'

'You're fine, because Michael Clayton has not been paying you any attention. He will know about you now. So –'

'The eye of Sauron?'

Nice. I like a woman who uses the same *Lord of the Rings* references as me.

'More like Saruman's spies, out there in the wild. I mean the man has used crows before, after all.'

'I will be careful, Sergeant Hutton,' she says, 'thank you for your concern. And for the tea.'

She turns. I watch her to the door, out into the short hallway, and out the front door. The sound of her footsteps quickly recedes. I am alone.

I get a strong, uneasy feeling that I may not see Police Constable Julia Rowan again.

31

I open the bottle of wine. Inspired by my brief conversation with PC Rowan, I also open The Cursed Woman and start picking out the edges. Occasionally I glance over at the window opposite to see if I can see her, but there's nothing bar a net curtain.

Maybe she's elsewhere and she lied about where she was going. Maybe, it occurs to me at some point, she's not one of ours, but is in fact acting on behalf of Clayton. Having had that thought, I care so little I don't even bother making a call to check. As ever with Clayton, I do not feel in control. Something will happen at some point. For now, all I can do is sit and wait. And drink wine.

The phone rings. Elise. I'm not drunk enough to want to see her, and I contemplate not answering, but she's a nice enough person for me not to be a dick about it, and I answer, putting the phone on speaker.

She's already laughing when I come on the phone.

'You got the cops on to me,' she says.

As I suspected she might, she obviously loved that I got the cops on to her.

'Someone came to see me last night after you left,' I say.

'I heard. Who *was* that?'

'Doesn't matter. What time did you go?'

She laughs again.

'Actually, I've just answered all these questions to one of your people.'

'Funny. What time did you go?'

'I don't know. About seven-ish, I guess. You were sound, didn't bother waking you. You don't mind, though, right?'

'Sure.'

'So who else came?'

'Just a guy. I don't know when he arrived. You weren't aware of anyone when you left the apartment?'

'You mean, someone else in the apartment?' She laughs again.

'Outside, in the vicinity, someone hovering maybe.'

'No, 'fraid not. I'm a terrible witness.'

'OK. Who saw you today?'

'Some, like, chief inspector or something.'

'It was OK?'

'It was hilarious!' More laughter. God, to be so young and take enjoyment in pretty much anything. 'I mean, I wondered if she thought I was like in league with some guy or something. Like, wow. And get this, she asked what I saw in you. I mean, like *rude!*'

She laughs again. Jesus, Eurydice really has made her day.

'I hope you told her it was my sensitive and caring personality.'

'Exactly. Then she asked if I had a crush on you, like, I don't know, like it's the nineteen fifties or something. O-M-G. Anyway, I think I held her at bay long enough to escape without a prison sentence.'

'That's good,' I say.

And just like that the end of the phone call is at hand, and we need to address the awkwardness to follow.

Or not, as it happens.

'Gotta dash,' she says. 'Places to be. You recovered from last night, by the way?'

'Think I've made it through, though it was touch and go.'

She laughs, she smiles – I can see the smile – she says, 'I'll give you a shout, Tom,' and before I can say goodbye, she's hung up.

The phone returns to its natural, silent state. I stare at it for a moment, consider whether there's anything that I need to look at on the Internet, decide there isn't, take a drink of wine, and then start looking methodically, once again, through the box for pieces from the outer rim.

*

A short while later. Almost through the first bottle of wine. Drinking too fast. War is coming, this much I know, but not just yet. We're in the Phoney War period, waiting for the other side to make a move.

Had a brief communication with Eileen. She called, checking in on me. She continues to do it, regardless of circumstances. She's sticking out the last couple of weeks for now. Taking it one day at a time, she said, then she laughed. Said she's busy tonight, not sure about tomorrow, maybe we could do something then. 'Firm up those Banff plans,' she said, and I said, 'I'll put an itinerary together,' like we're both being serious.

A long evening ahead awaits. What are the options? Go to the cinema and see Mission Impossible 27. Maybe Indiana Jones. Go out and sit on my own in a bar or a restaurant. Find a park, go for a walk. Stay in, get drunk, eat pizza, find a movie to watch on TV.

I think we all know it's going to be the latter.

My phone rings again, just at the moment I fit the first two pieces of the puzzle together. Can see it's Eurydice, contemplate not answering, and then decide to pick up. Having addressed the possibility of an empty, nothing evening head on, I'd been kind of looking forward to it. As long as I don't dwell on the fact that it will presage an empty, nothing life ahead.

'Hey,' I say.

'Going to send you a thing,' she says, an urgency in her tone. 'Take a look.'

I stare at the jigsaw pieces, nothing yet to be seen in the picture. I know immediately, since our vigilante has been releasing videos on a daily basis, that this will be another one.

'You'll likely find it online, but we're actively taking it down from everywhere he's already put it. So just look at what I send you. I'll call you back in five minutes.'

She hangs up. Immediately the phone pings with a message from her. I take a moment before looking. Drain the glass of wine, and then walk to the fridge, get the bottle, then tip the remainder of it into the glass. Take another drink. Deep breath.

'All right, then, you fucker, bring it on.'

I open the link. The video plays. We are in a basement. The lighting is not great. The camera lingers on a man manacled to the wall and the floor, his position familiar. I don't know who this is. His stomach has been slit open, his guts have been brought carefully into the open. They have yet to be attacked. He looks like he might not last until that happens, his head slumped to the side, though his eyes are open. He regards his captor, the cameraman, with hatred, but is in no position to do anything about it. His forehead has already been branded. No one is shocked to see that this time it has been marked with an E.

P-L-A-G-U-E it is.

I swallow.

This adds no extra value. Derivatives aside, there are no other words that begin P-L-A-G-U. We knew it was going to be E. If it's obvious it's Clayton today, it was obviously him last night, even if, as Clayton's lawyer would be quick to agree, he hardly has a monopoly on the word.

The camera moves on. A few yards, and another body comes in to view, another beside it. And the camera keeps going, one after another. Everyone in the same position. Everyone more tightly manacled than previous victims, although it is obvious why that is. And every one of them has been branded on the forehead, so that the viewer can read them off.

I-A-M-M-U-L-T-I-T-U-D-E-S.

The line of victims comes to an end.

Oh, piss off, you dickhead. *I Am Multitudes*.

I take half a glass of wine in one go, then set it down, swallowing harshly, spitting the word, 'Fuck,' at the day.

There's a loud croak from behind. As the camera pulls back to take in the crowd in one shot for the first time, they are all looking straight ahead as the noise suddenly starts to grow. Fourteen pairs of eyes, with blood running through them from the branding in the forehead, widen, as if on command.

I know what's coming even before I see any of them. You can hear them now, of course. Wherever they've come from, wherever they've been released from, now they come. Wary and curious at first, but hungry. These animals are always hungry.

Black crows. One, then another couple, and then suddenly a great rush. And, as with everything else that has approached the sundered bodies with caution, once the initial attack has been made, the initial hurdle has been cleared, suddenly the feeding frenzy begins, and soon the fourteen bodies are covered by a host of ravenous birds.

Quickly there is nothing to see other than the birds, there are so many of them. They fight each other. They rip at flesh and then fly up out of the way. Blood and the spatters of human remains fly around the room in bright light.

The camera fades to black. A moment, and then the legend I Am Multitudes comes up on the screen.

The video ends.

The phone rings almost as soon as the video stops playing, as though Eurydice was watching it again in tandem with me.

'You've watched it?'

'Yes.'

'Thoughts?'

'Who are the victims?'

'Drug gang from Possilpark. The man alone at the beginning, that's James Rankine. Drug dealer. One of those people that just escapes us, time after time. Every time we think we're getting him, he gets out of it, one way or another. We have a few of his crew in jail, but those turn out to be the lucky ones.'

'The rest of the victims are his current members of staff?'

'Nice way to put it. As far as we know, yes, though there are a couple whose names we don't know. I think at this stage it's safe to presume.'

'Where are the bodies?'

'Out near Rankine's territory. I'm heading there now. You want to join me?'

'Seriously?'

'You're still on active duty.'

'Speak to my chief. Tomorrow's my last day, and even that will just involve me going in to receive my happy retirement card, and eat cake. And neither of those things is actually going to happen. So... I'm sure you can manage without me.'

'I'd like you there. You were right about him spelling out the word plague, he's used crows again, and now we have this, this I Am Multitudes bullshit. One of my people thought that might be an allusion to some Dylan song, *I Contain Multitudes*. He did the Dylan thing before. This all points so obviously to our man Clayton, that either someone's trying some absurd stitch-up, or he is quite egregiously taking the piss out of us. I think it's the latter. I'm heading out there, and I'd like you to come and take a look. I want to talk to you about this guy, and we might as well do it there as delaying me at the office while I do this.'

'Fine, whatever. I can't drive though.'

'Jesus. It's... you were in work today and it's barely four o'clock, you can't have drunk that much.'

This senior detective has clearly never met an alcoholic. Really, she's just a bit wound up by events, not me, and she would probably take that one back if she could.

'I'm not driving,' I say. 'None of us want me to be in an accident in this state. Bad for business.'

'Jesus,' she says again.

I am a never-ending source of disappointment to some

people. Guess that's just the way it crumbles, cookie-wise.

'Send a car, or get your foot soldier across the road to come and get me.'

'What foot soldier?'

'Constable Rowan, the lesbian.'

Silence.

Well, look at that. Really, look at that. There is no Constable Rowan. Constable Rowan completely fooled me. I mean, sure, it occurred to me that maybe she was batting for the opposition, but I thought that was me just being paranoid.

'I don't have time for this,' says Eurydice. 'I'll pick you up in five minutes. I'll blue light it over there, so please be waiting outside.'

She hangs up.

I stare at the phone, take a moment, consider how the next five minutes is going to play out, find myself amused by the curious instance of the constable who wasn't, then decide, with no extra increase in the pace of my heart, to give in to this moment as required. Human flesh feasted on by crows? Nothing any of us hasn't seen before, right?

32

Eurydice drives scarily fast to the crime scene. My heart rate goes up at that, right enough. I outline what happened with Constable Rowan. She questions that Rowan definitely said she worked for her. I tell her what Rowan said about her, right down to the line about the reasons for her husband divorcing her.

She does not go ashen as such, but I can see that the personal targeting affects her all the same. She responds in the first instance by pressing her foot harder to the accelerator, and then backs off a little when she nearly loses control at a roundabout.

We arrive at the crime scene, somewhat surprisingly after that journey, in one piece. The area is already a clusterfuck of emergency vehicles, scenes of crime, and police officers. Lots of shouting, lots of equipment being hauled around. The perimeter is in the process of being set up, although we're on the edge of a small industrial estate, with the nearest homes a few hundred yards away. Anyone who's here has had to walk to see what's going on, so there aren't too many people. Still, there is a voluble argument coming from a chap who's having to be frog-marched away from the four-storey building which houses the slaughter shitshow in its basement. He's led past Eurydice and me as we approach through the line of coppers, and he looks me in the eye and shouts, 'Free country, man! What are you lot hiding in there?' A short while later we catch his, 'Fucking covert government experiments, man!' blown by the wind.

We come to a guy in police tactical gear, who's been running the operation up until this point.

'How's it looking?' asks Eurydice.

'It's unworkable in there,' says the guy. No name, nothing about him to indicate that he's anything other than a bloke ready to go into combat.

'How d'you mean?'

'There are hundreds of crows, ma'am. Maybe thousands. It's a horror movie. At the moment we're not getting near the corpses.'

Eurydice looks around, a quick assessment of where we are.

'You have gas,' she says.

'Yes. Was just waiting for your authorisation. But we need as much egress for the crows as possible. A couple of guys getting suited up. They'll go in there and open up this line of street level windows you see there. And by open up, they're going to have to bust them open. We'll leave the one door open, with access from there out of the building. We need to gas upstairs, so that the crows get the fuck out of the entire place.'

He pauses, he looks back at the site.

'It's going to get ugly. When we start we need to get everyone back. Plan is to try to clear them, let the air blow through, if any of the little bastards stick it out they're toast, so happy to kill any that we need, then get the place sealed up so they can't get back in. Then we can get to work.'

'We good to go then?' she asks.

'On your mark,' says the guy, like he's in a movie, and she says, 'Let's do it.'

Eurydice and I stand and watch for a moment, then the guy, after shouting a few instructions, turns back to us and says, 'You might want to move back a little, chief, this is going to be biblical.'

*

Fuck me, he's not wrong. With all the windows broken, they fire six gas cannisters into the basement. A moment, no more than that, and boom, there comes an absolute fuckrush of crows, squabbling and squawking and fighting and barking and crawing their way out of the basement, a great flight of desperation and anger, beaks dripping blood, a horror-fest of panic and smoke and wings and human flesh taking flight, everyone in the vicinity instinctively ducking down, hands and arms covering heads. The noise is cacophonous, terrifying, a blood-curdling grasp of sound at your throat and your heart.

Any sign of the crows looking to turn back, any sign of them deciding to linger and have a go at eating living human flesh, there are five armed operatives already authorised to fire into the air or the ground to scare them off, just no fancy-ass trying to shoot a crow off the top of someone's head.

A gun goes off into the midst of the stramash causing even greater panic. Another gunshot immediately follows.

The horror continues.

*

Much later DCI Hamilton and I stand in the basement, in full SOCO gear. A large area, like abandoned basements the world over. The concrete floor would have been dusty and dirty, with nothing else about it. Now it's covered in bird feathers, blood, and random pieces of dead meat.

The fourteen corpses are where they were left. The scene is one of schlock horror, like a pre-CGI movie bloodfest, the special effects guys given the entire film budget, running amok.

'Hard to believe it's real,' says Eurydice.

I have nothing to say.

'We're going to have to trauma assess the shit out of everyone here,' she says, a while later.

There's barely any noise, barely any conversation. There are seventeen scenes of crime staff in attendance, going about their work. They will be methodical and they will be quick, and they will then get the fuck out of here. The victims are long dead, and no one wants this scene to be allowed to linger. Nevertheless, with the number of victims so greatly increased, so too the chance surely that the perpetrator made a mistake. If nothing else, it's science. It's logical. With increased volume, comes increased opportunity for error.

'Seems a little clumsy,' she says, again words just appearing in the silence. 'The E, and then all the others.'

'Like he had to combine two murder events. Maybe he was due to do the gang leader one day, the gang the next, then something happened to make him bring it forward.'

We have no idea. Since it is all conjecture, with nowhere to go, words quickly run into the dust.

Conversation coming in fits and starts, so that when I start to say, 'I need a drink,' she's already cutting me off with, 'You never actually proved those original crows murders were Clayton, did you?'

Technically, that's true. I don't say anything.

'I know he confessed to you in the hospital, I've read the report, but how d'you know he wasn't messing with you?'

'Why come after me the second time, with those absurd

Dylan murders?' I say. Clayton was one hundred percent behind the Crows business, but I don't bother going there.

'You never even got a conviction against him on all of those murders,' she says. 'Ultimately, if you hadn't busted him in the process of kidnapping Eileen and the psychiatrist, we might never have had a case.'

I find myself looking directly into the bloody, brutalised, empty eye sockets of one of the dead. She is, of course, not wrong. The man can cover his tracks, you have to say that about him.

'You unearthed his other house, the house we never knew to search, and there still wasn't enough proof there to implicate him in any other murders.'

'Because he's good,' I say.

'Or maybe he had a vendetta against you, for some reason, then he dragged Eileen into it, he dragged the psychiatrist into it, making you think it was him all along, when it wasn't.'

'No.'

'He toys with you. He toys with the police. What is it about you that inspires him?'

'I really need a drink,' I manage to say uninterrupted.

'There will be time.'

Something in her tone that suggests she wants to be harder on me, but is holding off. But then, *of course* she wants to be harder on me. It's come to this. I'm an on-duty police officer at a crime scene in the middle of a fuck-awful investigation, and I'm openly saying I want to knock off and go and get drunk. Or more drunk, as I was already a little drunk when we arrived. Although, to be honest, there's something about a flock of human-flesh-infested, panicking crows flying past your head that's going to sober you up faster than finding out the woman you just slept with is twenty-two.

'What is it about you that inspires him?' she repeats.

Inside the covering of my NBC suit, my head twitches. She won't notice.

'I'm sport,' I say, voice suddenly on edge. 'I'm sport to the man, and that's it. The boss and I, DCI Taylor, we saw through him. I don't know what attracted him more to me than the boss, and what's kept on leading him on. Maybe it's, whatever, it's the same with all these women you don't understand wanting anything to do with me. I exude this something. An indefinable attraction. Some women inexplicably want to sleep with me, and

154

some psychopaths inexplicably want to toy with me, and mock me, and tear me slowly down, bit by fucking bit. I didn't make me the centre of this damned story. Jesus. Let me just go off and lie in a puddle of my own vomit, will you?'

'Inspiring words for a copper,' says Eurydice, but this time there's no judgement in her tone. 'Anyway, you may be right. You have something about you, sergeant. Even I see it, and you've driven me absolutely nuts repeatedly over the last couple of years.'

More silence. I have nothing else to say. I was riled for a moment there, passion and indolent disinterest coming in waves.

'What d'you think we should do now?' she asks.

'I don't know that I have anything other than what I presume you were already doing. You have his chosen theatre of operations,' I say, indicating the scene of devastation. 'He needs an abandoned building, preferably with a basement.'

'We've already been running a programme of identifying as many as we can find, setting up micro-cameras, and waiting. Obviously, we hadn't yet identified this place.'

'I'd suggest that he's way ahead of us. He will have identified *x* number of places, he'll have placed his own micro-cameras, and he'll only use a site which he knows we haven't discovered yet.'

'You're kind of in awe of his genius, aren't you?' she says.

'So should you be. He thinks of everything. More importantly, as the Constable Rowan incident illustrates, he is not working alone. God knows how many people he has on this.'

'And we cannot get away from the possibility that this is not Clayton at all,' she tosses in.

'You don't believe that.'

'Really?'

'If you did, I wouldn't be here.'

I get a glance now, but I'm right. I'm right about her motives, and I'm right about Clayton, and none of it puts as anywhere nearer finding the bastard.

33

Back in my spot. My safe place, sitting at my table by the window, jigsaw beginning to get going, a small plate of cheese and a piece of toast, a tomato, a couple of grapes, getting properly acquainted with the next bottle of Viognier. Bob's epic *Rough And Rowdy Ways* plays on Spotify. It's been three years, and I'm still listening to that album like it came out last week.

They know where I live, of course. That thought sits in the back of my head, but weirdly does not make me uncomfortable. I will deal with whatever comes my way, as drunk as I am able to get by the time it arrives. And this evening there are no women on the horizon who might possibly get caught in the crosshairs.

Of course, should Clayton wish to lure any women into the entanglement, he would have a way to do it.

I am, indeed, in his thrall, in awe of his complete command and control. He dominates the narrative. It would, I guess, be pretty funny if this all turned out to have nothing to do with him. But then, it would just be someone in his wake, influenced and inspired by him, and Clayton's name would still be all over it.

I drink wine by the jug, I do jigsaws of nudes. I contain multitudes.

I take a break from the perimeter of what by any measure, except Elise's, is the foreplay to a gangbang and open my phone, having a sudden curiosity about what the news media is making of the arrival of Mr Multitudes on the scene. They are, unsurprisingly, all over it, but for the most part feel the need to sanitize the worst of the awfulness. *A Multitude of Horror*. *Multitude Serial Killer Runs Amok*. *Cops Lost In Murder Spree*. *None Safe, As Death Comes To City*. (I feel we could argue the bit about none being safe, but the media does like everyone to feel that their own demise is imminent.) *A Murder of Crows*. Conventional. *Drug Gang Gets The Bird*. Oh, nice. Hats off to that guy. *Nessun Dorma As City Villains Wonder Who's Next*. Decent. *Bloodbath!* Yep, that one nails it.

I read a few paragraphs here and there. There's not a lot of inaccuracy, to be honest, and what there is, tends to be the media avoiding telling the full story because the full story is just so horrible. Basically, however, this is one story where the newspapers don't have to make anything up. The truth, even the slightly varnished truth they're getting from us, is quite batshit crazy enough for them to run with.

I learn nothing I don't already know. It doesn't, at least in media terms, look like there've been any new developments in the last hour or so, and so I turn the phone off and look back at the jigsaw.

Head not in the right place, it transpires, even though the jigsaw is of a perfectly agreeable subject matter.

I drink half a glass of wine. Realise how unexpectedly restless I am. A night in on my own suddenly, from nowhere, seems horrible. Is this it? Sit here? Do a jigsaw? I mean, the jigsaw, the quiet mindfulness of it, is all right. It creates a nice juxtaposition for the life of an officer. So brutal during the day, the jigsaw provides evening respite.

But what of this? What about when the job is over, and there's no longer brutality during the day? Then the jigsaw is no longer about respite, it's your life. This is what your life is, right now, and what it will be. Yes, sure, there was a surfeit of brutality this afternoon. A tsunami of it. But what about tomorrow? What about when Eurydice finally tires of me, what about when Clayton's work is done and (on the off-chance I'm not dead), he's gone, and I'm no longer of any use to anyone? What then will this jigsaw represent, regardless of the subject matter?

I get up, glass in hand, and look down onto the street. I quit today. Today was the day when I thought, OK, fuck that, enough. I'm gone. And so it doesn't matter what happens tomorrow, or any day thereafter. I'm done.

Glass to my lips, and unashamedly guzzle it. Shit, it's harsh when you drink it like that. I grab some of the cheese, pour another glass of wine.

Turn away from the window. Into the kitchen. Nothing for me here. Back through to the sitting room. Then the spare room, the bedroom. Nothing to see. Why would there be? It's not like I'm looking for inspiration, not like I think I'm going to find anyone to talk to.

Take a drink of wine. Leave the glass on the bedside table,

go into the bathroom. Get the shower running, take my clothes off. Look at myself in the mirror while the shower gets to temperature.

I get in the shower, and stand there, hating myself but warm, for the next fifteen minutes. The planet weeps at my excessive water usage.

I get out, dry off. Deodorant. Clean my teeth. Mouthwash. Drink some water. Stare at myself in the mirror again. What now?

I have no fucking idea.

*

I wanted to go home after the preposterously staged crows business. I mean, sure, that's going to be one hell of a terrific scene in the Netflix show, but fuck me, not a bundle of fun to be part of. And yet, what did I care? I'm done. This isn't my shit anymore.

Nevertheless, Eurydice refused to let me go. I would need to have just turned and walked away from her, and something, God knows what, made me bow to her authority, like I needed her permission to walk away. Until such times as it comes, I would be AWOL, feeling like I've run from the last of my responsibilities.

By the time we'd finished going over the minutiae of the case, and I had focused, and had had the undeniable feeling that I'd been of little use, the bodies of the dead had been detached from their bindings, bagged up, and dispatched to the lab, to go beneath the knife of Dr Fforbes.

Fforbes and I are quite familiar with each other's work, but I have not been sent her way so far this time, what with this not being my case. Nevertheless, I was on hand, as afternoon turned to evening, to accompany Eurydice on what has obviously been a daily trip to the morgue.

'Sergeant!' said Fforbes, upon my arrival, consequently registering as the first person to look pleased to see me since I was about six. 'I thought I might never see you again. At least, not until I have to dissect your liver while looking for likely cause of death.'

I laughed with her, beneath the DCI's curious eyebrow. Too dark for her, that one, obviously.

'Penultimate day,' I said, as we came alongside the

brutalised corpse of James Rankine.

'Have you had time to say I'm too old for this shit, yet?'

'Been saying it for years already.'

'Aye, join the club.'

I got a quick smile, and then she turned to Eurydice.

'Chief,' she said. 'Slightly different this time, though I'm not sure, again, how much use it's going to be for you.'

'Go on,' said Eurydice.

'I'm guessing, what with there being so many victims involved, that there had to be a greater level of control exercised by the perpetrator. Or perpetrators.'

'If nothing else,' said Eurydice, 'we see in the video, someone is filming the bodies, the camera is clearly hand-held and moving around, and then the birds appear as if by magic. The sound could've been edited, but it's as though they've been released. Someone filmed it, someone else was dealing with the birds. And putting that many people to the slaughter, just feels like the work of more than one person.'

'Rankine's been drugged,' said Forbes. 'Looks, on first inspection, like it was a cup of tea. Given the scale here, you might find that there was some sort of gang meeting, or a gang whatever. He'd eaten a little, but there's no immediate sign of alcohol or anything else in his stomach.'

'When d'you think that was?' I asked.

'Tough call, that one, as yet. Give me a few more hours, I'll get there. Maybe it happened this morning. Maybe it was a working breakfast, if a drug gang would have a working breakfast. That seems kind of anachronistic. I'll let you know asap if the others were all disabled the same way. If it happened this morning, then the killer would be able to revive them, but they're still going to be groggy for a long time.'

'That's one of the things with so many people in chains,' said Eurydice. 'You can be as on top of it as you like, but you just never know what might go wrong. The guy who can slip his wrist out of something, or the woman who can dislocate her shoulder, do whatever. Keep them all groggy, you're going to be able to stay in control.'

'Insurance,' said Fforbes. 'Thereafter, well, we've been here before. Stomach slit open, innards extracted, and then the finishing touch. Nasty tool a crow's beak, right, sergeant?'

She gave me a glance. Fforbes wasn't here back in those days, but we had the first-hand evidence of that statement in front of us. I didn't reply.

'OK, thanks, doc,' said Eurydice. 'We'll leave you to it.'

We engaged, the doctor and I, one last time. It was hardly a close working relationship, so no one was get teary-eyed over it.

'Lovely working with you,' I said, accompanied by a sad smile.

She returned the smile.

'What's the plan?'

'Going to walk across Canada.'

She kind of laughed at that, unsure whether to take me seriously.

'Isn't there a train?'

'I thought I'd walk. Got nothing else to do.'

'Well, that sounds exciting.'

'Sergeant Harrison's going to come with me.'

'Wow. I have absolutely no idea if you're being serious.'

'I think Sergeant Harrison might have something to say about it,' said Eurydice, with the tone of a mother on hearing that her kid is about to travel to the Amazon and go looking for lost Incan treasure.

'I'll send you a postcard,' I said, and Fforbes smiled again. We shared the kind of significant look that people share, while not necessarily having much idea what it was about, and then Eurydice and I turned away, and left the room.

Together we walked along a sanitized white corridor, past notice boards and pristine white tiles.

'Can I go home now?' I said, as we turned a corner, into another endless white corridor.

Eurydice didn't reply.

34

This is retirement. Nothing to do, all the time in the world to do it in.

The evening is pleasant, warm, so there's that. I walk to Glasgow Green, this end of it about half an hour from me. People sitting on the grass, couple of kids on bikes, someone pushing a pram, a dickhead playing a guitar.

I get to the river, lean on a railing and stare at the water. The river is edgy, though the evening feels calm, like the water knows something we don't. There's a storm coming, Harry, some shit like that.

I am lost. Unavoidably lost. And this will be my life, unless I grab something to give it direction.

That's why my ridiculous idea of walking across Canada has some currency in this discussion. Because you, the lay person who's never walked across a great land before, might think you can walk across Canada in a fortnight, but Canada is big my friends. It's an undertaking. It's full-on Frodo levels of shit, but with Vancouver at the end rather than Mordor.

No doubt I would absolutely hate it, but what the fuck. There might be occasions when I would look upon an endless prairie, or upon a vast lake or a giant-ass mountain range – if I got that far – and feel *something*. Wouldn't that be worth aiming for? Awareness. Feeling. Suffering, even. Because what did I feel today when our heads were surrounded by the beating wings of flesh-eating crows?

Aye, there we are. Fuck all, that's what.

'What are you doing?'

I recognise that voice. Didn't expect to hear it, to be fair. I turn. It's fake Police Constable Rowan.

Standing just behind me, with a couple of takeaway coffee cups. People always bring coffee, even when the moment demands alcohol. Or just nothing.

'This is a surprise,' I say.

For the last few hours I've assumed she works with

Clayton. I should probably leap into action or something, but instead, I just stand here, like a bit of a tube. To be fair, she's got coffee, not a machete or a Glock.

'Why? You know I'm watching you.'

'Eurydice said she'd never heard of you.'

She holds my look for a moment, and then reaches out with the coffee.

'Milk, no sugar.'

I take the drink, automatically taking a sip.

'Looks like I'm very trusting,' I say.

'I think you just don't care anymore,' says Rowan.

We turn away and start walking along the path by the river, in the direction of the centre of town.

In silence for a while. It's a nice temperature, the coffee and the air. Rowers on the river, lovers on a bench. There are a couple of trees along hear that smell great this time of year. No one knows what kind of trees they are.

'Show me your ID,' I say.

She fishes around in the pocket of her light summer coat, then hands me the card.

I don't doubt there are fake Police Scotland ID cards out there in the world, but this looks like the real thing. Police Constable Julia Rowan, ID number SP7156D. I hand the card back.

'You're internal affairs?'

'Yes,' she says. 'Sort of internal affairs.'

'Why the lie, then? I mean, I obviously mentioned it to Eurydice, and she obviously didn't know what I was talking about. We spent the afternoon assuming you worked for Michael Clayton.'

'I kind of fucked it,' she says. ''Scuse my language.'

'Oh, you're excused. That's pretty funny. So, who are you investigating? Me or Eurydice?'

'Why would we be investigating DCI Hamilton?'

'I don't know, but I'm not sure why you're paying any attention to me either. I'm literally about to leave. Like, tomorrow. I'm gone. I'm no one's problem.'

'OK,' she says.

Oh, there's a tone there. That was like her saying, *OK, but you do realise we know about you setting fire to the old Milsom place?*

'What does that mean?'

'What does what mean?'

'OK? Whatever OK means, it does not mean OK, not in this context. Tell me.'

We come to a grove of trees, and she turns along the path to our right, away from the river.

'My colleague asked me to describe you to her the other day,' she says, 'and I said it's like you were a figment of your own imagination.' A pause, and then, 'What d'you think about that?'

'I'm not sure what it means.'

'No, me neither. But I thought of it, and it sounded about right.'

'Wait, how long have you been following me?'

'Been on your case since you took early retirement. Just following you on and off.'

'I never noticed.'

'You've been too drunk most of the time.'

'Thanks.'

'You do get a lot of girlfriends.'

I don't say anything to that. Drink coffee, walk on. Still not sure why I'm under investigation, but she's talking now, and I feel we'll come to it eventually. Begin to realise that I might not actually want to know.

Nevertheless, when she doesn't say anything else, I can't help pushing it.

'I don't understand why you started investigating me only after my name was down for redundancy. Why didn't your lot make a push to kick me out years ago?'

Another long silence, and then, 'I'm not supposed to talk to my subjects.'

'Why are you talking to me, then?'

'Like I say, I screwed up. Out of nowhere, you were standing right in front of me. Like, boom, right there. I should just have outright denied everything. I mean, it's stupid, but you just look so haunted and sad and... God, I just want to give you a hug.'

She shudders.

'If they could hear me at the office, I'd be doing talks in primary schools by tomorrow afternoon.'

Haunted and sad. How attractive...

'Well, look on the bright side,' I say, deadpan, 'you're a lesbian, so you don't have to worry about doing anything dumb.'

'I'm already doing something dumb. And I'm not a lesbian.'

Well, this conversation is going well. I stop, touch her arm to get her to stop. We stand looking at each other in the middle of the path beneath the branches of a kind old tree.

A guy approaches on an electric scooter, scowling, veers around us, with a, 'Fuck's sake, man,' thrown into the light evening breeze.

'Just tell me what's happening, please,' I say.

'We're supposed to do this job anonymously.'

'Well, we're kind of passed that now, so what's the story?'

'I work for a unit, a sad, little unit in Gartcosh, not an elite unit, but a sad unit. And we're not, to be honest, proper police officers.' Another pause, she looks like she's descending to my level of haunted sadness as she talks. 'Basically, I'm currently compiling a dossier on you so that you get retrospectively kicked out the force, and you don't get your pension.'

Time passes.

'Sorry,' she says.

'How many people are in this unit?'

'Five.'

'And you go after your fellow officers to deprive them of their retirement?'

'Like I say, we're not really police officers, and therefore, we are not your fellow officers.'

'What a shit job,' is the next thing I think to say. 'No wonder you're not supposed to talk to me.'

She nods.

'Wait, wouldn't we know?' I say. 'I mean, wouldn't this be a thing? If there was this epidemic of officers getting shafted...' and I let the question drift off as she's nodding.

'People usually complain, then they get evidence put down in the front of them, then there's a bit of bargaining. Ultimately, very few ever get completely stripped of their pension, but always, always there's a reduction.'

'You don't have Eileen Harrison on your list, do you?'

'I don't know that name. Oh, wait, she's your friend. I've seen you two together. I don't think so.'

'You go after her, you and I are through.'

She starts to respond, and then smiles and stops herself.

'Look, I can save you a lot of trouble,' I say. 'We could just cut to the negotiation. I don't need much anyway, you know.

I'm going to walk across Canada.'

'Not my call, I'm afraid. I just have to watch you, and compile the dossier.'

'How's it coming along?'

'It's pretty thick, to be honest. You're going to walk across Canada?'

'That's the plan.'

'Wow.'

We stare at each other. She looks troubled. She looks around for somewhere to put her coffee, then hands it to me, and takes her coat off.

'I'm roasting all of a sudden. This is what happens.'

She's wearing a purple dress, low, round-neck cut. Great breasts. Large. You could bury your face in there. I fail in any attempt to not look at them.

'Really?'

'Sorry. Or not, I mean, you just took your jacket off *for a reason.*'

'I'm hot!'

'I know.'

Layers.

We both find it funny, weirdly enough, and she takes her coffee from me as we walk on.

'Stop it,' she says. 'Anyway, I've seen the women you sleep with. I'm not your type. Too old, too fat, too everything.'

We have learned something else about the detective sergeant this evening, people. I genuinely don't care about my pension. I mean, something would be nice, might be in a little trouble if I got no money, but I don't need much. I certainly don't need what I'm owed.

The other thing we learn, we already know. The merest mention of sex has me interested.

God, I hate myself.

'You look great in that dress,' I say.

'Thank you.'

'Seasalt?'

'You're full of surprises.'

'I don't think I am.'

She nods, staring straight ahead. Sort of says, 'I guess not,' but not particularly loudly.

We walk in silence, the evening frittering by as we go.

'Not sure why you're having to follow me,' I say after a

while. 'Surely there's already more than enough in the file.'

'Maybe it's because you've been given a pass so often in the past. They just wanted a cherry on top.'

A sardonic *great* is on my lips, but I leave it there.

'I'm going home to drink more,' I say. 'Want to join me? I mean, there's no more following to be done for this evening. I'm not working, I haven't arranged to see anyone. I'm going home, I'm going to drink wine and eat whatever I can scavenge from the meagre pickings in my fridge.'

Silence for a moment. We make another right turn, and start heading back, away from the town centre.

'I shouldn't.'

'I know. I won't tell. Ultimately, though, don't worry about it. If you think you'll get in trouble over it, it ain't worth it.'

We walk in silence for the rest of the way through the park. I know she's going to come to the house.

Multitudes 7

'Why are you here?'

Lord Ian Thewlis of Stenhousemuir, dumped on the floor, chained at the wrists and feet, stared grimly back at his captor through the half-light of the basement.

'I don't know,' he said.

'Why are you here?'

'I don't know. This will not stand. I am a sitting member of the Lords. If you are this madman, this supposed vigilante, then you have the wrong person. Let me go.'

'Why are you here?'

Lord Ian's head twitched. To be fair to Lord Ian, he genuinely had no idea. Seven years at Eton, a first in PPE from Brasenose College, Oxford, eighteen months working at a right-wing think tank in the city, followed by short stints as a SpAd to a variety of Conservative government ministers, before being elevated to the Lords at the age of thirty-one, was the kind of life that tended to lend one a certain level of entitlement. One did not try to do the right thing; rather, the right thing was defined by what you did. As a result, the impending murder of Lord Ian of Stenhousemuir was going to point to a new direction for his killer. Previous victims might all, under other circumstances, have been convicted of their crimes. Lord Ian, on the other hand, had lived a life of privilege, his years of exploiting the system for his own gain all ship-shape and above board.

'I have had quite enough,' said Lord Ian. Business-like, what appeared to be a genuine belief he wasn't about to be murdered. 'This is what we shall do. You will let me go, and you have my word as a gentleman, that I will find you the finest lawyers. I won't, obviously, defend you publicly myself, but this act of releasing me will, I can assure you, count in your favour. We all know that many of those you've previously killed were getting their just desserts. Up until this point, you have done some good work. Perhaps, in fact, there may be some sort of deal to be done with the security services for your further employment.'

The killer came a little closer. For the first time, Lord Ian seemed to flinch.

'What?' said Lord Ian.

'You know you're only thirty-four, right?'

'What?'

'You know you're only thirty-four?'

'Yes. Yes, of course.'

'Why do you talk like you're ninety-three and you're in an Agatha Christie movie?'

Lord Ian straightened his shoulders again, his head now resting back against the wall. The imperious look returned to his face. There was a line on his lips about the man mocking him, but he thought better of it. It would likely only induce further mockery. Instead, a sudden acceptance that he was indeed going to die. The killer recognised it in the look in his eyes, the tensing of the jaw.

'You can fuck off,' said Lord Ian, in his way.

The killer brought the knife forward, took a step closer to the prone body, and inserted the tip of the knife in the victim's stomach, just below the rib cage.

35

Well, that was exciting.

Commentators will note I'm on a good run this week. Unusual. I end up in a lot of erotic situations, although hands up, I do have to pay for it sometimes. It's been a while since that happened. A month. Maybe three weeks. But there can be a lot of shit sex, particularly when you just turn up at a bar, throw some money around, and see who's foolish enough to be attracted by it.

I thought after Kadri returned to Estonia, and I crawled home from hospital minus half a thumb, I'd curl up into a miserable ball of longing, and never want to have sex again in my life.

That's not how it panned out. The addicted part of my brain had other ideas. Rather than shrivel away into miserable nothingness, I found the need to go in completely the opposite direction, to compensate for my loss.

Some ill-gotten scenes have ensued, in the bedroom and other places. Oh, there was one particularly bleak incident on a bench in Victoria park. God, I don't like to think about that. But this week, for whatever reason, has gone well. And weirdly, though I think we all knew it was a possibility from the moment she decided to come and speak to me, Constable Rowan has now been added to the list.

Really, it's not a list. I have more respect for all these women than that.

What?

We lie in bed, staring at the ceiling, a single sheet draped vaguely over us.

'Did you pick me up?' I ask, breaking a comfortable silence.

'How d'you mean?'

'I just went for a walk, you came and found me. You chose to start talking to me. Did you pick me up?'

'You mean, with the intention that we'd end up here, in

bed?'

'Yes.'

Silence. Neither of us is looking at the other.

I'm better at this than I used to be. Lying in bed afterwards. I believe I used to be more of an asshole about it.

'Yes,' she says, after a while. Didn't expect that level of honesty. Or, indeed, for that actually to be the answer. 'Sorry.'

'I don't think an apology has been less needed in human history,' I say, and I can feel her smile next to me.

'It was unprofessional,' she says. Well, it was, but no one's complaining about it. 'Just got a little wrapped up in your life there for a while, sorry.'

Have nothing to say to that. Shit happens.

'Hopefully, and no offence, that'll be an itch scratched, and, you know…'

Hmm. Doesn't really work like that, I'm afraid. I mean, I'm not saying she's going to be banging on the door demanding more sex at some point, but the sex urge isn't really a turn on/turn off at will mechanism. That fucker will just come and bite you on the arse at any moment, and there's not a lot you can do about it.

Well, there's self-restraint. Some people have that, I suppose.

I feel her move, lift her head, a second, a low exasperated curse, and then she settles back in the bed.

'Shit, sorry.'

'What?'

'I've got to go. My husband's going to be calling shortly, asking what I'm up to. I said I'd be home by ten at the latest.'

'Husband?'

'Yeah. Don't wear the ring, but you know, I mean, I never wear it.' She giggles. 'I hadn't just slipped it off because I was on the pull. Started giving me eczema a couple of years back. Look, can I have a shower, is that OK?'

'Sure. There's a towel in that cupboard there.'

She squeezes my thigh, says, 'Thanks,' then gets up and walks to the cupboard. She grabs a bath sheet, then puts on the light and steps into the bathroom. Before the door is completely closed, she opens it again and leans on the doorframe.

She has the most fabulous breasts. Holy shit. A hundred curves, fabulous tits, and if she decides the itch hasn't been scratched, I'm here for her.

'This is the cleanest bathroom I've ever seen in a home of a single guy,' she says. 'Everything about you is wonderfully strange.'

'Thanks.'

She turns away. The door closes.

36

Confirmed last day as a police officer. It will, however, be a last working day after the fashion of Springsteen's *The River*. No wedding day smiles, no walk down the aisle and the like. Just a functional day at work.

Fittingly, given that I'm still getting paid for this, I've joined the general summons to go to Dalmarnock for the morning briefing on the Multitudes case. The media, and more importantly from our point of view, the police, are all in on Multitudes. No one really wants to give him his full name. I Am Multitudes sounds a little grandiose. Pompous. So, Multitudes it is.

I called Eurydice last night to tell her there was another story about Constable Rowan, and that we didn't have to worry about her working for, or with, Clayton. Eurydice seemed a little distracted. I got the impression she was otherwise occupied, which is fair enough. She has the shittiest job in the land this week, and if she needs to let off steam, then she should fill her boots. I thought I'd get more pushback on what the other story might be.

I do need to speak to her today, however. And, as I sit in amongst a throng of close on seventy officers getting the morning briefing, I'm contemplating one last act of grandstanding. Of making this meeting about me.

I mean, it's not really grandstanding. It kind of makes sense. Eurydice is up there, looking pretty tired and stressed and shot through, and she's giving everyone the broad sweep of instruction for the day, talking through the absolute horrorfest of the crows – which, I have to admit, I've largely managed not to think about since it happened, aided and abetted by Constable Rowan, the seductress – and she'll divvy up the day's tasks into whatever departments she thinks appropriate, and she won't have all the information to hand until I speak to her after the team talk is over.

'Anyone?' she says.

She's done. The final act of any wrap-up, giving the team the chance to speak. In this situation, it's really a hollow invitation. There are so many in the room, that really, everyone just needs to keep their mouths shut, because once one person pipes up, the floodgates have been breached, and you're liable to be here for the rest of your life.

Silence. It won't be allowed to linger, as she has the air of someone who wants to crack on with this.

I get to my feet. She takes a breath, regards me warily, throws a quick glance the way of her old ADC Sergeant Blumenthal, sitting by the door with a small folder of casework to be given to everyone present, and then indicates for me to talk.

'I hesitate, but please, go ahead.' A second, and then, 'If you could be brief.'

'I got a note pushed beneath my front door this morning. At least, it was there when I got up.'

I hold it up. Two words, hand-written. She won't be able to read it from up there.

'Tick-tock.'

She stares at it for a moment. Takes in the information, considers everything it implies, then nods, says, 'Thanks,' and I sit down. 'Speak to me after we're done. Everyone, well, it gives us a line, somewhere to go. We all know what this means. And let's put it out there again, a little more urgency now. He may well have sent out other notes at the same time. Otherwise, for now, let's run with what we've talked about. Get your folders from Sergeant Blumenthal, updates as and when. Let's roll.'

An instant tumult of noise, chairs being pushed back, conversations breaking out, footsteps and jackets and low mutters. I sit in my spot, pulling my legs in to make sure everyone can walk past. Eurydice goes to speak to the able lieutenant in charge of press matters.

Slowly the room is cleared, everyone heading off out into the world to tackle this Multitudes character head on. There are three of us left. I was about to walk to the front of the room, but as the last of the minions file out, Eurydice comes to sit in the row in front, and does that thing where she turns a seat around, straddles it, and leans on the back of the chair.

I hand her the note. She studies it, holds it up to the light, then lays it down on the chair next to her.

'I'll pass it on to Leah,' she says.

The room now emptied out, Blumenthal does not join the others, but instead comes to sit with us, parking his considerable girth in a seat in the same row as Eurydice.

'What d'you want to do?' she asks. 'This is your last day?'

'Yep. I mean, it doesn't have to be, but I feel like I've made the call. I need to leave.'

'I guess someone could be playing a joke, someone could be taunting you for badness, but if it's that, then we have to take precautions anyway, they'll just be a waste of time. We can put protection on you. You can leave now, and just get the fuck away from the city. You can tackle this head on. Maybe go on TV, speak to the guy. You did that before.'

'We could fit a tracker on you,' chips in Blumenthal. 'Leave you to your day. It's kind of using you as bait, but I'm guessing you might not mind.'

Eurydice looks at me while he speaks. She looks exhausted. Wonder what she was doing last night. I mean, let's not get distracted from the thing where she's pretty damned hot, by the way. Always has been. But she's been wrung out by that crows business yesterday in a way that I haven't been. To be fair, as they say on the football, hard to blame her.

'I'll go with Sergeant Blumenthal,' I say. 'But if you're really not trailing me, and you're really going to just have someone checking my location, you're going to have to bury this tracking device pretty deep, because assuming this is Clayton, he will find it, and he will remove it, and we know he'll have no qualms about how brutal he has to be to do that.'

'If this is Clayton,' says Eurydice, 'why d'you think he came to see you the other night, and then didn't follow through? Does that make sense? He had you right there. Asleep, drunk, naked.'

'I genuinely think that'll have been too easy for him. When he chooses, and he's clearly made a lot of choices with me in the past, but when he chooses to have it, he has some sort of code. Like the duellist who brings a gun to a swordfight, and who swaps his gun for a sword as a matter of honour. He would not like me as a sitting duck. He wants me to fear him.'

'And do you?'

'Sometimes. It's not dependent on him, it's dependent on me. I can be scared, I can happily not care. Right now, I don't care. Let's do what the sergeant says. Fit a tracker. Can we do some kind of movie thing, where you zap me in the neck? Like an implant.'

She gives me a *really?* look, then glances at Blumenthal.

The sergeant's phone rings.

'We can do that. Maybe as a decoy, though. I think the best thing to do at this stage, the least obvious, is to get the smallest device we can, and you swallow it,' says Blumenthal. 'If nothing's happened by the time it passes through, and this is still on-going, you take another one.'

'Fine,' I say, because really, that is fine, and kind of laugh saying, 'I shall look forward to examining my deposits to watch for its expulsion.'

'I think we can work around that,' he says, then answers the phone and takes a step or two away.

Eurydice and I look at each other. I suspect she's contemplating how this will actually play out, while I'm just staring at her, nothing to say.

'Tell me about Constable Rowan,' she says.

'Investigating my career to see how much of my pension they can pull.'

Her shoulders kind of slump, she shakes her head.

'Jesus, one of those. God, these people. They really do fuck with us.'

'You knew they did this?'

'Sure, it's pretty obvious if you pay attention,' she says. I look blankly at her. 'Obviously, you don't.'

'Nope.'

'How are you feeling?'

'Don't care.'

'Surprised she was honest with you.'

'Yeah.'

'How did that play out? I mean, that seems odd. I thought they were specifically tasked with not interacting with the subjects of their investigation.'

'I caught her off guard when she was running after me yesterday. She doesn't think on her feet, apparently.'

'One of those, huh? I suppose we should be glad she's not a real officer.'

'We've got another one,' says Blumenthal, slipping the phone into his pocket, and turning back to our conversation. He doesn't bother taking his seat. 'Got a call from a woman who reports her husband received a *tick-tock* note yesterday. He didn't take it seriously. Called it rubbish, tossed it in the bin. He took a call last night, didn't say from whom, went out to meet someone, hasn't come home yet.'

'We know the guy?' I ask.

'Not criminally, no. Actually, I've never heard of him, but he'll be on record. Lord Thewlis of Stenhousemuir.'

Eurydice and I take a moment to process that, then Eurydice gets to her feet.

'Jesus,' she says. 'So this call was from, presumably, Lady Thewlis?'

'Yes.'

'Send me the address, I'll get out there now. You,' and she points at me, gesturing for me to join her.

37

I read up about our potential next victim in the car on the way through to the outskirts of Larbert, reading out the relevant information as we go. It quickly falls into place.

Lord Thewlis of Stenhousemuir has no history in business whatsoever, nowt but a professional politician, albeit not one who feels the need to appear with any great regularity in parliament. Nevertheless, when Covid struck and the government were looking around in a panic for providers of emergency medical equipment, completely hamstrung by not being able to give contracts to British companies who could actually help them for reasons that have never been made clear, Thewlis was heroically there to help. He started a company, and the following week was given a contract for one hundred and forty-seven million pounds to provide syringes.

His company bought in supplies from Myanmar, providing the NHS with syringes with an estimated value of around twenty-one million pounds. They were found to be unusable. The Thewlis company provided nothing further. None of the money was ever paid back.

'God, these people,' says Eurydice, more than once, as I relate the narrative.

I stick the phone in my pocket as we speed along the outside lane of the M80 past Cumbernauld, blue light going, siren intermittently used as and when required.

Silence for a while, then I say, 'Interesting development.'

'You think?'

I smile at her tone. She's pretty frazzled. I wonder if I should say something. Not sure how it would come out, so probably just need to keep my mouth shut. Her driving is getting to the approximately terrifying stage, but I weirdly don't seem to mind. Enjoying the speed, and that vague curiosity about whether we'll actually make it to our destination alive.

'This is the kind of guy who'd think he's done nothing wrong,' I say. 'You can see him getting the note and thinking it's a prank. And, of course, he may not have done anything illegal, but there are going to be a tonne of people annoyed at him, and a tonne of people not in the slightest bit bothered when he gets his comeuppance, regardless of how brutal it turns out to be.'

She lets out a deep breath through puffed cheeks, nodding her way through it. Mutters, 'Come on,' at a silver Mercedes that dallies too long ahead of us.

'Where does it leave you?' she asks.

'How d'you mean?'

We left the office putting out the renewed call around the peoples of the earth. Contact the police if you receive one of these notes. Nevertheless, it wasn't like we hadn't already done it. The peoples of the Earth were already aware of the notes. But there is no escaping this one, undeniable fact. Most of the people are idiots. And this guy, this lord of the realm, he'll have got that note and thought nothing of it. Because for all his private school education, and his first class Oxbridge honours, and his work in government, he too is an idiot. Possibly dead already. Bring out the world's smallest violin.

'I get that you and Clayton have a history. I get that you played your part in his arrest, and that your methods have been questionable on a regular basis. But I'm not sure how the public are ever going to hear about you and think, ah, that guy had it coming. If his aim is to be some sort of weird populist serial killer – and let's be honest, nowadays that's hardly the strangest thing you'll find in the public realm – why take out a guy who's investigated, and cracked, a lot of high profile cases? I mean you're main faults are sex, alcohol and insubordination. You're like a maverick's maverick. The more details the public learn, they'll probably think you're amazing.'

I give her a bit of an eyebrow, which she catches with a glance over.

'Whatever. But I don't get it. The people you locked up deserved to be locked up. You've killed a couple of people, but it's been the right people, in the line of duty.'

I stare straight ahead. The road, the trees, the cars flit quickly by, a muddle, a confusion of shapes and colours. The past comes with it, on its grey horse, bringing death. Depression settles on me, insinuating itself, painting dark pictures.

She drives. Time passes. The road is a blur. She glances at me. I'm not looking, but I can feel her staring at me for a little longer than one would like in someone who's driving at over a hundred miles an hour.

The Larbert turn-off approaches.

'What don't I know?' she says, as she brakes sharply, coming off the motorway.

I don't answer. She glances at me again, comes quickly upon a slow-moving white something, swerves, brakes, curses, arrives at a sudden intersection, slamming the car to a stop.

*

'He didn't say where he was going?' asks Eurydice.

I haven't spoken since we got here.

'No, but that's not unusual,' says Lady Thewlis.

Lady Thewlis. That just sounds dumb. She's just some local lassie this bloke married. No kids, God knows what she actually does, barely in her thirties, if she even is. No airs and graces about her, which is a positive, of course, but calling this pair Lord and Lady Thewlis just shows you how stupid this system is. And they, of course, live in a nice, but fairly conventional home on the edge of a new-build estate, looking out across open countryside, rather than in some over-sized baronial mansion that's only one ill-timed, tax burdened death away from being passed on to the National Trust for Scotland.

Nevertheless, Eurydice is playing the game, addressing the victim's widow as Lady throughout.

Victim's widow may be getting ahead of ourselves a little here, but I think it's a fair shout. This fucker had it coming, and there's no doubt it'll have come already.

Lady Thewlis takes a drink of coffee. We all have coffee. Why not? It's certainly what Eurydice needs, so she can drive that little bit faster on the way home.

'Ian's in London every second week, of course, and often enough he'll go down for the night if he's needed for a vote. I won't say we have separate lives, but there's an element of... I often don't know what he's doing, and he certainly doesn't know what I'm doing. Or, perhaps I should say, he's not interested enough to ask.'

There's always the possibility that she was faking the whole thing, and that she'll have killed him herself, but we pretty much ruled that out, I guess, when she showed us the scrunched up *tick-tock* note retrieved from the basket in his office, and it's written in exactly the same handwriting as any others we've seen.

'So, he just walked out the door?' asks Eurydice. 'Did he say goodbye? Not saying anything sounds a little extreme.'

'He said it was a work thing.'

'Vague.'

'Yes.'

'Particularly since his work is in London.'

'Yes.'

'Did he look worried about it?'

'Worried? Why?'

'Did he think it might be related to the note he'd received, but felt compelled to go anyway?'

She almost looks confused by the question.

'No, I mean, you don't think it's anything to do with the note?'

'That's why we're here,' says Eurydice.

'Well, yes,' says Lady Thewlis. I think we're about to learn she's just as entitled as her undoubtedly dead husband. 'But I rather thought the police would be concerned about a missing peer, regardless of some spurious note. Even if the two are connected, there is absolutely no reason for this preposterous I Am Multitudes character to be targeting Ian. I mean, just none.'

Eurydice doesn't immediately leap in with the obvious, perhaps thinking of a way to put it diplomatically, so I just take the doubt out of the conversation.

'He never received any pushback for the Covid NHS contract?' I ask. My tone may be in the vicinity of no-fucks-to-give.

'Oh, please, we are not bringing that into it.'

'What else is there?'

'Sorry?'

'Why else would Multitudes be targeting him?'

'He's not! He's simply not! And why on earth would he target him because of that contract? Seriously? Are you two *actually* the police? Is this who they've sent? Because Ian knows people, obviously, he knows rather a lot of people, and when he turns up alive, your names will be getting mentioned.' She takes a furiously deep breath through her nose, and then gets straight back to work. 'Everything about that contract, and I mean *everything*, was above board. Ian was doing a public service, for God's sake. Frankly we were pissed off he didn't receive proper recognition.'

'He received a hundred and forty-seven million quid, how much recognition did you want?'

'Get out. You can get out.'

She looks harshly at me, then turns to Eurydice. Eurydice, today's good cop, seems to be not yet included in the demand. Eurydice nods at me, and I am only too happy to take my leave.

Being a contrary, obstreperous bastard, I take a drink of coffee. Lower the mug, take another, and then place it on the kitchen table and say, 'Thanks for the coffee,' get up, having thought of and decided not to end that sentence with, 'Your ladyship,' and then I'm out of the kitchen and walking up the elegant, minimalist hallway to the front door.

*

Eurydice emerges fifteen minutes later, looking no happier than she has the rest of the morning. I suspect, ultimately, she will consider this branch line to the investigation a waste of time. Nevertheless, she'll understand how this has to be. She's the detective chief inspector, and cannot be sending a lesser mortal to interview the spouse of a missing peer. Bad optics in our class-driven, class-riddled society. One simply must play to the establishment.

I'm leaning against the car, hands in my pockets, looking out across the fields. Somewhere over there are the Kelpies, but the view is nevertheless uninspiring. A nice day, though, with a pleasant summer's warmth.

'Going out all gun's blazing, huh?' she says.

Arms folded, staring at me. I'm leaning against the driver's door, or else I think she'd just be straight in the car and speeding off, regardless of whether or not I was in the passenger seat.

'Had enough of these people,' I say, without much tone.

'These people? Never done interviewing the nobility, are you?'

'OK, people. I've had enough of people. The reason this guy'll have been targeted is smacking everyone right in the damned face. I'm not here for their refusal to acknowledge that. No one likes truth anymore. That's what we, the police, deal in, and none of these fuckers care. This guy got what was coming to him.'

'We'll see,' she says. 'Can I get in the car?'

'I thought I'd drive.'

'Why?'

'You seem a little wired.'

I get a fabulous look of contempt. I mean, holy shit, she really does look like she wants to punch me, then she surprises me by holding forward the keys.

'Fair point. Scared the shit out of myself a couple of times on the way over.'

*

'So did you learn anything else in the fifteen minutes you had her alone?' I think to ask, about halfway through our drive home.

Eurydice needs to drag herself back from whatever world she's allowed herself to become immersed in, takes a moment to conjure up the question, then says, 'Said she thought he was having an affair, but wasn't at all specific on the detail. Didn't give me a name to speak to. She said he had lovers, and so wasn't at all surprised or bothered that he hadn't come home. He did, however, miss his tee time at the golf club this morning. That was unusual. That was why she called. Nevertheless, she's still persuading herself he's likely been derailed by some wanton succubus.'

'Did she use the term wanton succubus?'

'Yes.'

Can't help smiling at that.

'What d'you think?' I ask.

'Oh, she's lying to herself. But I suspect she'll continue to lie to herself, even if our friend Multitudes goes on live TV and says I killed this guy cause he's a corrupt, money-grabbing bastard.' Barely a second of a pause, then she says, 'Tell me.'

I don't say *tell me what*. I know what she means. The question has been sitting there waiting to be asked, and it was me, right enough, who was stupid enough to re-introduce conversation to the silence.

And it's not like I've not been thinking about this since it came up.

'I killed a guy in Bosnia once,' I say.

'I've read your file.'

'That shouldn't be on my file.'

'It's on your file.'

Fuck me.

Speak to a doctor, they said. Tell her anything. You'll be good, she's literally a doctor. It doesn't get written down, no one gets to hear about it.

'I killed a guy,' I repeat.

'I know.'

'Shot him in the back of the head. Unarmed civilian.'

'I know.'

'Then you know there are mitigating circumstances, but that doesn't amount to a hill of beans in the hands of a professional. The fact is I killed him. I could have turned the bullet on myself, I could have turned it on the, whatever they were, bandits. But I did what they asked.'

'You saved those women.'

'Far as I know.'

'You did.'

'You've read my side of it. I have no idea what happened to those women. I also have no idea how Clayton found out about the whole thing, but maybe he knows more than I do. He can easily make something of it so that I'm the bad guy here, even if his motives are more about his own personal revenge.'

Sitting in the inside lane. Strangely, my driving is the complete opposite of Eurydice. Slowing to below sixty as I go, just wanting the day to be over, and it's not even eleven a.m.

She doesn't speak. Maybe she'll like the slightly longer break of a slow crawl back to the station. She looks like she needs the time even more than I do. Of course, she has a sense of responsibility in this, while I have the sense of an ending.

'I don't even think it's revenge,' I say some time later. 'Like I said before, it's sport, that's all.'

'You don't have to let him win,' she says, just as we're lapsing into another silence.

38

The last video and testament of Lord Thewlis of Stenhousemuir appears online as I'm driving between Dalmarnock and Cambuslang. I've swallowed my tracker, and I've been fitted with two others which are more obvious, in the forlorn hope this might throw Clayton off the scent when he comes for me. And I've been sent out into the world. I am bait.

I walk into see Hawkins, just as she's watching the video. I know as soon as I see her face what she'll be looking at. Everyone working the case has been expecting it.

She closes the file, looking at me as I close the door and stand on the other side of the desk.

'Have you seen?' she asks.

'There's another video?'

'Lord Thewlis.'

'Well, we knew that was coming.'

'And you haven't seen it?' she asks again.

I shake my head.

She swallows.

'I think I might be sick. There's just something about this one.'

'Really? How much worse can it be?'

I'm curious now, in my defeated, ready to walk away and drown in a barrel of white wine way.

She turns her screen around, brings the file up, and presses play, turning away as she does so, so she can't see the screen.

Lord Thewlis's guts are being eaten by a couple of infant chimpanzees. After every small mouthful, they look round, their eyes occasionally catching the camera. A look that says they think they shouldn't be doing this, but they're starving, so they'll take the opportunity while it's there.

They look almost human.

I watch for a second, then reach over and stop the file.

I don't say anything. Hawkins is still staring darkly out of the window. A moment, then she turns back. Trying to be annoyed by it, rather than haunted. Possibly by the thought that this feels one step away from Multitudes having a feral, starving child doing his dirty work for him, and the sudden awful thought that he might have it in the pipeline.

'We need to catch him,' she manages.

'Yes.'

'You're still… I don't know, sergeant… You're aiming to leave after today?'

'Yes. But that's been superseded in any case.'

'By what?'

'I received the note. *Tick-tock*. And we know our guy there got his yesterday morning. If our vigilante hero is working to the same schedule, then I should be due to get taken some time today or this evening. And then,' and I end the sentence dragging my thumb across my throat.

Hawkins looks concerned. Glances over her shoulder, as though there might be something outside the window to answer her question.

'What does this mean? Eurydice's put a tail on you? You have protection of some sort?'

'I'm bait.'

She straightens, she cannot be surprised.

'You've just come out into the world, and will wait to be accosted by this monster?'

'Pretty much.'

'Eurydice is worried that if you have a tail, the killer would be scared off.'

'Yes. Well, I articulated that before she did, but that's about the size of it.'

I choose to skip the bit where we also discussed what to do about Constable Rowan, on the off-chance she's still keeping tabs on me, because if Clayton discovers her, then either she's dead, or this meagre plan we're hatching is a bust.

'They fitted you with a tracking device?' and she shakes her head as she says it. 'That's going to be obvious, and fairly easily removed.'

'I have two decoys. One on my ankle, one injected into my neck. The active one, I swallowed. Plus I've downloaded the app so I can track the device myself. In the off chance I off-load it before I'm taken, then I'll be able to tell, and I can take another one and start the process again.'

'What are you going to do now?'

I hold my hands out to the side in a bit of a *there's nothing left* gesture.

'I thought I'd see if Eileen was available for lunch, then I'm going to come back, clear out my desk, and leave. Sit at home and wait for the coming horseperson of the apocalypse.'

'You're liable to be drunk when he arrives,' she says.

'Not out of the question. To be fair, I have done some of my best work while drunk.'

'Sergeant.'

'I don't know, boss, what d'you want me to do? This is how it's playing out. He's going to come for me, and then we'll deal with it. I'll deal with it. Whatever happens will happen.'

'Most likely this time tomorrow you'll be in one of those videos and I'd rather you weren't.'

'Well, that's possible. I mean, obviously it's possible. But at least I'm going to know it's coming, and there's something about this guy. This is Clayton, one hundred percent Clayton, and he'll give me a chance. It's who he is. He put a gun in my hand the last time, remember. He did it then, he'll do it again. He'll do something again, something that's not straightforward, something that's not what he did with all these others. History suggests that it doesn't matter whether I'm drunk, sober or somewhere in between. I'll deal with it.'

I don't bother with the other side of the coin. The one where I don't deal with it, and I just don't care.

'I need to head out shortly,' she says. 'I won't be here when you get back from lunch.'

'OK.'

Then I realise what she means.

'Oh, right, I see, sorry. This is goodbye.'

'Yes.'

She takes a deep breath, and lets it slowly go.

'I thought we'd be doing a bit more than this. You've had such a long career, it feels wrong to just be –'

'I've spent the last few weeks intending not being here on my last day at all. You know me well enough to know I just want to go.'

'Yes.'

We hold the stare. There's some line to be said about how easily we'll be able to see each other if either of us wants to, but it doesn't seem right. That's not who we are, despite the testy relations that thawed so much we ended up in bed this week without either of us being drunk.

Well, we were both a bit drunk.

'I should go and grab Eileen before she vanishes.'

'Yes.'

Something in her look that still doesn't let me go, then she walks round the desk, stands in front of me for a moment, puts a soft hand to my face, and then kisses me. She lingers a moment on my lips, and then pulls away and returns behind the protection of her desk.

'That was very unprofessional.'

I'm definitely here for all these female fellow officers being unprofessional. Today, though, my spirit is so doused in guilt and melancholy, that it doesn't mean much. Perhaps it will in the future.

'Thank you,' I say. 'I hope the Geneva thing pans out.'

She nods. A last sad smile, and then I turn away.

*

'Oh, shit.'

Eileen and I in our spot. Our usual spot, the café in the precinct. Club sandwiches, crisps on the side, water. Befitting my last day in the office, I got myself one of those mini bottles of wine. Thought I'd make it prosecco, but weirdly they didn't have that. I mean, every bastard drinks prosecco these days.

I've just told her about the Thewlis death video.

'It's bad enough seeing a chimp in a cage in a zoo. I mean, the poor little fellas, just looking so sad. So aware.'

She looks at her club sandwich. I take a bite out of mine.

'And worse, what option will they have but to put them down when they catch them?'

Hadn't thought about that yet, but fair enough. Can't be letting feral, flesh-eating chimps run wild in Scotland. Someone would complain.

She finally takes a bite of sandwich, but doesn't look very happy about it as she does, like she too is eating sweetbreads of Thewlis.

'Eurydice looks strung out,' I say. 'Must be tough being in charge of this. I wonder if she's been given the shoulder tap. Get results, or else, curtains for you. Particularly now, with the blessed nobility targeted. Hey, there will be a lot, *a lot* of rich people who've benefitted from government corruption over the years, getting on their private jets to wherever.'

She doesn't answer, staring away across the precinct.

It's a beautiful early afternoon. Lovely temperature, a light breeze. This is not, never has been, never will be, an attractive spot, but the café does what it can, and the summer sun, and that fountain there, which is remarkably actively spouting water, give the place a nice ambience.

'I've seen her the last three nights,' says Eileen.

Well, I guess that's been apparent, but I've been too busy wrapped up in my own shit to think about it.

'You and Eurydice?'

'Yes.'

'You're sleeping together?'

'Yes.'

'Good,' is all I say.

She continues to stare vaguely at the large birch tree by the walkway, then she finally looks at me.

'Is that it? No, is there video? No, can I come? No, tell me everything, that sounds amazing?'

I give her the same sad smile I'm giving everyone today.

'Well, obviously, all of those. But…,' and I let it go.

She can read me well enough, and she knows. She'd kind of been joking in any case. I don't think, under the circumstances, she was really looking for that much of a reaction.

'How is she anyway?' I ask. 'She's looking pretty frazzled.'

'That's the word. She's wound round the axle. I was hoping I might help, but I'm not sure I am. You'd think,' and she smiles self-deprecatingly, 'I mean you'd think having me in bed would be enough to distract anyone, right?''

'God, aye.'

'Well, she still needs alcohol, and she was doing coke the last two nights. And a bit too much of it.'

'Coke?'

'Yes.'

'Eurydice?'

'Yes.'

'Shit.'

'Yes.'

'Did you?'

'Nope. Never have, never will.'

'Yeah, me neither.'

'I mean, don't get me wrong, she was pretty sensational on that stuff, but it wasn't like she wasn't also sensational without it.' A pause, a small shrug. 'I don't like the effect it has on people. You don't know who they are anymore.'

'It's like alcohol, multiplied by something batshit.'

'Yes. Which is its obvious appeal, just not for me.'

That dismissal of drug culture happily dispensed with by us two boring old farts in our fifties, we take a bite of sandwich and a meandering look around the square. The usual suspects are in attendance. Not necessarily the same people, but from the same groups, nevertheless. The young mother, the couple, the kid in a pram, the dog lapping at the fountain water, the greetin' bairn, the old guy looking miserable. The sun is out and all human life is here.

'So, what's the story?' she asks. 'You really done today?'

I don't immediately answer. I need to tell Eileen the plan, and she's not going to like it. This is going to be like when Tom Cruise tells health & safety on a movie that he's going to free climb up the outside of the Shard, his naked body smeared with grease, while fighting a gorilla.

'I don't like that silence, Tom,' she says.

'I got the note,' I say quickly. Not looking at her. Eyes on a woman and a dog on the other side of the precinct. Dog on lead, sniffing at some weeds. The woman in a light summer dress, looking at her phone. I think of Elise and her dog walking. Almost smile thinking about her reaction to Eurydice calling her. Her enjoyment at being questioned by the police in a murder enquiry. The raw, innocent fun of youth.

I wish I'd had that. I wish I could have it now, like there was a version of it for the nearly-60s.

'*Tick-tock*?'

'Yes.'

'Look at me, Tom. You can't have her.'

I turn.

'Can't have who?'

'The woman you're staring at in the red dress.'

I smile, I kind of shrug. May as well get on with it.

'I got the note. I let Eurydice know. We agreed I'd be bait, and that I wouldn't be tailed. I swallowed a tracking device. Should I, you know, get rid of it before anything's happened, I have an app on my phone to alert me, and I can swallow the back-up.'

'You agreed you'd be bait.'

'Yes.'

She holds my look for a few moments, then looks at her lunch. She's upset, she likely wants to argue, but she knows, nevertheless, that it makes sense, and that it's obviously the kind of thing I'd do.

'Would you consider allowing me to sneak into your apartment prior to you going home, so that I'm there with you when this, whatever it is, actually happens?'

I don't answer, but she knows the answer.

'I can't believe Eurydice isn't just going to flood the vicinity with officers.'

'He'll know,' I say. 'You know he'll know. I have two fake trackers on. Hopefully he finds the obvious one, thinks, that's *too* obvious, then identifies the other hidden one. Doesn't realise there's a third. He takes me somewhere, he's obviously giving his victims time to say *something*, which means there'll be time for the team that's on standby to intercept him before we get to the gullet slitting.'

'And what will you be doing while you make yourself available for capture, disembowelment and animalistic feasting?'

I smile at her beautiful delivery.

'You're sweet,' I can't help saying.

'Fuck you, Tom. What are you doing?'

'Just started the *Cursed Woman* jigsaw.'

'You're going to sit in your flat and wait for the angel of death?'

'Pretty much. I can't put anyone else in danger.'

She has the words *I'd happily put myself in danger* on her lips, I can see them there. But she doesn't say it.

'Honestly,' I say, 'I don't think he comes this evening. It's always possible he doesn't come at all. It's him toying with me. That would be just as on brand. But even if he's coming, then he might well leave it a night or two. I equally wouldn't be surprised if he's sent out another few notes, confident that most of the people who receive them won't contact us.'

'Why wouldn't someone contact the police if they got what amounts to a sentence of death?'

'Thewlis didn't contact us, cause he didn't think he'd done anything wrong. And there will be people who know exactly what they did, but they won't know how anyone else knows. And they won't want to go to the police because it's an admission that there's a reason for this guy to come after them.'

She doesn't say anything. I tap the side of the head.

'We know our boy,' I say. 'Warburton aside, and he was just as guilty in any case, the first round of victims were all people in the public eye. People who'd been accused, arrested perhaps, and had avoided justice. This is a different round. He can taunt them just the same, but knowing they won't come to us. In fact, he's taunting them better than the others. The others had no idea what was coming. Now though, all recipients of one of those things, they're in the crosshairs, they know it, but they won't want to tell anyone. Top tier taunting.'

'Don't sound so impressed with the damned man,' she snaps.

Silence joins us at the table. Not a lot to be said after a conversation that's pretty much gone along the lines of, 'Death paying me a visit this evening,' 'can I help?' 'nah, we're good, I'm happy to invite him in, see how it plays out.'

'You working this afternoon?' she asks after a melancholic while.

'I'm done. Going back up to the office, collect my jotters, and that's that.'

'Anyone else know?'

'The boss. We said goodbye. I guess everyone else'll work it out when they realise after a while that I'm not there.'

I get another significant look, sad and knowing and annoyed and let down, then she drags her eyes away and stares grimly across the square.

'Jesus, Tom,' she mutters after a while.

39

Do I believe myself? Do I think our anti-hero, the elusive Mr Clayton, will have carefully selected a host of undiscovered crooks and predators, sending them notes he knows they will never report? It's going to be a very specific type of person who doesn't report it, especially after Lord Sparky there got nailed. The undiscovered bad 'uns of the earth won't think they've done anything wrong anyway, and will happily push their way to the front of the queue to get police protection. There's also the possibility that Clayton isn't as smart as we're all taking him for, and he makes a mistake. Goes after someone who is, by all measure, even his own, completely innocent. But then, surely that person would contact the police, as they'd have nothing to hide?

Basically, nobody knows, so let's everyone just calm the fuck down. It'll play out as it plays out. Like it always does.

I return to the station for twenty minutes. I shred a few things. I log out of my account. I have nothing to collect. There is, in fact, no clearing out my desk. No photos, no memorabilia of any sort. Just a pen that DCI Taylor gave me a long time ago, my final remembrance of him, that I slip into my pocket.

Emma's in position, so I stop for a moment.

'Hey.'

She looks up from her screen. She's currently touch-typing a report at a hundred and seventy miles an hour.

'You OK?' she asks.

We've not had much to do with each other the last couple of days. Or weeks, in fact.

'I'm off,' I say.

'Oh, OK. See you tomorrow?'

'No, I'm off.'

'What? For good?'

'Yep.'

'Gosh. I didn't know. Wait, there wasn't like a card or a thing? Like drinks, or a leaving present? I mean...'

I kind of shrug and give her a look, and she quickly nods, accepting the way things are. She is a detective after all.

'You just want to walk out with no, like, fanfare or anything.'

'Yep. And this is me doing it.'

'What are you going to do now?'

The honest answer is in my head, but she doesn't need to know about the note and the tracking devices and the whatever, and so I say what I've been saying to everyone, and to myself when I lie to the mirror, 'Walk across Canada.'

'You're going to walk across Canada?'

'I'll pack first.'

'Wow, that's amazing.'

The credulity of youth. I wish I shared her certainty I was being honest.

'Yeah, should be. Bit of planning to do first, so, you know, not going this evening.'

If I just went tonight, I wonder if Clayton would come and find me in the middle of Newfoundland?

'Wow. Well, super-impressed, sarge. You should set up an Insta, I mean, that shit'll be amazing.'

'Insta. Sure.'

We share a look that says I have no intention of setting up an Instagram account.

'Take care of yourself,' I say, by way of goodbye. 'Get out before it kills you.'

'Sure. I'll give it another two, three years tops, then I'll find something else.'

I nod, we smile, I turn away.

As I get to the door to the open-plan, I look over at Eileen. I stop for a moment, we stare at each other, I make an *I'll call* sign, and get the merest acknowledgement in response, and then I'm out the door and walking past reception.

Ramsey, the only other person in my police career to whom I care to say goodbye – and even then, I don't care that much – is on the phone as I walk past. I stop, I look at him, thinking there's a significance in my look, I guess. He raises his eyebrows at me, still listening to the call. I salute with mock formality, then turn the salute into a goodbye wave, he gets it, and gives me a nod, and then I'm gone, and that's it.

I step out of the office, and walk down the stairs outside the building, and then I'm walking through the precinct, and I stop for a moment.

I look back at the office, as though expecting I might see something. There is, of course, nothing to see. The only windows on the station on this side are high up in the wall, and there's no way there could be anyone standing there, tearfully waiting to wave me off. Not, of course, that that would happen in any case.

Turn back and look around the familiar scene, the Cambuslang precinct on a sunny July early afternoon. And that's it. My time in the police is over. No walk down the aisle, right enough. Thirty-odd years, a few bumps along the way, and off we fuck to Neverland.

The world is your lobster. Could do anything, go anywhere.

We all know where I'm going.

I turn back, walk through the small passageway to the rear carpark, get into that same old shitty Ford that's been defying MOT failure predictions for fifteen years now, and head for home.

Via the off licence.

Heading up onto Main Street, turning right, and starting down the hill it finally creeps up on me. Not sadness at the end of my career, a life-changing moment in which I'm investing absolutely no interest. It's that other thing. What the evening holds. Because as from now, having left the station and headed home, I'm on my own and on watch.

I don't think for a minute that Eurydice will undermine her own plans, and suddenly crack and instigate surveillance. I am let loose, and this thing will play out as it comes. All it remains for me to do is fortify myself with alcohol in preparation.

One of Marcus Aurelius' that one, I think.

40

I sit in my spot. There's an empty wine glass before me. The bottle is in the freezer, chilling. I'm going for wine, rather than vodka. Vodka's great 'n all, but the trouble is that I drink a double vodka tonic in under ten minutes. Drink six of those in an hour, that's twelve units. Start drinking at four in the afternoon, let's say aiming to head to bed around midnight, that's a potential ninety-six units of alcohol before bedtime.

Some might point out that I can easily drink a bottle of wine in an hour, and that's nine units, and that ain't a whole lot better. Thing is, I tend to slow down with wine as time passes. It starts to taste bitter. Soon enough I'll not be enjoying it, more than likely I'll start to feel unwell, and while I might not have the common sense or the wherewithal to actually stop drinking, at least the rate of consumption falls. Vodka tonic is, on the other hand, a far more potent brew, and one that my taste buds can tolerate for a much longer period.

My gangbang jigsaw hasn't really got going, but I've got all afternoon to sit here and crack on, while I wait for a visit, and I find myself only vaguely wondering how that visit will arrive. Will I know it's coming, or will I not realise until I'm waking up in the cold darkness, nothing for company but strange noises from an unseen cage on the other side of the room?

I eat crisps and cheese and apple as stomach lining.

Apple. Ha!

I stare at the empty glass for as long as possible. Once you start, you're gone, that's just the way it is. Like pushing your brakeless go-kart down the side of the hill. There ain't no stopping until you crash.

I try not to think about work. About the police. About that shitshow of a career just ended. About the coming storm. Any of it. My mind is constantly plagued by so many incidents and accidents, so many times I've screwed up over the years. So many times I fucked it, fucked other people, dropped the damned ball, disappeared into the abyss of alcohol, used women and hurt women and fucked women in all the wrong sorts of ways, all those times that I've just so completely and utterly fucked up jobs and cases and interviews and lives and opportunities and everything, everywhere all at once, everything in extremis. If there was something there to be fucked up, something to grab hold of and ruin, then I've been your sergeant on duty. The most colossal, gigantic disaster of an officer there has likely ever been on the force, and every single one of those senior officers who looked at my career and voiced out loud their incredulity that I was still in a job was absolutely spot the fuck on.

Never takes much for my brain to pluck a random thought out its arse. An error, an embarrassment, a life flushed away, a chance gone, a fellow human trodden underfoot.

And yet, sitting here, when I most definitely don't want to think of any of it, it somehow makes it easier to ignore. There's just so damned much to choose from. Like a WWII Atlantic convoy, there is safety in numbers. If there was just the one incident, I might be constantly haunted by it. But there are so many, so gargantuan in number, it's as though they have created a giant ball with an impermeable surface.

Sure, should I somehow manage to live through the twin dangers of alcohol and Clayton, the random one-offs will continue to pick me off at unexpected moments throughout any given day, even when I'm striding across the plains of Ontario. But sitting here, trying not to think about it, it is easier.

I have my crisps. I have my cheese. I have my apple. The wine awaits me in the freezer. I have my cursed woman being taken by three men.

I crack. I retrieve the wine. I pour the glass. I take my first drink of wine at four-thirteen. God, it's good. Crisp, chill, fresh. Perfect.

I let it sit in my mouth for a moment. Close my eyes, the wine on my tongue.

I swallow.

Fuck me.

I take another small drink.

I look at the painting on the cover of the box. The woman and her three lovers. What makes that so erotic, I wonder. It's not like I want to be in that situation. I would not want to be one of three men in a foursome. I can see the odds being in her favour, given that she'd still be able to out-orgasm the three blokes combined, but I wouldn't want to be one of them.

Hmm.

Constable Rowan. I can see her in this position. She could take it. She's got the body for it. I can see the man kissing her, his hand on her right breast; the next caressing and sucking her left breast; the third between her legs.

I drink more wine.

I imagine the look on Rowan's face. She came loudly. And she said *fuck* a lot. I feel women really ought to say fuck while orgasming, it's important. She grabbed my hair a couple of times, that was nice. Really hurt too, but the whole thing was so intense.

I wonder if she's out there now, somewhere, watching the window. Looking up at my profile. I hope not. I hope Eurydice's managed to get hold of her.

I drink wine. I settle back in my chair, fantasizing about Constable Rowan being fucked by three guys. That is a pretty erotic thought. The sounds she makes, the look on her face. The tongues licking her breasts, the cock sliding inside her, while she takes another in her mouth.

Maybe I could take up writing porn novels, there must be a market for that. Hmm…

I sit back, staring at the painting. Fingers resting lightly on the stem of the wine glass, mind drifting away in a delicious erotic fantasy, one in which I'm a spectator.

The phone rings. Silence shattered.

Pull it over towards me, stare at the name. DCI Hamilton. Well, reasonable she would call at some point. Let's hope she hasn't started drinking and snorting coke yet, am I right, kids? I mean, you can't trust people when they do that kind of shit.

'Eurydice,' I say.

There's a pause while she mentally addresses the fact that I just called her Eurydice for the first time. But that's the new reality, sports fans. I'm done with the police.

'Sergeant,' she finally says. 'How are things?'

'I'm good.'

'You're at home?'

'Yep.'

'Nothing to report?'

'No bowel movement,' I say, and I smile to myself at the terrible joke, and I can see her give me the rueful look down the phone.

'Nothing to report?' she repeats.

'Nope. You?'

'A few things,' she says.

Her voice sounds heavy. Not alcohol-induced heavy, though. It's exhaustion. Hopelessness.

'I'm here for it all,' I say lightly, and she doesn't immediately respond. I can hear the quiet sip at the cup of coffee, the placing of the mug back on the table.

'I have an update on Constable Rowan.'

'I was just thinking about her,' I respond, and the latent sixteen-year-old boy in me, which ain't buried all that deep, let's be honest, sniggers quietly.

'There is no Constable Rowan.'

Oh.

'Interesting,' comes glibly from my lips.

'Yeah, interesting.'

'Is there not even a unit taking down the pensions of well-meaning officers?'

'Oh no, we have that unit, don't you worry. There will be someone somewhere looking to cut your pension in half, of that you can be pretty sure.'

'Good to know.'

'Just not Constable Rowan, as there is no Constable Rowan.'

I stare at the cursed woman and think the same thing I was thinking before the phone rang. The fake Constable Rowan in this position, getting gloriously fucked.

Still stands, to be fair.

I take another drink of wine.

'What d'you think?' she asks.

'Is she an agent of Michael Clayton? Frankly, yes, I guess. I mean, I must've pissed off an absolute tonne of people along the way, there could be God knows who crawling out of the woodwork to take a crack at me, but this? Now? Way too much of a coincidence for it to be anything else. And the storyline, the fake ID card, it all plays beautifully. It's a quality set-up.'

'So, we haven't talked about her much today. You saw her again last night, right? She told you she worked for the pension squad?'

The pension squad. Doesn't that sound like the shittiest TV show you ever heard of?

'I went for a walk. Just decided to get out. Fresh air. She

approached me in the park, started chatting. Spilled the beans.'

'But there was no attempt to molest you in the park?'

'Molest me?'

Can't help laughing.

'Sergeant, please. I'm tired. I've had enough of this shit. You know what I mean.'

Her tone speaks to me. Her feeling of just needing to do what has to be done.

'She brought me coffee. I drank it. If she'd wanted to drug me, I was there for the taking. Though, to be honest, we were at the Green, so not sure what she'd have done with my slumped body on a park bench. There were plenty of people about.'

'You chatted, you drank coffee...'

'Came back here and had sex.'

Silence.

Well, she knows enough about me. She's read my file. She won't be surprised.

'The first time,' says Eurydice after a while, 'the first time you encountered the Plague of Crows, he used one of his agents to seduce you, then you were attacked when you were naked and vulnerable and completely off guard.'

'Yes.'

Taser in the erection, my friends. We must thank the brain's inability to recreate pain. One can wince at the memory, but not actually feel it.

'The second time, he filmed you having sex and used that against you.'

'Yep.'

And we're all still talking about it now.

'So, if this was the same set up, if this was him once again using someone to seduce you, what was the point?'

I stare straight ahead at a blank bit of wall on the other side of the sitting room. The phone is on speaker. A couple of fingers of my right hand rest lightly on the stem of the wine glass. A couple of fingers of my left softly tap out the three-four beat of *My Own Version of You*.

'I don't know.'

'How did it play out?' she asks.

There could be layers there, and there could be some glib question to be asked about how much detail she's looking for, but the conversation has taken on a lot more weight than that.

'We were in the park, walking and talking. I said I was

going to go home, and did she want to come. I always knew she was going to say yes, but it didn't feel wrong. I mean, she'd searched me out in the first place.'

'A totally random women offering to jump into bed with you is just part of your life, eh?'

I don't answer that. There are quite a lot of them turn out to be not so random.

'You got home, you made love... then what? She hung around, you had cocktails?'

'We lay in bed for a while, then she said she had to go as her husband would be wondering where she was. She took a shower, she left.'

'Nice detail. Was she wearing a ring?'

'Said she never did cause it gave her eczema.'

Another lifting of the mug at the other end, the quiet sip, the settling of the mug back on the desk.

'I'm not sure it makes sense,' she says.

'Nope.'

'You got a good look at her ID?'

'Took it out of her hand, studied it. If it was a fake, then –'

'It was definitely a fake.'

'They nailed it. It was bang on.'

A long sigh at the other end of the phone. I picture her rubbing her forehead. A tired, anxious face.

'I don't know,' she says eventually.

'Well, she knows where I live,' I say. 'I can ask if she shows up.'

'She won't.'

'No, I don't think so.'

Silence threatens to return. I recall she said there were a few things on the agenda. I don't ask. They'll be coming soon enough.

'I got replaced,' she says.

Holy shit.

'You fucking didn't,' is the way my mouth chooses to react to that.

'I did. And not relegated either. Removed altogether.'

'Fuck me.'

'I don't know that I will, but thank you for the offer.'

'Well that was dumb. Who've they put in charge?'

'Guy called Faraday. Through from Edinburgh. I presume you don't know him.'

'Nope. But, well we've all been there. Nothing the suits upstairs like more than to put an Edinburgh copper in charge, like they're kryptonite or something.'

'Exactly.'

We sit in collective silence for a moment or two. I've never not liked Eurydice, though we haven't ever really shared a moment before. Other than moments when she was being exasperated with me, or moments when she was handing me my arse.

'I'm sorry,' I say. 'You don't deserve that.'

'Well, thank you, but I'm not so sure. I mean…'

She lets the sentence go with a sigh, then finishes with a depressed, 'Shit,' thrown out into the world.

'Who should I report to, now, then?'

Another silence. I can see her staring blankly into nothingness. I'd been picturing her in her office, but I wonder if she's gone home already.

'This isn't going to sound great,' she says, and I can't help laughing. I mean, when what you're expecting to happen is that you get immobilised by some means, and then you get your gullet cut open, you get disembowelled, and then your viscera eaten by a hungry pack of rabid baby sloths or something, the bar is pretty high.

'I'm here for whatever it is.'

'I passed everything onto Faraday. He knows about you, he's not interested. He expressed the opinion that you'd probably sent the *tick-tock* note to yourself.'

'Ha!'

'Upon hearing you were on the verge of retirement, he was of the opinion that you were likely making the investigation about you, for one last narcissistic bite at the cherry.'

What a prick.

'So, I told him about the tracking devices, he expressed incredulity, and indeed triple incredulity when he learned that I'd wasted – his word – three devices on you, and that they would not be getting tracked.'

'He can't be that much of an asshole.'

'Oh, he can.'

Son, you're on your own. To quote *Blazing Saddles*.

'Look, I spoke to a couple of people. It's not just me and Sergeant Blumenthal who believe you. Someone'll keep an eye out. I just won't be able to stay on top of it.'

'Are you… wait, you're not suspended or anything?'

'God, it's not that bad. I am about to leave, however, and tomorrow morning… well, it's not like the rest of the city is keeping its head down while this Multitudes character goes about his business. Still plenty for a DCI about town to be getting on with. However, I am not taking a leaf out of your book. I'm done with this case. I'm sure DCI Faraday will do a fine job without me.'

'You seeing Eileen this evening?' I ask. Not thinking straight. Should probably have kept that question to myself.

I can picture her looking a little taken aback, she scowls, she decides to ignore the question.

'Stay safe. Anything suspicious, call Sergeant Blumenthal. You've still got his number?'

'Sure.'

A pause, I guess because neither of us really knows what else to say, then the phone goes dead.

I stare at it for a moment, then push it away across the table. I lift the glass and drain it, then walk through to the fridge for a top-up.

Multitudes 8

Clayton looked around the grim basement, situated beneath a derelict building in Rutherglen, under the M74. At some point the building had been earmarked for destruction, and at some further point the funding for that had been withdrawn.

As locations went, it was perfect. Buildings located under overhead motorways are like space. No one can hear you scream.

The cages of giant huntsmen spiders were lined up against the far wall. If they'd all been crammed into the same cage, there might have been some cannibalism. Animal species could go different ways. So there were a hundred and nineteen spiders spread through twenty-three cages. There had been some fighting, but most of them were intact. Unlike some of the other ravenous beasts who had swarmed over the warm, disembowelled bodies, Clayton wasn't sure that all the spiders would immediately flock in the direction of the spilled viscera. But enough of them would, as it'd be the only food readily available. Eventually they would all come.

He'd contemplated the complete opposite. Rather than a host of spiders, how about one giant, pregnant female, looking for somewhere warm and soft? He imagined Hutton's terror as this huge spider crawled up onto his torso, then burrowed into his insides to lay her eggs. But then there would be the three weeks waiting. Three weeks making sure Hutton didn't die from his wounds. Three weeks trying to keep him alive, while the mother ferociously defended her new patch.

'Nice idea,' he said to himself, with a smile. 'Not practical on this occasion.'

He didn't have three weeks. He was about to leave, having done what he'd set out to do. He'd compiled a list, while in prison, of people who in his opinion deserved more than he did to be in jail, and had taken vengeance upon them. Not for himself, obviously, but for their victims. For society. Then the preposterous Lord Thewlis had been a bonus victim.

Yes, there were many more like him, but as soon as one got taken, the rest of his sort were going to be on guard, and with only one person to help him in his operation, he was never going to be able to waylay another host of crooks. Nevertheless, they would live in fear for a long time, and it would be very easy to stoke that fear. Messages left on the Internet, messages sent in the mail. There would be a lot of people very scared. It would endure. It had been a magnificent week, he thought, but logistics had got in the way of it being even more spectacular.

A succession of articulated lorries rumbled by overhead, and then the sound finally quietened to the more regular drone of three lanes of traffic.

'Hmm,' said Clayton, looking around the small room. Everything in its place, the usual meticulous planning having done the job. The following morning he would be travelling by first class train to London. Two nights in the capital. The National Portrait Gallery was on the cards. He was looking forward to the McCartney Beatles exhibition. Then a matinee of *Hamilton* on the second day. And then, after a two-night stay at the Dorchester, the Eurostar to Paris, then the Orient Express to Istanbul. From there, a short trip to the remote island in the Thracian Sea, where he would rest up for the remainder of the summer, into the autumn.

So many future plans to be made. The world of multitudes, I Am Multitudes, was only just beginning.

41

I'm bored.

Not sure I'm going to be very good at this retirement bullshit.

What's it been now? Three hours?

Lift the glass, don't even take a drink before setting it back down on the table.

I've got that restless boredom, the kind that almost makes you anxious. You need something to do, and there's nothing you can think of to meet the need. I even checked out the website of the Canadian Great Trail. Looks pretty decent, by the way. I could do that, I thought. But then, I couldn't look at the website for more than about ten minutes without getting bored, so two years walking across the land might not fit the bill.

Of course, this is different. There is no settling down this evening. I'm waiting. At home, right where Clayton will know I am, a sitting duck.

Managed to string that bottle of wine out a long time. Now only about halfway through the second. That's not bad for me.

Took a long shower, like I need to be clean to die. Decided that sex might be a worthwhile pastime. Invited in a little bit more self-hate by calling Elise, seeing if she was free for the evening. This was, of course, reckless. If Clayton is coming here for me, then Elise shouldn't be involved. But then, on the other hand, she was here the other night and he must have known about it, and he didn't touch her. Hopefully he just left her out of it because he's not interested. He's killed widely and indiscriminately in the past, but this time he's following some sort of moral code. Elise will be safe.

She ain't coming anyway. She apologised, said she was busy. *Other plans*. Not the same lightness of tone this time, and a quality that suggested she was done with me.

We hung up. I was embarrassed. I downed the rest of a glass of wine at that point and felt stupid. Classic loser move. Get a good thing, (wrong but good), then keep pushing for more when it's obviously done.

I want to have sex though, that's the trouble. That's why I've slowed down. Don't want to be paralytically drunk.

Let's talk through the options.

So, we have Fake Constable Rowan. She was great. And, importantly, I've been sitting here imagining her getting fucked for the past couple of hours. She is the specific reason I'm currently horny. To be honest, I called Elise because I can't call Rowan, not knowing her number.

Yes, we have the tricky part where she's not who she says she is, and is consequently more than likely a working agent of Multitudes. But the sex! And we did it yesterday and she didn't deliver me to evil.

However, we cannot deny the massive stumbling block. I have no idea how to get in touch with her. So she's as out of the picture as Elise.

Moving on.

See, this is something. This is fun. An activity to alleviate the boredom while we wait for the apocalypse.

Chief Hawkins. Hmm, now there's a thought. And that was an unexpected and rather lovely goodbye kiss she gave me. Still, it doesn't feel right. Not sure why. Maybe I have too much respect for her.

What?

Whatever it is, however one would explain it, calling the chief feels wrong. And perhaps I just know she would one hundred percent say no. And I would be embarrassed again.

So, what other options are there? There are the ladies who never say no, so long as you're paying the right amount of money. It's been a few weeks, but there are plenty of them to be found, and it's not like I don't know where to find them.

Fuck it, I could even pay the extra to get one of them here. That might work.

Hmm.

Trouble is, there's another idea in my head, and it's been there for a while. It's erotic, coupled with being dumb. Those are the best ideas. Self-destructingly dumb at that. Everything about it would be so gloriously stupid, it almost demands that I do it. And the very worst part of it would be that I'd be taking the best relationship I have left, the one good thing to come out of my career in the police, I'd be taking my only true friend on all the earth, and I'd be pissing her off. I'd be inserting myself in her life. I'd be saying, you know how you think I'm a self-absorbed twat who has to make literally every situation about himself? Well, I'm here now. Here you are, having an affair with the DCI, and I was just thinking about how amazingly horny that is, and I thought I'd join you. We cool?

Not going to go well, is it?

Add on that I'm going to have to drive over there, and multiply that by the fact that they may well not actually be at Eileen's place anyway. They could be out. They could be at Eurydice's house, and I don't know where Eurydice lives. And the very fact that I know, I *know*, that if I call and ask where they are so I can join them, Eileen would be so mad at me. She would be off the scale pissed off. And quite rightly too. So, I shouldn't go. No way should I go.

Obviously this calls for a Pugh Matrix.

As soon as I have the thought, I realise I've never paid attention to what a Pugh Matrix actually is. So we'll settle for old fashioned pros and cons.

Cons:

Dick move.

I'd be bringing them into the firing line.

My best friend will hate me.

Eurydice won't want me there any more than Eileen.

Driving while under the influence of alcohol.

Someone wants to kill me, and while I'm hardly impregnable sitting here, at least I'm on home turf. Walking out there, out into the great outdoors unprotected, would be dumb.

And number one bears repeating. It's a really, really dick move.

Pros:

I potentially know where two hot women are having lesbian sex.

You can see my dilemma.

42

Solid start.

Well, on the plus side, I made it here. I may not have driven terribly well, but I arrived untroubled by agents of law enforcement all the same. Now, of course, for the first time in thirty years or so, I don't have a police ID to hide behind.

Yes, whatever, I'm still technically on the books for another few days. But the paperwork's done, left my ID at the station, I turned over my metaphorical .45 Magnum.

Outside buzzer pressed, bit of a gap, was beginning to think maybe there was nobody home, which would have been both a relief and a crushing disappointment, then Eileen answered.

And like I say, a solid start. I said, 'It's me,' and she said, 'Shit, Tom, is everything all right?' and I hesitated because I hadn't planned this *at all*, and also I have no sophistry in me, pretty gormless really, and all I could say was, 'Just thought I'd come over,' and now I'm standing outside the front door of her building, staring drunkenly at the intercom, waiting for her to say something. Waiting while she processes me being here, and why I'm here. And she'll know. Eileen knows me, after all, better than anyone.

She hasn't hung up yet, so at least there's that.

She doesn't speak. The door buzzes, I push it open and walk up the two flights of stairs.

Nicer block than mine, this one. Newer. I contemplated buying here when Eileen did, and we didn't have all the emotional shit between us back then so I could've done it without it being weird or awkward, and I should have done it, but ultimately I didn't because of reasons entirely related to the effort involved.

There's always a reason and it's rarely good.

The door is ajar, so I knock and enter. There's a short hallway, leading to the open-plan kitchen diner. No one immediately evident. I close the door and stand for a moment, suddenly crushingly aware of being somewhere uninvited. Out of place, out of my depth in my way. Like I've invited myself to a dinner party when there's no place at the table.

Even drunk, I'm no party crasher.

Eileen comes out of the bedroom wearing a long T-shirt – but not that long – carrying a glass of sparkling white. She leans on the wall, about seven or eight yards away, the other side of the open-plan, where the other half of the small corridor leads to the bedrooms and the bathroom.

Her hair's just the right amount of messy. Standing like that, pissed off, obviously interrupted, maybe a little bit sad, alcohol to hand, bare legs all the way up, she is hot as fuck. She is not here for me thinking that, of course.

I take a step or two closer, but that's a damned strong forcefield she's got in place, by the way.

'What d'you want, Tom?'

I should maybe have given this some thought beforehand, although under the circumstances, I doubt even Sorkin's coming up with a decent line of dialogue.

I've got nothing.

She asks the question again with eyebrows raised, and a bit of a, 'Well?' gesture.

'I was bored.'

'Right. Well, I'm glad you had good reason, my friend. Seriously?'

'Sorry.'

'You drove over here drunk?'

'I'm not *that* drunk.'

'Have you seen your eyes?'

I think of saying something about being fine, but don't bother. No one thinks I'm fine in any case.

She sighs, she looks around the open-plan as though it might present her with an idea. Silently mutters a *fuck me* beneath her breath.

'You should, I don't know,' she says, indicating the sofa, 'sit down, stick on the tele or something. You shouldn't drive home like that.'

Movement behind her, and Eurydice comes out. Eurydice is hammered. Or Eurydice has been at the nose candy again.

Uh-oh. *Nose candy.* All right, grandad.

Eurydice has thrown on a shirt, eschewing doing up any of the buttons. She's buzzing, a glass of prosecco in her hand. She stops by Eileen, caresses her bare backside and kisses her, and

Eileen may be currently mad, and may not want to be a performing lesbian for my benefit, but she's obviously in some sort of thrall to Eurydice, and can't stop herself enjoying the kiss.

I swallow. I need some of that fizz.

Eileen breaks away, closing her eyes. The DCI lets her caress linger a little longer on Eileen's bottom, and then turns to address me. High as a kite, she pirouettes away from Eileen, her shirt flies round with her, I stand here like a dumb fuck, getting exactly what I came for, staring at her breasts as she moves, and then she's in front of me, smiling a little stupidly, and giving me a mock curtsey.

'Mr Hutton!' she says. 'How wonderful of you to realise that two women are completely incapable of enjoying themselves without the help of a man. If only more of your fellows could display such chivalry.'

She laughs. I have nothing to contribute. I mean, I really didn't think this through. Of course, it's not in my power to do anything. I have no agency in this situation. I've come over here, I have presented myself, and the women can do with me what they will. Eileen's already got the ball rolling by suggesting I can watch TV. Eurydice's state of intoxication may be more promising, although that ain't going to play well with Eileen.

Eurydice reaches out and rests her hand beneath my chin, like she's examining me. I risk a glance at Eileen, who's watching unexpectedly warily. Not that I'm surprised she's wary, but I was expecting more full-throated annoyance.

'What are you bringing to the party, Mr Hutton?' she says.

She sniffs. She laughs.

I start to say, 'What would you like me to bring to the party,' but haven't got very far when she cuts me off with a kiss, leaning into me, her lips lingering on mine.

Mindful of Eileen watching, I respond to the kiss, but don't reach out to touch Eurydice.

She pulls away, she's smiling.

'You've been drinking, sergeant.'

The Mr Hutton thing didn't last. I'm not sure we can really expect much consistency.

Time to relax.

'I may have made a start,' I say.

She kisses me again, more quickly, this time running her hand over my groin as she does so, and she laughs again.

'Well, I think we all know what you're bringing to the party. You must drink, sir! Follow!'

She walks back towards the bedroom, stopping again beside Eileen to kiss her, lingering on her lips, this time her hand resting lightly on her breasts, and then she smiles, glances over her shoulder at me, and says, 'Wouldn't have thought you needed too many invitations.'

I look at Eileen, desperate to go in there. In fact, there's nothing stopping me, but I'm aware enough to hope I get some sort of approval from Eileen before it happens.

She's not looking terribly excited, but Eurydice obviously has some power over her, and she gives me a *well, what are you waiting for* look, and ushers me into the bedroom.

I come up alongside her. Stop for a moment, and we exchange a significant look from two feet apart. No going back from this, and no idea what the two of us will look like on the other side. But then, it's been pretty rocky this side, so is there that much to lose?

I usher her in ahead of me, and can't stop myself saying, 'You look gorgeous like this,' and she turns away, leading me into the bedroom.

There's music playing quietly. Not sure. Gotan maybe. Got a bit of a rhythmic vibe, perfect for being absolutely fucked out your face. Eurydice is swaying side to side, and she smiles as we enter, then reaches out, puts her arms around Eileen's neck and kisses her. God, that's hot.

I watch. I kick off my shoes, reach down, remove my socks. Eurydice breaks the kiss, then smiles at me.

'What've you got, then?' she says.

She kisses me again, completely in charge, her hand running over my groin, and then she's undone the button and the zip, and she bends down, taking my jeans and NASA technology briefs with her as she drops, and then my already damp erection is springing up and she grabs my thighs and takes the end of my cock into her mouth.

Jesus Christ. That escalated quickly. And fuck, that's sensational.

Close my eyes, my hands in her hair. Open them again quickly, look at Eileen.

She's standing behind her, watching. Unsure, possibly, what to do.

Eurydice, though, is controlling the narrative, so it barely matters, acting like she has had the scene planned out in her head beforehand. She stands, she quickly kisses me, then pulls away, whips her shirt off, then falls back on the bed, her legs slightly parted.

She looks up at us both, as we stand by the bottom of the bed.

'What are you waiting for, sergeants? Take me!'

Eileen removes her top, and then, ignoring me, lies down beside Eurydice. She kisses her first, her hand automatically caressing her soaking pussy, and then she moves down and starts to lick and bite her right breast. I follow, lying on her other side, kissing her straight away, enjoying her soft moans, and then moving down and sucking her breast.

Eileen does not hesitate now that she's here, now that the moment has started. Back where she was when this idiot first turned up and interrupted them. She moves down Eurydice's body, then starts licking her pussy, Eurydice grabbing the back of her head, pressing her in more deeply. I watch for a second, then move up, kiss Eurydice deeply again, and then kneel beside her, and she reaches out, grabs my erection, and takes it into her mouth.

Oh, my God, that is glorious. She sucks me so hard, takes me as deep into her mouth as she can, and then pushes me away for a second while she gasps for breath, moaning loudly as she does so, and then immediately takes me back into her mouth.

And Jesus Christ, I get to do this. I get to watch this, and I'm part of it, this wonderful, fabulous threesome, one of them fucking me with her mouth, moaning in increasing ecstasy all the time.

*

Sometime later, not too much time, I don't suppose it lasts all that long, but sometime later I'm on the bed, and Eurydice has fucked me, and she's fucked Eileen, and then Eileen is kneeling beside me, and she's still horny, and I can see the moment when she just thinks, fuck it, we're here now, and she kneels over me, hesitates, and then slowly lowers herself on to me, gasping as my cock slides inside her, and an, 'Oh, God, Tom,' is out of her mouth, and she leans into it and starts fucking me, and Eurydice, who has directed this erotic drama with the skill of an experienced porn movie director, is forgotten.

43

I leave a little over an hour after I got there. That will go down in history as one of the best hours of my life. Oh my God. Sensational.

When we were done, Eurydice disappeared off to the toilet, and Eileen and I were left there, post-coitus, looking at each other. I'm not sure she really knew what had just happened. Having ejaculated, I was once again taken by high level imposter syndrome, having invited myself to join lesbian sex. Who the fuck do you think you are?

'You should go,' said Eileen, although there was no particular judgement in it. It was just the right thing for me to do.

I nodded, I had nothing to say.

Clothes thrown on, I stood at the door of the bedroom.

'I'll call you tomorrow,' I said.

She was lying in bed, a white sheet loosely draped over her. She didn't reply.

The bathroom door opened as I was stepping out the front door, I didn't wait to see Eurydice, and then I was gone.

Driving home, still obviously way over the limit, but far more sober than I was an hour ago.

I just fucked my lesbian best friend. Process that on a bottle and a half of wine.

Turn the corner onto my road, and I see her sitting by the entrance to my building. Slow automatically, as though I may decide to turn around before I get there, and then I come alongside the building, there are always places to park along here, and then I'm out of the car and approaching the entrance.

Elise, sitting on the pavement, her back to the wall, has watched me from the moment I turned into the road. Something about her, looking way more unhappy than every other time we've spoken to each other. Have a not unexpected feeling of relief that she might be here for someone to talk to, rather than for sex. Sex addict or not, sex as good as the sex I've just had is going to keep you sated for a while.

'What's up?' I say.

She shows no particular urge to get up. Her eyes on me, she raises the front of her jumper. She's not wearing a bra, so that she shows me her breasts, though that's not what she's actually showing me. She's been whipped across her stomach and lower chest, five ugly, bright welts. A moment, then she lowers her jumper, as I say, 'Jesus, where'd you get that?'

'Just some guy,' she says. 'Just some prick.'

I offer her my hand, she picks herself up off the floor, we take a moment staring at each other, and then I lead her into the apartment block.

*

'Tell me.'

We're sitting almost formally at the table, albeit we have a glass of wine each, and the snacks are still here, as is the gangbang jigsaw, so it's not like it's that formal. I washed, I brushed my teeth. Thought that was best, given what I've just been doing. One must bring some standards into one's life of unbridled, careless hedonism.

'The guy's one of my clients, you know? Owns a Schnauzer. Little bastard. The guy's rich, entitled, used to getting what he wants. I fucked him last week some time, you know, before you and me. Anyway, he calls a couple of days ago and asks me over, and I'm like, sure, why not? He's got a bit of a weird cock, you know, but what the hell, right?'

I drink wine and let her meander to the point. She is, at least, safe for now. I have quite forgotten, for the moment, that my own head is on the chopping block. Then again, perhaps it's not. The fucker let me walk out of here, drive drunk, have sex, drive home. If this is captivity leading to certain death, bring it on.

'I get to his place, and there's something about him. Like, he had been really, really looking forward to me coming. I mean, that can be nice, you know, but he was wired. Maybe he'd snorted something. Jesus, people, right? You have no idea who they are. They lose themselves, right?'

This young woman fits right into the gang with Eileen and me.

Hmm, that gives me an idea.

Not now, genius, she's got a grim story to tell. Focus!

'He gives me drink, which is cool, right, fine with that. He says he wants to show me something, and then boom! I get his bondage cupboard. The guy is buzzing. I mean, that is straight up Fifty Shades shit, except this fucker ain't, you know, grooming or setting me up nice and slow, and when it comes to it, he's not giving me any option either.'

She stops talking, she shivers. Takes a drink of wine.

'Did he rape you?'

She doesn't reply. She lifts a large crisp from the bowl, takes a large crunch out of the large crisp.

'Did he rape you?'

'I'm not going there. Listen,' she says, and then I get a kind of desperate look, and she reaches out and quickly squeezes my hand, then pulls away again. 'It got ugly for a while, obviously, and there are more welts on my leg, but I got away. I'm not here, I'm not coming to you because you're a police officer. I guess I just wanted somewhere I knew I'd be safe.' Another pause, another careful drink of wine, a small head shake. 'I don't think I even want to talk about it, sorry. I just want... I don't know, maybe we can watch a movie or something. Like, you got Disney? We could watch, like, Wakanda or something. A leave your brain at home.'

I swallow. The alcohol's beginning to catch up with me. I think that must be because I stopped drinking for an hour or two. It never does to stop drinking. I take a drink, and feel that first hit of nausea take a more substantial hold.

It'll pass.

'I have Disney,' I say.

'Wow, that's cool. I don't think I really expected that.'

'I got it so I could give me daughter the password.'

'Oh, that's lovely. What age is she?'

'Twenty-six.'

Her eyes widen a little, she awkwardly bites her bottom lip.

'OK,' she says. 'Well, that's nice that you got her Disney+, right?'

'Sure, it's nice.'

Shit, that feeling of nausea ain't passing with a couple of sips of wine. Where the fuck has that come from?

Shit, I don't want to vomit again. I hate vomiting. If I vomit twice in a week it'll be like I'm seventeen.

'You OK?'

She looks a little concerned.

'Yeah, I'm good. Too much to drink.'

'Maybe a cup of tea with the mov –'

And I'm up and out of the seat and running into the bathroom, barely making it to the toilet in time before the afternoon and evening's intake is spewed forcefully into the bowl.

Now that I'm here, the vomiting does not stop. From nowhere all hell breaks loose, the floodgates are opened.

Oh my God.

At some point in the horror show I think this is what you get. You've just had the sex you've dreamed off, you just got to fuck your best friend you've been wanting to sleep with for years, with a bonus sensational fucked-out-of-her-face blonde thrown in. Now, here you go. Pay the price, you fool.

Time gets lost. Maybe time just gets vomited up along with everything else. I forget I had company when I came in here. The vomiting, which I manage to flush away, soon enough turns to me sitting on the toilet, the other end playing catch-up.

Liquid streams forth, my insides obliterated by the gargantuan stomach bug from hell. As I sit there, unable to pull myself away from the bathroom, the vomit rises in me again, and there's nothing I can do. I can't get up, I can't turn round, I can't reach the sink.

Vomit surges up and out of my mouth, spewing across the bathroom floor. Another retch, another, a fourth, and then I'm slumped forward on my weak and shaking legs, as the stream of liquid diarrhoea finally comes to an end.

I'm panting, emptied out within what can't have been more than a few minutes. Exhausted, my limbs utterly shot, mouth open, eyes streaming, nose streaming.

'Sorry about that.'

I look up. Didn't lock the bathroom door, of course. Elise is there, leaning on the door frame, looking down at me. She looks a little sympathetic, but not quite as sympathetic or concerned – or, indeed grossed out – as one might expect.

'It's not your fault,' I manage.

I retch again, but nothing comes. Once again, then the feeling passes.

'Well, you know, you might want to reconsider that statement,' she says.

I don't know what she's talking about. I kind of look at her, but I can't think, and I feel better when I close my eyes. So I close my eyes.

'Since I put that powder in your wine when you went to the bathroom earlier, and this is as a result of you drinking the wine, one could say that technically, yes, it is my fault.'

I let the words sink in, and that in itself isn't easy, then I finally manage to lift my eyes again.

'What?'

She shrugs, she walks forward.

'You think you're done?'

'What?'

'You think you're done? I think maybe you are. That's what the boss said, you know. He described it as a short, sharp punch to the digestive system. He'll be here shortly.'

I notice she's holding something in her hand, and she lifts it now. A pack of wet wipes. I can't think straight. Why does she need wet wipes? She hands me a few.

'Clean yourself. And mind, we have strict instructions to not flush the toilet after your explosion there, so make sure you leave it. But like I say, clean yourself.'

I automatically start to clean myself. I have no idea what's going on, like my mind has just been shat out of my body along with everything else.

Elise whips her jumper off, naked beneath, revealing those thick ugly red welts across her stomach and chest. I watch as she takes a wet wipe to them, and they disappear.

44

Walked into that one.

Let's look on the bright side. I mean, sure, that's tough to do when you're sitting in a darkened room, a basement presumably, beneath a motorway.

Not like I saw where they brought me, but that's definitely a motorway up there. And we did not travel far, so I'm guessing it's the M74. M8 not out of the question. The number, the motorway, the location, don't really matter, do they?

Naked. Manacled at the wrists and ankles. No other sound but the rumble of traffic. Have a sense of something in the room with me, but I can't decide if that's because I know there's going to be some creature lurking in a cage, or if I can feel something more tangible. Something I can sense that does not obviously present itself. Maybe that's the same thing and not an either/or. Not thinking terribly straight.

Oh, aye, the bright side. We were supposed to be looking on the bright side. So, what is that exactly?

The sex. I mean, Clayton could just have taken me out of the game at any time in the last few weeks, or months. The nights when I'm drunk and borderline incapacitated have been legion. I am easy meat for any animal. The position I'm in now is not so metaphorically different from my usual state. And yet, he chose to seduce me. He gave me someone young and sexy as fuck. I mean, I doubt he had anything to do with the rest of the past week's sex, but at least I was allowed the time.

So, that's the bright side. Plus, I've stopped vomiting and shitting, so there's that. Hadn't quite stopped when I started cleaning myself up, but it didn't last much longer. Made a determined effort to turn quickly and flush the toilet, flush that tracker away so it started moving somewhere, but I was wrung through, incapable of rapid movement. She caught my wrist, fast and hard. She has moves, Elise.

It occurred to me at some point that no one checked up on me when I went to Eileen's, so the chances are no one's paying any attention in any case. Nice that the bad guys felt the need to clear out my system just in case.

Clayton arrived soon enough. Ran a quick scanner over my body, identified the location of the tracker in my neck, cut it out. Removed the one from my ankle by breaking my ankle, and fracturing my heel. That was unpleasant. That part wasn't the bright side.

So, here we are. Bound, not gagged, beneath a motorway. About to die. Completely strung out, my insides fantastically puked and defecated forth, my lower left leg and ankle useless, but dull. He gave me an injection so that I wouldn't feel any pain down there. 'We don't want your death to be a relief,' he said, as I grimaced anew at the needle being thrust into my leg. 'It'll already be a fucking relief,' I spat at him, and he laughed.

I want to talk to Eileen. That's interesting. Eileen and I had sex. Penetrative sex. There was a third party present which altered the dynamic somewhat, but ultimately there we were, old friends, best friends, fucking. And her a lesbian.

I don't know. I guess she got lost in the moment. Was that it? Carried away.

Given my current circumstances, moot point, perhaps, but chances are that's us done. I can see it. Friendship over. Another woman pushed away. Another relationship ruined, like every other one I've had. Perhaps the end of the line for Kadri and I wasn't my fault, but her leaving just prevented me messing it up. We all know that. And, despite not voicing it, I'm sure she knew it too. She led us to a glorious and fitting conclusion, then disappeared off into the night.

And now, a nasty end imminent, it's Eileen I want to see. It's Eileen I want to burst through the door, guns blazing. But that's not going to happen, and ultimately I'm not going to be around for Eileen and me to not speak to each other again.

Clayton dumped me here and left. I'm not sure where he's gone, or why he doesn't just get on with it. Perhaps he has something to do. Perhaps he's toying with me. All part of the game he plays with his victims. Leaves them in silence. Allows them to stew. The psychological horror of sitting in the dark is pretty intense in itself.

I want to be able to kill myself. If I could, I would. If nothing else, it would be a good way to avoid my swift decline into a sex, alcohol and boredom spiral. Mainly it would be a good way to avoid being eaten alive by whatever the fuck sits in the cage just out of my sight.

But it's been a hell of a week, right? The alcohol part, the part that will actually kill me, if Clayton doesn't, that's not been too solid. I've felt pretty shitty by my own hand, even if the worst of it was because of Elise and her magic potion. But the sex? Oh my God. If I wasn't to die, I could look back with some enjoyment. Elise, the chief, the fake Constable, Eileen and Eurydice. Wow. It's like I made it up. It's like I dreamed it.

In my wrung out state, I begin to wonder if maybe I have. In reality, I've been here the entire time. My part in this drama started with Clayton beaning me over the napper, taking me captive and locking me in a basement. I've been here for days. That's all there is. The rest of it has been a delirious invention. It would certainly explain every time I've had sex, as each of them oughtn't to have happened. Each of them was ridiculous in its own right. As are these preposterous murders committed by Clayton. As is Clayton not still being in prison.

Is this where we are? Bobby Ewing times a thousand. An episode of *Dallas* with added slaughter, gore, disembowelment and fucking?

God, I can't think straight.

How could I kill myself? How can anyone kill themselves, without the use of their hands and feet, without being able to go anywhere? Can't just hold your breath. I could, I guess, try to smack my head off the wall, but I don't think I have that in me. Don't think I have the strength, and I just don't think I could do it. It's one thing stepping off a cliff, one thing running a blade across a wrist, or putting a noose around your neck and kicking away the chair, another altogether causing yourself that kind of pain. It's the sort of thing that would need to be done in desperation. And I'm not desperate. Too washed out for that level of feeling. Just sitting here, logically thinking that the best thing that could happen is that I die before this pathological eejit returns.

I rest my head back against the wall. For the first time I think about spiders, wondering if there might be one on the wall. I fucking hate spiders. It's still midsummer, so too early for actual spider season, but I'm in a basement. Basement spiders don't have a season. They're just here all the time. Big and bored and interested in whatever life happens to find its way into their vicinity.

I want to move my head, I think about it, my brain tells it

to move, to lift myself away from the wall, but nothing happens.

Fuck me. I wish this stupid bastard would just get on with this.

45

'What d'you think is in the cages?'

Time passes. Darkness. No dreams. If there are dreams, I forget them. Unless the women were in dreams. The deaths were in dreams. Clayton being out of prison was in dreams. I remember those dreams.

'What d'you think is in the cages?'

There are words in the air. Moments pass. I reacquaint myself with where I am.

I don't know where I am.

A loud rumble of noise, and then it dies away. Another, not quite as insistent. Silence.

The motorway. It's the middle of the night. Must be. I have no idea how long I've been here. How many days. Maybe this is the same day, the same night, as the one when I left.

The sounds of traffic come intermittently. Eventually the day will pick up. Perhaps I will recognise rush hour.

'What d'you think is in the cages?'

That voice. That's what woke me up.

I open my eyes, even though I don't want to. I don't want to see anyone. I don't want to know why I'm here. I just want this over with.

It'll come soon enough.

There's a figure, though I can't make out too much. He's shining a light at me. In the light I can see a string of small cages in a semi-circle. I couldn't see them in the dark, but here now, in this strange half-light, they are close. Shuttered at the front, so I can't see what they hold.

Small though, they're all small. And they emit no sound.

Oh Jesus fuck, we are not going to be gifted the quick death by the teeth of a wolf, that's for sure.

For the first time in forever I feel fear.

'What do you think?' he says.

Clayton. I can't see him properly, but I'd recognise that voice anywhere, under any circumstance. So there's to be no shock, no deus ex machina, no surprise character in off the sidelines. His able lieutenants, both of whom completely fooled the shit out of me, they're the crime novel surprise packages. Big whoop. I expect others saw them coming far more clearly than I did.

Maybe I was too close to the action. Couldn't see the wood for the trees. Maybe I'm just shit at this.

Well, there's a thought.

'Your mind drifts, doesn't it?' says Clayton. 'That's what everyone says about you. More than a few invoke Walter Mitty. Very dull, of course, very predictable. Poor Walter, they'd probably diagnose him with ADHD nowadays. Ha. But not you. I don't think you're ADHD, are you? A troubled soul, that's all, about to be put out of his misery.'

'Are you still talking?'

I can picture the sharp look, though I can't see his face.

'What d'you think is in the cages?' he says, with a little more edge.

I have to summon up the strength to speak, everything being such an effort. God, I'm dehydrated. Hadn't realised how bad that was, but the thought is in my head now, and Jesus, I'm thirsty as fuck.

I rub my fingers together, can feel the wrinkling of the skin, the texture of dehydration.

'Miniature giraffes,' I say, voice flat.

Not really here for playing games. The thought of what could be in there is starting to make me very uncomfortable. What's the worst thing it could be? The very worst? Because he'll know, this fucker will know, and whatever the worst thing is that I could think of, this will be it.

Don't think of it.

'You're not playing, sergeant. I suppose it's understandable, one can hardly expect you to be in the mood for fun given what's happened to you. And is about to happen. But really, I have given you a bit of a send-off, haven't I? You've had fun this week.'

'I had fun without anything you did,' I say, hating that I'm getting in to a battle of words. I owe him nothing but silence.

He laughs at that.

'Oh yes, you did, didn't you? Quite the Lothario. A fitting end to a long career in the saddle. If only there was a Hall of Fame for which you'd be eligible. Sigh...'

Oh, just fuck off.

'Well, my preferred course of action here this morning would be to leave you for a while. I might enjoy that. A long period in the dark. Two or three days, perhaps longer. You're a little dried out after all the sickness, so you likely wouldn't last too long without water, but we could hydrate you, then lock the door and walk away. Extraordinary the way the mind works when that's done to a man. However, my old friend, my time here is limited. I really ought to be getting on. My new career as vengeful superhero is off to a flying start, now I need to leave everyone to stew in their own fear. I shall return at some point, but for now, lying low is the best defence.' A pause, and then, 'I was rather pleased with the way I dispatched the drugs gang, weren't you? The horror of the crows. Gosh, that must've taken you back, sergeant.'

I give him nothing, having belatedly decided to keep my mouth shut.

'I keep calling you that. Sergeant. Except, you're not a sergeant anymore, are you?'

I want to get him to shut up. I want to taunt him into just getting the fuck on with it. Except there's something in those cages there, and it scares the shit out of me.

'Oh, how disappointing,' he says. 'I had such high hopes for this. The last act. The final, you know, the final thing between us. It's been such a long and glorious partnership. Like, Rodgers and Hammerstein, or perhaps you would prefer Bond and Blofeld.' He laughs stupidly. 'But if you're not going to talk, then we may as well bring the curtain down on everything once and for all. Such a shame. Let us meet your killers, shall we?'

There's a click, and the shutters at the front of the cages all rise at the same time. I get a judder of fear, until I realise that behind the shutters there is close-knit mesh, and that the creatures inside are not yet free. This is just another level of taunting.

And it is, I have to say, as the breath stalls in my throat, top level fucking taunting.

Clayton gives a little squeal of delight.

Huntsmen. Cage after cage, stretching into the darkness around me, of huntsmen spiders. Big bastards. Big bodies, long, powerful legs.

Oh my fucking Jesus.

The feeling of nausea comes out of nowhere, induced by fear.

Fuck, fuck, fuck.

He giggles.

'Perhaps you want to talk now, or shall we just press on with the entertainment?'

I can't take my eyes off them. Some alone, some enclosed together, four or five to a cage. Some pressed against the front, some sitting in corners, some on the bottom of the cage, waiting. Waiting for the door to be opened.

Huntsmen aren't poisonous. Huntsmen won't do you any harm. Sure, but then, neither will Shih Tzu Inu puppies. And like those damned little handbag dogs, these spiders are going to need to feed.

Oh my God.

The light is bobbling around me, in my eyes and out of my eyes, and then he's set his phone in a stand, so that it's directly front on.

He steps to the side of it, and I can now, in the half light of the periphery, see his face. The same face I first looked upon more than ten years ago. The same face that's haunted me since. The face that hasn't changed.

He turns to the camera, sets it going, then turns back.

'Why are you here?'

Dumped on the floor, chained at the wrists and feet, I drag my fearful gaze away from the spiders, and back to Clayton, hiding behind the bright light of the torch.

'No,' I say.

Another peculiar noise, like a laugh, but not. Like a squeal, but deeper.

'Oh, interesting. No? What do you mean?'

'I'm not playing your shitty game,' I say. 'Why am I here? Because you're a dickhead. How's that?'

'Oh, rude. Very rude. There's nothing you want to confess to? Nothing that happened say, in Bosnia for example. It's a while ago now, of course, but these things... well, they're out there, aren't they? They've been done. They happened. They can't unhappen, no matter how much time has elapsed. Perhaps you might like to get it off your chest. I don't know, what d'you think? No?'

'Fuck off.'

'Well, well, how disheartening. Since this one, this

particular indiscretion of yours, isn't in the public eye, I may have to issue a written statement along with the video. Obviously a piece to camera would be better,' and he laughs stupidly again, 'but we're not there yet. Yes, there are digital technologies we could use, but let's not fritter around with that. Life's too short.' A pause, then another laugh. 'Yours certainly is.'

I look back at the spiders. There's one of them, just one of them, moving. With barely anywhere to go, it slowly lifts its legs, crawling across the base of the cage. Big, ugly, horrific, and hungry. Alone in a cage, because it would be quickly done, presumably, with anything unlucky to share with it.

It stops by the front panel, its two foremost legs up against it. It's been able to sense me all the time I've been here. Now it can see me and it can smell me.

'Fuuuuuuuuuuuck!' comes suddenly from my mouth, unplanned, unthought of, just there, coming from the pits of my stomach.

I swallow, the fear crawling up my stomach, panting breaths heaving from my guts.

'Oh, fuck, come on, then! Open the cages, you fucker! Come on!'

Here we go. Such an inglorious end. Gullet slit open, eaten by spiders.

Oh fuck, oh fuck.

'Come on!'

'Oh, such desperation. It's quite thrilling, really. And I thought you'd be much more, I don't know, disdainful perhaps. Or urbane. But no...'

'Fucking shut up! Shut up! Just fucking do it you festering piece of shit!'

A sigh, an ugly, *I've had enough of you* sigh.

'You are so disappointing. But then, that's who you are, isn't it? A bitter disappointment to everyone you've ever known. The long suffering Sergeant Harrison, for example. How many times do you think you've let her d –'

'Leave her alone!'

'Such passion,' he says softly. 'If only you could have lived your life with such controlled fervour, applied yourself to things that mattered rather than the fripperies of alcohol consumption and the breaking of lady's hearts.'

'Fuck off! And you fucking leave Eileen alone!'

'Well, I might.' He giggles. 'No, I'm kidding, I am one hundred percent not going to leave Eileen alone.'

'Fucker!' I scream, pulling against all the bonds, and now that lower left leg, broken and twisted, stabs me with pain, and another high, guttural scream escapes.

'Eileen remembers me, I'm sure. Such a lovely naked body, I recall. I must see that again. I wonder if the thought will excite her.'

I scream again, and then the look on his face changes, the supercilious, smug, pompous twatery vanishes in a snap of the fingers, like a veil is drawn across it, and then he stares darkly at me, finally with the face of the man he really is.

'Sergeant, you have saddened me to the end.'

He pulls something from his pocket, straightens it out, the mask of Multitudes, and then pulls it over his head, so that the look of evil is gone, replaced by cartoon devilry.

'For my short interlude in the spotlight,' he says.

'Fuck off!'

He reaches behind him and takes the knife which he's kept tucked into his trouser belt. He steps forward, bends down, and then places the knife at a point just beneath my rib cage. A piercing stab, and I flinch, an ugly, desperate sound escaping my mouth.

'Last chance, you coward,' he sneers. 'Confess your pathetic sins, all of them, all of your mindless, shameful crap, and I might not rape Sergeant Harrison repeatedly before I kill her.'

I jerk forcefully, and with it, he pushes the knife further in, and then does what he's done with all the others, drawing it quickly down my stomach.

I stop moving instantly, my body slumping back. *Fuck* judders into my mouth, but does not make it all the way, finishing in a desperate gasp, new pain shooting all over my body.

He draws the knife down to the top of my pubic hair, the pain of it piercing me all the way, and then he stops, takes a second to check his work, and then lays the knife down to the side.

He takes something else from his pocket, as I lie there, wrung out and impotent, a bloody slit down the middle of my stomach. Gloves, this time. Nitrile, as used by scenes of crime officers worldwide.

'Now the fun part,' he says. 'Buckle up, lover boy.'

He puts his fingers to either side of the wound, takes another moment to enjoy my horror, my feckless incapacitation, and then he starts to slowly pull the sides apart.

I scream. I scream and try not to move.

He reaches inside, cups his hands around as much of my viscera as he can manage, and then slowly lifts them out of my stomach.

Head against the wall, my mouth open, tears streaking my face, my nose running, awful panting breaths coming from my throat, I have nothing. This is the fucking end, and I have nothing but fear and pain and horror.

I almost scream again, but it breaks quickly into a heaving sob, and he looks darkly up at me. A warning. A don't move too much or your dead, mate.

But I want to be dead. I need it, now! Move! Come on! Move! Move more!

And now I find I cannot move.

My insides rest on the top of my body. Grotesque beyond imagination. Jesus Christ. I feel sick. I need to be sick.

Clayton straightens up, standing by my legs, looking down on me imperiously.

'Sorry, I was premature before. *Now*, now is the fun part.'

He steps back, he holds a small clicker in his hands.

'I'll just be over there. Just need to put a little more light on the subject, then we're good to go. The wonderful thing about all these creatures, is that you just never know how long they'll take. Well, except the wolf. And flies. Flies land on any old thing straight away. And the rats, I don't suppose they were going to be skittish. Oh look, it would appear I was talking through my head.'

I'm gasping, horrible breaths, wanting desperately to die, but I don't feel it, not yet. I don't feel myself fading, I don't feel the oncome of *anything*.

A brighter light comes on, although not illuminating the whole of the room. Clayton removes his mask, his gloves already stuffed into a small bag that was lying behind him somewhere.

I look around at the spiders. They sit where they sat. Seemingly neither interested nor agitated.

Still.

Patient.

Menacing.

The fear crawls once again across my skin.

'Goodbye, Sergeant Hutton.'

He purposefully holds the small device in front of him, ready to press. I stare pathetically back. Lost, broken, utterly laid waste. And fucking terrified of what's about to be crawling unchecked across my face.

'Fuuck!' from my lips again, and that will be the fitting, final word.

Click.

The doors of each of the cages springs upwards, hinged along the top. One spider, attached to the front, comes with the movement of the door, and scurries off, disappearing out of sight. Fear courses through me, and I wish I would die. Now! I've been disembowelled! Die! Now! For fuck's sake!

'I'd love to stay and watch, but there's about to be rather a lot of scurrying. These things are absolutely terrifying. But don't worry, I'll be sure to wat –'

Phht! Phht!

He falls, stone cold dead in a second. Two bullets to the head. Gun with a silencer attachment. He clatters forward, knocking two or three cages, and immediately there's a scampering of legs and bodies, spiders on the run, as Clayton's overweight body crumples to a final rest.

A huntsmen up over my leg, and I yelp, pathetically. Big fuckers. More movement to the side.

Then footsteps quickly across the floor, and then into the light comes Constable Rowan.

'Oh dear, you do get into some scrapes,' she says, from nowhere like she's in an episode of the Famous Five, and she swipes the spider from the top of my leg, stands on another, squishing it dead in an instant, and then she puts a bullet in one, then another.

'Jesus,' she mutters, staring down at me.

More movement of legs, more scurrying.

Phone out of her pocket, she whirls around the confined space, in total command. Call connected, she begins to bark instructions, rapid fire. At the same time, bends, lifts the small remote from Clayton's pale dead hand, clicks the button, and the doors of all the cages slam shut. She scans the floor, steps forward, one spider squashed, then another, and another. Looks quickly around the room, identifies five more and shoots them in a couple of quick snaps of the fingers.

She turns back, bending down beside me.

I am lost. So fucking lost.

'I'm not going to touch you. I'm sorry, this is beyond my skills. But I suggest you don't move. Help will not be long. Sorry I didn't get here earlier. I got detained unexpectedly by your friend's helper. That young lady had talents beyond her years,' she says, the last words delivered in an almost rueful tone. Then she adds, 'Dead now.'

Movement. My eyes swivel, the fear begins to catch in my throat, and before I can utter a sound she's turned and put a bullet in the body of the hopefully last surviving loose huntsman in the pack.

'Tricky buggers,' she says.

She looks down at me, resting a hand gently on my arm.

'There's one thing I can do for you,' she says, and she pats her pocket. 'I can knock you out. Trouble for you is, given your wounds, you might not wake u –'

'Do it,' I manage. 'Please.'

'Good call. You need to lie as still as possible, so…'

She takes a small metal case from her pocket, flicks open the top, selects one of three syringes, pulls the plunger, holds it poised at my arm, and says, 'Ready?'

Yes. Ready to die, in fact. Not sure I really wanted saved this time, though nice to be protected from the huntsmen.

'Thank you,' I say.

She smiles.

Needle to the arm, senses heightened, hurts like fuck, and immediately, another snap of those fingers, everything is gone.

Two Weeks Later

I didn't die. I guess I can say that much. Induced coma. They sewed me back up. Out of the woods. Still groggy, still sleeping most of the day. Only just started getting out of bed with assistance, but they say it's time I was doing it, several times a day. Some shit about muscle atrophy and bed sores and dying of sepsis.

Eileen arrives. I haven't spoken to her yet. I wanted to yesterday, and I think the day before, but I couldn't get my mouth to work. This morning, I spoke to the nurse. Big guy. He told me to stop being a pussy when I winced at having to get out of bed.

Yesterday afternoon I lay with my eyes shut, drifting in and out, listening to Rebecca, my daughter, chatting with Eileen.

'I never know whether I should call you like Aunt Eileen or something.'

I imagined the look on Eileen's face.

'I'm still nominally a police officer for three more days,' she replied. 'If you call me aunt, I'll have to arrest you.'

Rebecca laughed. She has a lovely laugh.

'Anyway, I slept with your dad just before he ended up in here,' said Eileen, 'so you might want to hold off on the aunt.'

'I think that might be too much information,' came after a pause.

'Yes, sorry. Obviously I needed to share.'

Another pause, and then Rebecca said, 'I thought you were gay.'

'I am.'

I could imagine Eileen's small shrug.

I think Rebecca said, 'Well, love knows no boundaries, I guess,' at that point, although maybe I'm projecting, because that's what Eurydice said.

I drifted off to sleep. When I woke up, Eileen was still here. The nurse says she's always here.

'Hey,' says Eileen.

My eyes are open. Properly awake today for the first time since she's been visiting.

'Hey,' I say.

'The nurse said you got out of bed this morning.'

I conjure up the words.

'He used to work for the Stasi.'

She smiles, she pulls her seat a little closer to the bed.

'How are you feeling?'

'Head fuggy. Not sore, but I think that's... still on morphine. They probably need to get me off of that shit.'

'They're reducing it every day.'

'That makes sense.'

'How's the leg?'

'No idea. I wasn't walking on that one. They've ruled me out the next three World Cups, though.'

We look at each other. A familiar melancholy, as though everything is lost. Except, it's not. Well, with the exception of the police careers. Up until this point we've been two sergeants in the police. Now what are we? What will bind us?

'So, what did you think?' I ask.

She gives this a moment, can't decide what I mean, and says, 'What did I think about what?'

'The sex.'

I get the deadpan stare.

'Really, Tom? *That's* the first thing you're asking me?'

'It's important.'

'Well, I suppose it is.'

I get another familiar look from her. The one that says I'm incorrigible.

'When are you going to stop doing this?' she says. 'I mean, every damn time you end up in flippin' hospital. *Every time.* Why can't I be the one in hospital, with you sitting here? We can get some equanimity.'

'You're not a detective,' I say, and I get an eye roll in response. 'Anyway, I don't want you to end up in hospital.'

'I don't want you to end up in hospital!'

'Well, we're done now,' I say. 'Clayton's actually dead, right?'

Clayton. Have been trying not to think too much about him, trying not to think that he might turn up here, standing beside my bed, to either pull a plug, or put a pillow over my head, or to taunt me, to say, 'Until the next time,' before disappearing into the night. But I saw him die. This isn't some shitty horror movie. Getting out of prison is one thing. Outrageous perhaps, but still logical, still possible. Not dying with two bullets exploding in the brain, not so much.

'Yes. Very, very dead. You're not worrying about him are you?'

'No,' I lie.

She reaches out and squeezes my hand.

'He's dead, Tom, you're OK.'

I look into her eyes. I think I believe her. I saw him fall. He fell onto the spiders.

A shiver courses through me. She feels it, and she squeezes my hand again.

'It's OK.'

'That was the spiders,' I say.

'Sorry?'

'I thought of the spiders. That's why I shivered.'

'The spiders also got taken care of. You're OK.'

'We're not going to Australia,' I say, and she smiles.

'I'll take that off the list.'

The first smile comes weakly to my lips, and leaves again.

'Who was that…?' I begin, then struggle for a moment to formulate the question. 'The constable? She was like… wait, what *was* that about?' A moment, and then, 'Constable Rowan.'

'I'm not sure her name was Constable Rowan.'

'No. What was her name?'

'I don't know. She stuck with Constable Rowan.'

'Who was she? I mean…'

I think of the end. What was supposed to be the end. My end. I mean, you'd think the damned end would come some day, some time. But it never seems to.

'Security services. I think. I'm guessing, don't really know.' She kind of shrugs, then says, 'She said she'd be in touch with you just to wrap everything up. Apologised for not being able to stick around, though she has called me a couple of times to check up on you. Which is nice. I suppose.'

This all makes perfect sense, apart from the bit about her being in the security services, and that she was following me, and that she was involved in the story in any way whatsoever. So, apart from all that, everything fits together.

'I don't understand.'

'She said she'd been sent to write a report on you, with the possibility of recruitment.'

I'm still groggy. I'm probably not hearing her properly.

'Recruitment to what?'

'The security services, I presume.'

'Me?'

'Yes.'

'That's not real.'

'That's what she said. You're the right personality type for a certain sort of job.'

'She said that?'

'Yes.'

I hold her look and then finally turn away, staring down to the bottom of the bed. At the bump made by my feet.

'I'm not sure how I feel about that.'

'You don't have to feel anything. I'm afraid she said she wouldn't be recommending you. You can forget the Aston Martin, schmancy hotels in exotic locations, and cool gadgets like packs of cards that taste of vodka and double as tactical nuclear weapons.'

'Ah. Too bad.'

'Right? She also apologised for sleeping with you, by the way. Said it was unprofessional.'

I don't say anything to that. Some unprofessionalism is welcome.

'She said she had a husband,' I think to say.

'Did she? I have no idea. I think you probably have to presume she was lying about everything. I'm glad you got to sleep with her, though,' she says deadpan. 'Was that before or after you had your gullet cut open?'

We smile together at that. I move my hand towards her, and she takes my fingers into hers. I squeeze her hand.

I don't think of anything else to say.

Twilight On An Autumn Day

This is where the story ends.

Clayton is dead. That's the end. The fucker played the system, used every opportunity presented to him, used the best lawyers he could buy, and got out. The plans he put in place thereafter were already in the making, with the aid of Elise, a young woman he'd met in Cornton Vale. A young psychopath, perhaps would be a better way to put it. She played me like a kipper. Played her part to perfection, right up until she lost her final fight.

Still, I remain convinced she wasn't faking all those orgasms.

She'd completely bought into Clayton's agenda. Zero coercion on his part. Go after people the public were going to be more or less happy to see dead. Strike fear into the hearts of other criminals. Then they spread the love with the murder of the Covid exploiter, Lord Thewlis. That would've set another few hearts racing. Subsequently, Clayton was about to do the sensible thing. Disappear for a while, leaving fear in his wake, only to return when the fear had begun to subside. A pretty impressive terror campaign, with criminals and corrupt parliamentarians as its victims. This guy could've been the Robin Hood of serial killers. This guy would've been getting played by Brad Pitt in the Netflix adaptation. Except, he fucked it. Tagged me on at the end for no real reason. Sure, I have something from my past to confess, and my police career was somewhat chequered, but the public wouldn't have cared.

His final act was purely personal on his part. A conceit, and he paid for it. Of course, he wasn't to know about the fake Constable Rowan. Even I didn't know about the fake Constable Rowan, and I'd slept with her.

She called to ask how I was doing. I guess we had a similar conversation to the one she'd had with Eileen. She even apologised for the sex again. I said she really didn't need to do that. I asked her what her real name was and she said her name was Julia Rowan, and then she said she's like James Bond, she tells everyone her real name straight from the off. I still didn't believe her.

Sure enough, though, she said she hadn't recommended me for her office. That was what she called it. Her office. Maybe it's all a scam, and she works in the HR department at Waitrose. She did have some moves though. I commended her on her ability to take out fifteen huntsmen spiders in under a minute. She thanked me.

And there she goes, never to be heard of again.

My police career done and dusted. Eileen's too. I got out of hospital after a month. All sewn back up, everything where it's supposed to be, screws and plates and other medical hardware fitted to my foot and ankle, and it looks like I'll be adding a world-weary and windswept limp to my litany of scars, melancholic eyes, and half a thumb. 'Hell of a thing to survive,' said the surgeon. I think I said something dumb like, 'Ain't that the truth.'

Several weeks at home recuperating, getting my shit together. Eileen stayed with me. I needed her there, and of course, we had to plan that trip to Canada everybody's been talking about.

Plan made, everything booked, we got the train from Glasgow to Southampton. Queen Mary 2 to New York. Spent three nights in the city, then took the train to Toronto, and then trains across Canada. Not so much walking. And I mean, as you get the train across some long, flat, dull-ass plains when it's pishing with rain, you're kind of thinking to yourself, pretty happy I'm not walking this, by the way.

And now here we are. Twilight on an autumn day. We arrived an hour ago, and we've been in our suite at the Banff Springs Hotel for forty-three minutes. We're sitting on a sofa, looking out of the window at the pine forest stretching away to the mountains, which are already snow covered. Perhaps they're always snow covered. I might just sit here in this position until next summer to find out. This is like getting pleasurable relaxation injected straight into your eyeballs.

Bottle of Champagne on the table, on ice. Glass each. Eileen and I together on the sofa, looking out at the view. A comfortable silence hangs over the room. We lift our glasses, take a drink, set them back down.

'How long d'you think we can afford to just sit here?' asks

Eileen. 'I mean, our pensions are pretty decent, right? We can take this room for several months at least.'

'Sounds like a plan,' I say. 'Though I need to be back in the UK in time for the next general election.'

I smile to myself as I say it, and she gives me a wary look.

'Go on.'

'Well, we've been talking about what we're going to do with our lives. We need a plan.'

'Yes…?'

'And we were having that *who the fuck is there to vote for any more* discussion?'

'Yes.'

I glance at her, do something with my face.

'You're thinking you might run for parliament?'

'Thought it'd be worth a shot. As an independent, obviously.'

She smiles, looks away, back to the trees and the mountains.

'What's your platform?'

I take another sip of champagne. This is nice stuff. I make a banner headline gesture, indicating my campaign slogan, and say, 'Running for parliament because everyone else is a cunt,' and she laughs and elbows me softly in the side.

She's still being very gentle with me. One day it'll be nice if she gets a little rougher.

We drink champagne. Minutes pass. The sky imperceptibly darkens with time. The comfortable silence returns. Peace settles upon us like lightly falling snow.

Despite the comfort of the silence, I want to say something about the view. I want to say something about being here with her. I want to find the words to sum up just how perfect this moment is. I've given up on myself so many times in the past, and if she'd let me, if Eileen had given up on me, then we wouldn't be here now.

I told her I loved her as we sat in John's Coffee Shop on the corner of 2nd and 44th, eating pancakes and maple syrup for breakfast, five days ago. I wish I hadn't said it then, so that I could say it now for the first time. Given that that's already out there, this moment demands something even more profound than I love you, and I have nothing. No one wants to sound like some dickhead romantic poet, looking at a Swiss mountain just before he dies of consumption.

'Fuck me,' says Eileen out of nowhere.

I glance at her. She has the same look on her face that I know I have. I turn away again and look at the view.

'That's just what I was thinking,' I say.

By Douglas Lindsay

DI Buchan

Buchan
Painted In Blood
The Lonely And The Dead
A Long Day's Journey Into Death

The Barber, Barney Thomson

The Long Midnight of Barney Thomson
The Cutting Edge of Barney Thomson
A Prayer for Barney Thomson
The King Was in His Counting House
The Last Fish Supper
The Haunting of Barney Thomson
The Final Cut
Aye, Barney
Curse of The Clown

Other Barney Thomson

The Face of Death
The End of Days
Barney Thomson: Zombie Slayer
The Curse of Barney Thomson & Other Stories
Scenes from The Barbershop Floor

DCI Jericho

We Are the Hanged Man
We Are Death

Pereira & Bain

Cold Cuts
The Judas Flower

DI Westphall

Song of the Dead
Boy in the Well
The Art of Dying

DS Hutton

The Unburied Dead
A Plague of Crows
The Blood That Stains Your Hands
See That My Grave Is Kept Clean
In My Time of Dying
Implements of the Model Maker
Let Me Die In My Footsteps
Blood In My Eyes
The Deer's Cry
A Winter Night
I Am Multitudes

Stand Alone Novels

Lost in Juarez
Being For The Benefit Of Mr Kite!
A Room with No Natural Light
Ballad in Blue
These Are The Stories We Tell
Alice On The Shore

Other

Santa's Christmas Eve Blues
Cold September

Printed in Great Britain
by Amazon